Best Wishes
Jerry

The Fenian Season
A Canadian Historical Thriller

Jaroslav (*Jerry*) Petryshyn

 FriesenPress

Suite 300 - 990 Fort St
Victoria, BC, V8V 3K2
Canada

www.friesenpress.com

Copyright © 2017 by Jaroslav (*Jerry*) Petryshyn
First Edition — 2017

Cover image of John A MacDonald Courtesy of Library and Archives Canada

ISBN
978-1-5255-1151-6 (Hardcover)
978-1-5255-1152-3 (Paperback)
978-1-5255-1153-0 (eBook)

1. FICTION, HISTORICAL

Distributed to the trade by The Ingram Book Company

For the usual suspects with love.

Buffalo, Late February, 1866

John Rourke lit a fat cigar as he made his way up the sloped street toward his abode. Expelling a conspicuous cloud of smoke, he increased his stride anticipating a cup of tea and a warm embrace from Molly, who, as was her habit, would be waiting for him near the heat of the hearth. She made it a distinct pleasure to come home from the late night sorties he was obliged to make of late into frost-starched back alleys. Tonight, he was in an especially good frame of mind. Perhaps, he would even celebrate a little – if Molly were not too tired.

Rourke indeed was feeling exceedingly fine – flushed with success. After almost one month of hobnobbing with scheming lunatics, listening to their morbid tirades against England and profuse toasts to the 'Emerald Isle', he finally ferreted out their dastardly plan – or at least part of it.

Admittedly, his informant, a wretched example of Irish manhood if there ever was one, had heard it second hand, no doubt while in a state of blissful intoxication, but Rourke was confident that it was genuine enough. After all, more than a gill of rum was riding on the man's veracity (besides, Rourke doubted that O'Bannion had the imagination to formulate such a convincing story).

More than satisfied with himself, Rourke resolved that come first morning light he would compose an urgent dispatch to McMicken at Windsor informing him of the sordid conspiracy the vainglorious bastards had concocted. McMicken would take the appropriate action – on that one could depend …

Rourke felt his ears tingle. Although the day had been spring-like for the time of year, the night air was cool. Ice formed over puddles and a gentle snow had been falling for a good portion of the evening. He was almost there, however - a red brick row house adjoined to other red brick row houses that he and Molly discreetly cohabited since late summer. It wasn't the most fashionable part of town but then the rent was affordable and no-one asked questions.

At the door, Rourke reached deeply into the pocket of his ulster producing a key. He then threw down his cigar, crushed the glowing stub with the toe of his boot, wiped his crystallizing moustache with the back of his hand and stooped to insert the key into the lock.

At that moment a voice accosted him from behind, "Mr. Rourke."

The startled man dropped his key and swung around. Regaining his composure, he said, "Tis not polite to address a man from his backside in the wee hours of the sleeping city. Come out of the shadows where I might see you and state your business."

"You 'ave been condemned, Mr. Rourke," the stranger said, making no effort to show himself.

"Who are you? Show yourself man." Rourke took a couple of steps toward the muffled form a few feet away.

"Stand fast, Mr. Rourke."

Rourke hesitated. "Who are you?" he repeated, chagrined and frightened both at the same time. "Is it my wallet you be wanting?"

"I be a friend of liberty and your money will not save you."

"I – I do not understand. You know my name but …"

"Methinks you do. You 'ave been found out you 'ave, Mr. Rourke. We knows who you be an' what you're after."

Rourke squinted into the darkness, his thoughts racing wildly as he realized the import of those words. "No, wait!" he cried, raising his hands, taking a step back.

"'Tis much too late for that now Mr. Rourke – much too late."

"Noooo!" Rourke screamed as he heard the metallic click of a pistol being fully cocked.

Two shots rang out, the noise seemingly to explode in Rourke's head. He dropped to his knees, his bowler settling in the gutter after a brief jig across an ice patch. Convulsively, he attempted to pull himself up but fell backwards. He lay awkwardly, his right hand slightly extended, his left leg pinned beneath his torso, blood oozing from his mouth and other parts of his body.

The assassin stepped forward and for a few seconds looked down at the sprawled body and the pool of red forming on the snow. "Green above red, Mr. Rourke; Green above red." With that the executioner hurriedly crossed the street and disappeared into the darkness.

CHAPTER ONE
Ottawa, Late April

Popping an English peppermint into his mouth, John Alexander Macdonald rose from his desk, rubbed his hands vigorously and began pacing about his cluttered office in the Eastern Departmental Building. His tall, almost gaunt figure attached to a rather narrow face, punctuated by a large, spade-shaped nose and mass of curly black hair projected the image of a brooding, austere man – a man who could easily be provoked into a vindictive outburst. On closer inspection, however, the twinkling blue eyes and wide, generous mouth unveiled a softer, more charming personality – the kind that could just as well entice children to laughter and women to take second notice.

At that moment he was inclined neither to overt vindictiveness nor charm; his gut was roiling in unmitigated indigestion and he had just run out of his favourite relief – Beecham Pills for Bilious Nervous Disorders. The peppermints he was copiously consuming were clearly not an adequate substitute. Moreover, he was cold – bloody cold. His teeth chattered and his fingers were numb. Result: a mountain of correspondence was left unattended. How could one write sitting in an icebox! To think that two million dollars had been spent on the Parliament Buildings and not have adequate provisions for regulating the heat! Last month he had lamented that it was unbearably hot. Today, he wished he had worn a pair of long johns under his dark blue civil suit.

Under the shaft of silvery light that cut through the Gothic window, Macdonald paused, arched his back and cracked his knuckles; crunching

5

hard on the peppermint he resolutely returned to his desk. The warming confines of the Russell Hotel, tempting that it was, would have to wait for an hour or two; matters of state took precedence. Plopping down unceremoniously onto his Elizabethan chair, he once more stared ruefully at the stack of papers before him. Like the heating pipes of Parliament, the business of the United Province of Canada had taken on a decided chill.

First, there was the confederation stalemate. Stalemate courting disaster, thought Macdonald darkly. As things stood there was no way New Brunswick was going to proceed with union. And without New Brunswick the project was dead not to mention his ministry, which was inextricably tied to it.

Tilley, Tilley, Tilley ... The thought of New Brunswick's former premier raised Macdonald's temperature a degree or two. Tilley's normally well-oiled brain had rusted momentarily when he called an election without legislative approval of the Quebec Resolutions. Predictably, given the popular sentiment against the scheme, Tilley lost. That was back in March '65; now almost a year later the cursed anti-unionists were still firmly entrenched in Fredericton.

Feeling every measure of his fifty-one years, Macdonald could only hope that Her Majesty's government through the Lieutenant-Governor would apply enough pressure in the 'loyalist' province to force the diehard anti-confederates to acquiesce or resign. But judging from the correspondence he had been receiving the whole affair seemed tangled beyond comprehension and assurances from Tilley notwithstanding, Macdonald was deeply worried.

But that was only part of his troubles. As Attorney General of Canada West and Minister of Militia Affairs he had more immediate concerns. The American Civil War was over (thank God for that at least) but there were now within a cock's stride of the Canadian border, soldiers from the world's largest army milling about with not much to do. Among the boys in blue, moreover, were the Irish nationalists who belonged to the Fenian Brotherhood. Founded by militant radicals in 1858, the Brotherhood made no secret of its objective – to liberate Ireland from English rule and establish an independent republic. Until now the Brotherhood had done nothing of a revolutionary nature except engage in vehemently anti-British rhetoric. Indeed, Macdonald had considered it an 'Old World' problem. Suddenly, all that changed.

Across the border there were strident speeches exhorting battle-hardened Irish patriots to take up arms anew against England. Fenian 'generals' came to the fore advocating the seizure of British North America since it was evident that no uprising could be expected in Ireland. Ludicrous! And yet the idea struck a responsive chord at Fenian conventions in major Northern cities.

And where did the American government fit into this? Aye, where indeed. The answer bothered Macdonald. Washington, he believed, could not be trusted to stop them. The assassination of President Lincoln had left the administration weak and spiteful; in any case, it was not well disposed toward Britain nor its North American offspring what with the accumulated grievances against the mother country during four years of Civil War. Republican politicians, he knew, needed Irish votes and what better way to get them than to, at the very least, turn a blind eye while the Fenians organized for mayhem and murder.

The Fenians were planning an invasion, of that Macdonald was convinced. The evidence was in front of him in the form of reports from Gilbert McMicken, the diligent magistrate at Windsor who organized a detective force along the American border and who established as a result a wide network of informers and spies.

"Be at all times on the lookout," warned McMicken. "A desperate advance and attack will be made along the whole frontier on or about the seventeenth instant. You may depend that a struggle is at hand ..."

The seventeenth of course was the logical date. Indeed, a symbolic day for a march on Canada. It was St. Patrick's Day. What better opportunity to strike!

There was no reason to doubt McMicken's reports, especially since similar reports were flooding in from the British Minister in Washington and from British Consuls in the larger American cities.

What alarmed Macdonald most was McMicken's postscript attached to his latest intelligence. One of his men had been murdered in Buffalo. Although it was not certain that the Fenians were involved, McMicken confided that John Rourke at the time of his death had infiltrated the local Fenian hierarchy. What information he managed to obtain unfortunately perished with him; evidently he did not have a chance to pass it on. "We lost a good man," concluded McMicken. "I will keep in touch. Meanwhile, are there any further instructions?"

Macdonald leaned back and caressed his distinctively cleft chin. Buffalo, as he recalled from some of the earlier reports, was the home of the 69th Irish reserve and a hotbed of Fenian activity. But that was about all he knew … What were those scoundrels up to? It would be prudent Macdonald decided, to discuss the whole sordid affair with Thomas D'Arcy McGee and George-Étienne Cartier before issuing further instructions to McMicken. McGee, the government's Minister of Agriculture, knew more than most about the Fenians, having been in his more reckless past implicated in the Rebellions of '48 (from which he barely escaped to America disguised as a priest). George, in his capacity as Attorney General for Canada East, of course, would be vitally interested. Both were trusted friends, moreover, whose judgements Macdonald valued.

Scribbling a quick note to both, not at all sure whether the honourable gentlemen were still on Parliament Hill given the lateness of the hour, Macdonald was about to summon Hewitt Bernard, his private secretary, when three decisive raps permeated through the door.

A trifle annoyed since he had left instructions with Hewitt that he did not wish to be disturbed while catching up on his correspondence (apparently he had not been emphatic enough!), the lanky politician strode across the chamber and brusquely opened the door. Standing before him was the compact figure of George-Étienne Cartier.

Speak of the devil… "George! Mon Ami! What a pleasant surprise. You're not per chance a mind reader?"

"Dat power no-one 'as accused me of possessing," replied the nonplussed Montrealer. "Although," he added wryly, "at times I wish I could."

Macdonald ushered his colleague inside and hastily shut the door. It was colder in the corridor than in his office – if that were possible.

Cartier was one of Macdonald's closest political confidants and co-premier of the province from '57 to '62 (give or take a couple of days). A robust, energetic man with guile and tenacity, he was indispensable both to Macdonald and the grand ideal of a federated British North America. When he set his sights on a goal he was like a juggernaut meeting head on anyone who stood in his path. That was one of the characteristics Macdonald admired in the man. The other was Cartier's political acumen; like Macdonald, he practiced it with relentless aplomb. Despite their divergent personalities they worked well together and had grown fond of each other.

"Well, my inquiry was not entirely facetious," Macdonald chortled, "I was about to seek you out—"

"Moi aussi," replied Cartier, "I too 'ave a matter to discuss."

Macdonald nodded, suspecting as much. Unlike some of his other colleagues, Cartier was too officious a minister to simply drop in unannounced for no apparent reason.

The Montrealer eased himself into a brocaded armchair and ran a hand through his mass of brushed back silver hair. In the late afternoon light he appeared less than his sturdy self; the square face somehow sagged and his usually clear, keen eyes had an uncharacteristic dullness. Macdonald guessed that on closer inspection they would reveal a bloodshot tinge.

"You look a little haggard," Macdonald ventured, rolling his r's ever so slightly.

"Tired but nutting more," Cartier reassured his political cohort. "Late evenings …"

"Ah …" Macdonald was well aware that Cartier was an incurable work monger who often toiled into the small hours of the morning. "Don't overextend yourself unduly, *mon ami.* Save a little for the Rideau Club." He gave Cartier a sagacious wink.

"I always save a little for such soirées," Cartier mused. "As for my 'ealth … never felt better. *Et vous?"*

"Fine …fine …" Macdonald gave a dismissive wave of his hand. "My constitution is fit."

"Bon …" Cartier hesitated, clearing his throat before continuing. "Speaking of constitutions, I gather d'ere is still no news from Fredericton?"

"Is that what you wished to discuss?"

"Non," replied the French Canadian, "another matter entirely … but I keep 'oping of a breakthrough 'owever – some good news from Monsieur Tilley. The situation 'as left me most anxious. Our opponents in Quebec are gathering new strength from events in New Brunswick."

"I sympathize," Macdonald said with a touch of weariness, settling into his chair again. "But thus far there's nae a peep – though Tilley says the anti-unionists are squirming. 'Tis only a matter of time before that disagreeable government is forced out."

"*Mon Dieu.* How long can we wait! Wit' the opening of the legislature only a couple of months off and Monsieur Brown, for one, thundering against the ministry our position will become most precarious."

Macdonald sighed deeply. "Ah yes, Mr. Brown. If only he were more flexible ... There is something about our earnest Grit that prevents him from looking ahead—"

"Baboon," muttered Cartier. "A dangerous baboon!"

"I understand your anger George ..." And indeed he did. It was Cartier who had wooed the influential Grit leader into the government to form the highly touted Reform-Conservative coalition in an effort to forestall the crippling political deadlock in the United Canadas through a wider union of Her Majesty's North American colonies. This was done at some risk to Cartier politically since Brown, the avowed 'papist hater', was a liability in Quebec. That was back in '64. And, indeed, their relationship seemed to blossom. As Macdonald recalled, during the Parliamentary sessions of '65, Cartier rose frequently to Brown's defense when he was attacked by disgruntled Grits and Rouge alike. But Brown, upset over the ministry's trade policies and at odds with some of the government's leading members, resigned from the coalition at the end of '65. Since then, he had been hammering away at the government through his newspaper, the formidable *Toronto Globe*. Cartier, passionate, as he was dedicated to the cause of confederation, was not a forgiving soul.

"At least," Macdonald continued with a sardonic smirk, "he has not renounced confederation."

"Humph ..." Cartier snorted, "just the ministry. And over what! Petty politics! Because 'e didn't like dis or dat particular policy ... By attacking us, he attacks confederation. He undermines the possibility of its achievement."

"Nevertheless," Macdonald leaned forward, thrusting back with a well-practiced hand a lock of curly hair that had strayed out of place onto his high forehead. "I wouldn't worry too much about Mr. Brown. We will best him yet. Haven't we always?" He gave his friend a placating smile.

"I only 'ope you are right. Here we have constructed a Westminster in the wilderness worthy of *une grande nation* only to be endangered by ... by petty politics!" Cartier repeated again, shaking his massive head in disgust.

There was a pause. Cartier appeared spent momentarily from his minor tirade against Brown. Before he could rally for another verbal volley Macdonald diverted the subject.

"Aside from confederation there is another matter of lesser importance, though no less pressing at the moment, I wish to discuss with you."

"Oui, of course ..."

"The Fenians."

"Those lunatics. Wot have dey been up to?"

Macdonald snatched McMicken's latest report from atop a pile of papers and handed it to Cartier, who scanned it quickly picking out the pertinent passages.

"*Mon Dieu!* Wot madness!"

"Aye and mark my words, that fellow Rourke," he pointed at the report in Cartier's hands, "was murdered by them."

"*Sans doute.*"

"We will, of course, make preparations for any overt military action on their part, have the militia at the ready, reinforce the frontier – though God knows, that will be difficult – and fortify the constabulary in Toronto and Montreal for St. Patrick's Day parade. That, however, may not be enough. I fear we may be up against something much more sinister than some half-pissed Irishmen hell-bent on tasting English bullets."

"Because of M'sieu' Rourke's death?"

"Precisely. McMicken thinks he was on to some nefarious scheme the ruffians had hatched – perhaps as a diversionary tactic in advance of the seventeenth."

"'Hmm ... quite possible," Cartier said cautiously, giving the report one more studious survey before placing it on Macdonald's desk. "Dis group is capable of almost anyt'ing."

"Let's speculate for a moment." Macdonald suggested, his wide mouth tucking downward at the corners. "The Fenians would want to make a dramatic gesture – they are, after all, as most Irishmen, grandly theatrical. The question is what?"

"We must presume dat wotever their plans dey would aim for maximum military and political effectiveness dat will weaken our defences and undermine our morale. We therefore cannot rule out sabotage or – God forbid – assassination."

Macdonald nodded gravely. "Aye, those were my thoughts."

Cartier shifted uncomfortably and began drumming his fingers along the curved arm of the chair. "Wot of the American government?" he asked. "Our difficulties aside, dey would be in the best position to ascertain wot the Fenians are up to and take action. Perhaps if we conveyed our concerns ..."

"A point well taken," concurred Macdonald. "I will, of course, write to the British Minister in Washington and urge him to approach the Secretary of State on this matter. Unfortunately, in the past such undertakings have produced no satisfactory results. All reports to date reveal that the Yankees are not willing to take any official notice of a Fenian conspiracy until an actual breach of law has been committed. Nay, I'm afraid that the Republicans are not inclined to take any measures – *that* they have amply demonstrated."

" Den it is strictly up to M'sieur McMicken and his detectives?"

"I think so," replied Macdonald with a grunt as he got up from his chair and made his way to the window now well etched with growing frost. "Meanwhile," he continued, again rubbing his hands vigorously as he stared out onto the hard whiteness of the parliamentary grounds, "there is still the question of preventive measures ... Any suggestions as for what or whom we should provide extra security?"

"Well ..." Cartier said, "if dey are planning sabotage one obvious target would be the Parliament buildings. Most assuredly dere are many Fenians who, as a result of their Civil War experience, would possess an adequate knowledge of explosives—"

"Ah! Good thought – so they would," acknowledged the Minister of Militia. "And," he added, "it's been attempted before – in the mother country." Guy Fox's gunpowder plot sprang to mind. Fenians, he assumed, read history books too.

"Not to mention," Cartier appended with a touch of sarcasm, "our own Tories who, if you recall, in '49 burned down the seat of government in Montreal."

"Aye, I remember it only too well." Macdonald turned to his colleague with a bemused expression. "Different circumstances but an effective bonfire nonetheless. I'll make arrangements for the Civil Rifles to patrol the grounds 'til after St. Patrick's Day parade. They've had little to do since their transfer from Quebec City."

"Dat would be wise."

"Good, that's done then. Now, the odious possibility of an assassination attempt. I think we can agree on the most likely candidate—"

"Lord Monck," Cartier stated flatly

"Aye, Lord Monck. The Governor General must be considered the most likely target both as Her Majesty's representative and the fact that he is, after all, a prominent member of the Anglo-Irish landowning class. His personal safety for the next fortnight or so must be our highest priority."

"Agreed," Cartier said.

"Then I will send a dispatch to him in Montreal and—"

"I can save you dat trouble," Cartier interjected. "You 'ave much to preoccupy yourself with here in Ottawa and Montreal is my domain. I will be going back dere the day after tomorrow and I will see him on my arrival."

"Oh?"

"I promised to convey to him in some detail de state of repairs to Rideau Hall."

"Ah… And how is Government House coming along?"

"I 'ad a look at it last week. I believe the Governor General will be agreeably surprised. It should be ready for occupation by late April, early May."

Macdonald nodded. Rideau Hall was an eleven-room regency villa leased from a mason contractor. In order to make it suitable for the Governor General's permanent residence in the new capital, workmen were feverishly completing an additional two story wing.

"Be dat as it may," Cartier continued after his explanatory digression, "I will underscore to 'im and Lady Monck – who has no small influence on 'er husband – our concerns for his well-being. All measures will be taken to guard his person and staff from calamity."

"I leave it in your hands then," Macdonald said relieved that Cartier had assigned himself the task.

"*Bon.*"

Macdonald clasped his hands behind his back and returned to his chair. "Aside from the Governor General who else would be of special interest to the Fenians?"

Cartier pursed his lips and shrugged. "The other most likely candidate is M'sieu McGee. Has he not been raging about the seditious, pagan leprosy of the Fenians?"

"Aye, D'Arcy has been a strident detractor of his wild countrymen for some time ... Nothing like a converted rebel to give hard knocks for a former cause." Macdonald said this with some relish being fully aware that Cartier himself was once a fugitive for his support of Papineau. "He has been receiving threatening letters for over a year now ... Could they have actually put a death sentence on him?"

"A most unpredictable group of fanatics," Cartier said simply.

"Hmm ... I'll speak to D'Arcy first opportunity about watching his backside – at least 'til after St. Patty's day."

"Den again, we cannot be sure," Cartier thought aloud. "Anyone could be a target, perhaps even you – or other ministers of the government. It would be impossible to safeguard everybody. Wit'out more information ..." he trailed off.

"That's that then," Macdonald said. "I will instruct McMicken to give this matter top priority, drop everything and put his best men on it. Spare no expense. For the next ten days or so all concentration will be on ferreting out the Fenian plot! Buffalo is the key. Someone will talk – has talked – otherwise Mr. McMicken's man would be alive today. Besides," Macdonald suddenly smiled with convincing alacrity, "we do have one advantage."

"Oh ... and wot is dat?" Cartier gave the Minister of Militia a skeptical glance.

"We're dealing with Irishmen and I haven't met one who didn't have a loose tongue. Law of nature."

Cartier's face wrinkled into a shallow laugh. "You may wish to try out dat proposition on M'sieur McGee."

Their discussion on the Fenians apparently at an end, Cartier reached into his vest and extracted an Ingersoll pocket watch. Giving it a quick glance, he said, "Forgive me, the hour is late but I had hoped to talk to you about another matter altogether."

"By all means." Macdonald had forgotten that Cartier had originally come to his office with something of his own to discuss.

"It concerns the Grand Trunk Railway," the Montrealer said, pocketing his timepiece.

Inwardly, Macdonald groaned. He was not sure he was up to listening. The complicated machinations of the company and Cartier's vested interest both as Grand Trunk's solicitor and promoter guaranteed a long harangue on the company's difficulties and its enemies. There rarely was a politician who did not dabble in railways but Cartier seemed at times totally subsumed by the iron band. And as chairman of the Railway Committee of the United Province of Canada, he wielded immense power, which in his explosive, bullying way he did not hesitate to use. No doubt he had crunched some sensitive toes and now was approaching Macdonald to mend fences – probably in Toronto or Kingston.

"Undoubtedly, this will take some time?"

"*Oui* – a little," Cartier replied crossing his legs and settling down into his chair more comfortably.

Macdonald rose from his desk and made his way to the coat rack. "Well, *mon ami* – shall we go?" he said gathering up his Angola coat, Prince Teck scarf and stovepipe hat.

"Where?" asked the perplexed French Canadian.

"To the Russell House of course – for a good meal and some claret or perhaps burgundy. There you can proceed with your discourse on the unfolding fortunes of the Grand Trunk."

"*Bon.*" Cartier rose and proceeded to the door. "I will get my t'ings."

"Fine." *But be quick about it,* thought Macdonald, *I'm freezing and in dire need of some fortification. The correspondence will have to wait for another day.*

CHAPTER TWO
Washington

Mr. Michael McQuealy, unofficial Fenian 'ambassador', was primly attired in a long black suit (significantly stretched around his rather prominent belly), an expansive collar with a green bow tie attached, a light vest and a pair of striped trousers. His bearing of a proper gentleman not-withstanding, William H. Seward, Secretary of State for the United States, did not at all like him. If it weren't for the Irish vote the petulant little man would have never gotten through the door.

McQuealy possessed an irritating, high-pitched voice which, for the last half hour – since the beginning of his 'courtesy' call – had been shooting off in bursts like a Gatling gun. Moreover, it was difficult to get to the meat of what the Irishman was saying. He now was hinting broadly that the 'duly elected' Fenian executive had embarked on a 'dramatic' enterprise to liberate Ireland. Seward, making a Herculean effort to keep his impatience in check, finally decided to intervene and ferret out something of substance before he got lost in the rhetoric.

"What sort of enterprise?" The question caught the ambassador in mid-sentence. There was a pause while he adjusted his thought patterns.

"One of a delicate nature," he replied.

Seward gave him an icy stare. "Let me make this point clear Mr. McQuealy; if it is true that your organization intends to do violence to a neighbour country then this government cannot condone it."

The ruddy-cheeked, pug-nosed Irishman smiled from his teeth outward. "Our organization contemplates no breach of American law, nor would we be dragging the Union into any imbroglio for the sake of Ireland."

"Good ..." Seward said coldly. "Our neutrality laws cannot be violated."

"No, Mr. Secretary, I can appreciate that of course ... nevertheless," he quickly added, "perhaps bent a wee bit ..."

When silence greeted him, McQuealy delicately moistened his thick lips and continued, "Mr. Secretary, I need not remind you of the contributions made by Irish Americans during the Civil War ... I just express the hopes of all Irishmen that when the day of Ireland's trial comes, that America would not forget the many brave Irish hearts who marched to death beneath the starry banner."

"What is it that your organization wants?" Seward asked curtly.

"We need moral support and certain assurances."

"Such as?"

The Fenian ambassador tightened his mouth into a half smile and shifted ever so slightly in his chair. "If we were to obtain a ..." McQuealy hesitated searching for the proper word "a foothold, yes, a foothold on Canadian soil on which to plant the Irish flag – we should expect to be recognized by this government as belligerents."

Well, thought the Secretary of State, *finally a blunt statement of substance.* About as blunt as a diplomat could express it and he supposed McQuealy was a diplomat of sorts. "And your exact purpose?"

"Entirely compatible with American policy." The Irishman again flashed an insincere smile. "We wish to twist the British tail as it were ... and at the same time liberate Canadians from the tyranny of English rule."

"I see. How do you propose to do that?"

"Persuasion ... yes, by persuasion if possible and a wee bit of agitation for our cause. There are many Irishmen in the British North American colonies willing to take up the cause."

"Yes, I'm sure there are," replied Seward with no conviction registering in his voice.

"Mr. Secretary," McQuealy intoned in a confidential, conspiratorial manner. "It is no secret that the British North American colonies are weak, especially if their union scheme is prevented, which is one of our objectives.

It is also no secret that a strong body of American opinion, which your party cannot ignore, favours the annexation of Canadian territories. And although it may annoy those who do not support our cause, the hard truth is we can still deliver the votes. As you are aware – and no malice intended – an anti-Fenian stand would hurt the chances of Republican candidates come voting time … Many an Irish-American firmly believes that having helped preserve the Union a debt is owed them in their struggles to liberate their homeland."

"Yes, Mr. McQuealy, I am well aware of the sentiments you have expressed," *to the point of annoying redundancy,* thought Seward. "But in no way can this administration officially support your movement. It would be … incompatible with our interests at the moment."

"We are not ignorant of this fact, sir. I have requested this audience on behalf of the Brotherhood because of your government's pro-Irish sympathies in the past. And although approval cannot be publicly given, private assurances are sought that this administration will, at the very least, not hinder our Canada crusade. Again let me assure you, Mr. Secretary, that there are between one hundred and two hundred thousand souls in the colonies – all true sons of liberty – who have a burning desire to drive from this continent the last vestiges of British power and monarchial institutions."

"Indeed, Mr. Quealy, but I cannot ignore the fact that General Sweeny, whom you purport to represent, has publicly stated that with four hundred thousand dollars and an army of ten thousand men, an invasion of Canada is feasible."

"If it is the only way by which Britain could be forced to liberate Ireland," McQuealy admitted with a shrug.

"The United States cannot be seen to be party to such a scheme," Seward emphasized again.

"We are well aware of that Mr. Secretary."

Seward nodded. "Then Mr. McQuealy, perhaps we can reach an understanding…"

Later, after the porky ambassador had taken his leave, Seward mulled over McQuealy's not so cryptic words. He disliked the man even more after the meeting, likening him – no matter how unfairly – to the wretched conspirators that plotted and assassinated Lincoln nearly a year before and almost did the same to him. "Fanatics, crazed fanatics, all of them," he muttered darkly to himself as his left hand involuntarily traced the deep scar on his right cheek and throat, the aftermath of the knife blade used by his would-be killer on the same night that the President was slain. The Secretary of State's forehead formed frowning lines, puckering his tangled grey eyebrows and extending those lines downward to create a scowling face as his thoughts turned to the events on that fateful day ...

He was in bed, quite incapacitated recovering from a serious carriage accident – broken jaw, broken right arm and assorted scrapes and bruises. Served him right, he later mused with a wince of pain; instead of staying inside the cab he sat up front with the driver in order to enjoy one of David Swisher's fine cigars. Apparently, there was a collision of some sort – thrown clear and knocked senseless, he had no recollection of the details. His convalescence was becoming acutely uncomfortable, he recalled, not because of broken bones and internal injuries but because he couldn't smoke and was in the throes of withdrawal, dying for a long drag ...

At first, he did not hear the commotion outside his door. He wasn't aware of anything amiss until a large man in a long dark overcoat burst into his chamber, Bowie knife in hand.

What occurred, he subsequently learned, was that the assassin knocked on the front door. The address would not have been hard to find since the Sewards lived in a large, three storey home on fashionable Lafayette Square across the street from the White House. He pretended to be bringing a bottle of medicine ordered by his doctor. William Bell, the household's young black butler, was puzzled since the doctor had just been there less than an hour ago and he didn't recognize this man. He offered to take the medicine but was quickly rebuffed by this stranger who emphatically declared that it had to be delivered in person.

When Bell insisted that he had strict instructions not to disturb the Secretary of State, the visitor, already in a "high state of agitation", according to Bell's testimony, figured the ruse was up. He brushed by the startled butler and bound up the stairs to the second floor pulling out a revolver only to be confronted by Seward's son Frederick. Meanwhile, Bell's confusion turned into terror and he rushed out to the street yelling "Murder! Murder!"

Seward was relieved to learn that the gun misfired when the assassin aimed it at his son at the top of the stairs although the 'poor boy' sustained a frightful pistol whipping. In fact, Seward was grateful that everyone in his room survived, which included his daughter who got punched in the face and his attending army nurse cum bodyguard who suffered a slash across his forehead and forearm along with other nasty lacerations ...

Seward remembered the onslaught of panic that seized him when the looming shadow leapt onto his bed and began swinging the knife at his head and throat. How fortunate and ironic, he realized only much later in his less painful moments of recuperation, that he was wearing a metal and canvas splint on his jaw and a neck brace as a result of his previous accident, which saved him by deflecting the most lethal thrusts.

The assassin, Lewis Powell – or was it Lewis Paine – it now blurred in Seward's mind since the man employed a number of aliases, then hurriedly left thinking that he had accomplished his mission. But not before inflicting further injury. His other son, Augustus and a State Department messenger, who happened to enter the hallway on official business just as Powell/Paine ran out, were also stabbed. The messenger received the worst of it with wounds that crippled him for life.

In the hunt for Booth and his fellow conspirators, Seward's attacker, a Confederate soldier and member of the Confederate secret service, as it turned out, was apprehended three days later. He was duly tried, convicted and executed along with six others at the Washington Arsenal. The only good that came out of the whole affair, Seward rationalized, was that he could justifiably continue to smoke his cigars. After all, smoking had saved his life, albeit indirectly ...

Seward snapped back into focus from his brief, sordid reverie. McQuealy and the Fenians, with their network of secret societies were no better than those malevolent miscreants who planned the murder of Lincoln and himself. And yet, as crazy as their scheme was – to free Ireland from British rule by conquering the British colonies in America – it could have useful side benefits whether they succeeded or not. At the very least, it could prevent the 'confederation project' and the consolidation of British power to the north. Shifting uncomfortably in his chair, Seward summoned his secretary and chief but wholly informal advisor.

21

"You know, Baxter, there's method to these madmen."

"Sir?"

"They are cunningly attempting to exploit us and the American populace for their own political purposes."

Seward flipped open the file again that the bespectacled and spindly Baxter had placed on his desk for perusal in preparation for the meeting with the Fenian ambassador. The secretary stood by impassively, knowing that his shrewd boss had not yet said his piece on the matter.

"It says here that Thomas Sweeny is the Fenian Secretary of War," Seward turned over the page, "and that he still holds the rank of an officer in the U. S. army?"

"That is not quite correct, sir. According to our latest information Mr. Sweeny has been recently dismissed from the 16th U. S. infantry – for absence without leave."

Seward pursed his lips. "That so … What was his rank?"

"Colonel, I believe, sir."

"Hmm … calls himself a general now. What else do we know about him?"

Baxter furrowed his gullied face and thought for a few seconds. As chief purveyor of the official correspondence that reached the Secretary of State's office, he was exceptionally well-informed, especially since he had the unique ability to retain all that he read – an ability Seward found indispensable. "Colonel … General Sweeny is a bit of a peculiar fellow, sir. Came to this country as a child. The story goes that one day he fell overboard while the vessel he was on was in full motion. His rescue and recovery partook so much of the miraculous that ever since he believes that he is reserved for a certain destiny."

"What kind of destiny?"

"He is convinced, apparently, that his destiny is connected with the salvation of the homeland."

"Ireland."

"Yes, sir."

"And what about our ambassador, Mr. McQuealy?"

"There is practically no knowledge of him other than he is or was a solicitor in New York. He has no army record."

Seward closed the file and raised his head affixing pale eyes on a point somewhere just beyond Baxter's right shoulder. His heavy eyebrows wrinkled again into a familiar caustic scowl sharpened by shallow cheeks that gave way to deeply etched grooves on either side of his protuberant nose. At the corners of his mouth similar lines ran forth folding neatly into his jowls and a small, puckered chin. 'Uncle Billy' (as he was sometimes called in private by friend and foe alike) was annoyed at his own indecision regarding the Fenians. Were they to be encouraged, made use of or discarded as unpalatable miscreants? In themselves they were galling and yet … appealing as instruments to further the Union's grand design …

"Baxter, what do we know about the Fenians' current activities?"

"Sir, according to our intelligence there is no doubt that the Brotherhood is planning military action against the Canadians. When cannot be accurately determined but reports from Chicago, Detroit and Buffalo indicate substantial preparations."

"What are their chances of success? Any indications?"

"Not very good according to the most reliable information. They are not as highly organized as they claim. They need more men and arms and it is certain that the vast majority of Irish in the Canadian colonies do not support them."

"Hmm … would a sudden infusion of men and money alter the balance in their favour?"

"Highly doubtful and ill-advised sir, considering our neutrality laws—"

"Yes, yes I know Baxter." Seward gave a wave of his hand, which seemed to take in the whole room. "I don't mean it that way. We could channel funds from – ah – let's say the Secret Service Fund to promote the nonmilitary activities of the Fenians … All quite unofficial."

"Y–yes sir," Baxter bobbed his conspicuous Adam's apple up and down a couple of times as if swallowing distasteful medicine.

Seward ignored the look of apprehension that followed. "If these Fenians wish to use this government for their own ends, perhaps we can exploit them for ours."

"I'm not sure I understand, sir."

"Just a thought Baxter, just a thought. For now we will do nothing to encourage or discourage their plans. Let them carry on. With luck perhaps, just perhaps they will disrupt the colonies' proposed federation."

With a groan, Seward rose from his seat and reached for his ivory handled walking cane leaning against his desk. That he needed it was due to his carriage accident rather than the assassin's attack although Seward always thought of the latter when reaching for it. "As you know, Baxter, I have always thought that it is our manifest destiny to govern the whole of this continent. With the abrogation of the reciprocity treaty we have, I think, severely damaged the British Canadians economically. By disrupting their scheme for political union, the Fenians may well drive the colonials into our arms. Meanwhile, I want to know every move Sweeny, McQuealy and the Fenian War Consul make."

"Yes, sir."

Seward made his way to the door, Baxter a stride behind. "Have the Secret Service assign agents to the Fenian leadership," the Secretary of State said over his shoulder. "I want to know precisely what they are going to do before they do it. It may be in our interest to remain in the background or actively intervene in the course of events."

"Yes, sir."

"Oh and make sure they are not connected to Mr. Pinkerton's Detective Agency," Seward added with pronounced distaste bordering on distain.

Allan Pinkerton was the well-known detective who had been hired during the war by General George McClelland to ferret out and catch Confederate spies. He somehow evolved (wormed Seward believed) from a private contractor to 'Chief of Union Intelligence' and by the end of the war was passing himself off as 'Chief of the United States Secret Service' – all of which affronted Seward because it was presumptuous, over reaching and totally unofficial.

At the heart of Seward's dislike of the "snooty little Scotsman" was the influence he managed to attain not only over General McClelland but Lincoln himself. On those occasions when he met with Pinkerton to discuss security issues, Seward found him to be full of himself, exaggerating his contribution to the war effort, claiming to be on the verge of exposing all manner of dangerous assassins, spies and other "credible threats". In particular, Seward did not appreciate Pinkerton's front and centre handling of Lincoln's security which, far from a discreet service, inflated Pinkerton's image as the Union's indispensable detective, spy catcher and secret agent rolled into one.

This was especially true of his highly publicized role in preventing an assassination plot on the President's visit to Baltimore at the beginning of the war – the plot, the Secretary of State suspected, was more about the aggrandizement of Pinkerton and his agency than an actual threat to Lincoln. And where in the hell was he or his vaunted detectives when the President was assassinated and he himself and members of his family almost murdered?

"Sir?"

"We have competent agents that can operate under the cloak of secrecy without resorting to Pinkerton's detectives, do we not?"

"Yes, sir, of course." Baxter was somewhat puzzled by his boss's negative tone toward Pinkerton and his detectives who were often contracted to perform such clandestine work.

"Use them then to shadow key Fenian figures, and the agent assigned to McQuealy report directly here. Understood?"

"Yes, sir." Baxter blinked rapidly through his spectacles not fully comprehending. "I will put together a list of who we should be watching."

"Good, and have 'our man'" Seward emphasized again the possessive content of his request, "report directly here rather than go through the so called 'Chief of the Secret Service'.

"Yes, sir."

CHAPTER THREE
Windsor

Oliver Lynch was a handsome man, not quite six feet with a good carriage and military bearing. He possessed opaque blue eyes, a straight nose and firm chin. His regular features were given a masculine imperiousness by a neatly trimmed moustache and a shock of thick, curly brown hair that showed no sign of grey despite his mature forty-one years. The only flaw of note physically was his right ear, the top third of which was missing and now covered by a few, loose locks.

Lynch had long since reconciled himself to the missing piece of his anatomy and hardly thought about it at all except on a day like today. As he crisply made his way up the staircase of the Essex County Court House, his partial ear ached. It was always like that when the weather turned nasty. He placed his palm over the affected area and gently rubbed as he turned right and proceeded down the corridor to an imposing oak door. There, that was better; a little heat did the trick. He curtailed any further massaging, hauled open the door and stepped inside.

A cherubic, acne-faced clerk straightened himself from a wooden filing cabinet on the far side of the office and tugged nervously at the corners of his rather threadbare blue suit. "Good morning, sir," he chirped, hastily closing the cabinet drawer.

"And a pleasant morning to you – Mr. Spense, is it?" Lynch replied.

"Why yes, you must be Mr. Lynch."

"Quite correct. Your memory is as good as mine."

"I have the advantage, sir. Your name is in the appointment ledger." Spense cast a glance at a large, black book on a desk opposite the cabinet.

Lynch smiled. He had met Mr. Spense briefly the last time he visited the court house some four months ago. It always surprised people that he could remember their names even after the most perfunctory parley. Lynch, however, made it a mental habit to register names with faces. Spense had the kind of flushed, nervous face that made an impact, albeit a negative one. "Well, it's good to know that I'm expected."

"Indeed, you are."

"I hope that I have not kept Mr. McMicken waiting," Lynch said shedding his overcoat and placing his gloves into his bowler already in hand.

"Right on time, sir. Here, allow me." The plump clerk took the apparel still dripping from the snow and hung the outer garment on a nearby coat tree that wobbled precariously under the weight. The hat replete with the gloves was deposited on top of the cabinet. "Foul weather out there."

"A real mess," declared Lynch smoothing his collar and straightening his tie. "Can't say as I appreciate all this snow."

"'Tis a bit inconvenient, especially for travel I'd imagine." Spense led Lynch toward the door to an inner chamber.

"Treacherous both for man and beast to be sure."

"Travel far?" the clerk inquired casually.

"No, not far – Detroit."

"Ah, Detroit. A nest of Fenian activity I understand. I trust your mission was satisfactorily concluded?" he asked with a smile that seemed to Lynch too solicitous by half.

"Yes, it was an interesting visit," Lynch replied with no further elaboration.

"Well then ..." There was a brief hesitant pause as Spense realized that there would be no further conversation. He knocked on the door, listened for an affirmative response, opened it and announced the arrival of Lynch. After showing the visitor through, he closed the door quietly behind him.

Lynch found Gilbert McMicken seated behind a large mahogany-topped desk. Attired in his heavy, black, broadcloth suit, the bearded Chief of the Canadian Secret Service looked every inch the punctilious magistrate. His long, deeply lined face bespoke of his fifty-three years, giving the impression of a serious if not stern man. Lynch did not know McMicken well; their meetings were infrequent and strictly business.

Making a cursory survey of the surroundings Lynch noted that the room was the epitome of function without a token of personal effects. The most obvious evidence of McMicken's interests, Lynch supposed, were the thick roles of legal books prominently displayed on sturdy shelves behind the Chief of Detectives: Russell on Crimes, Addison on Torts and Contracts, Bullen and Leakes on Precedents, Taylor on Evidence, Roscoe's Criminal Evidence, Smith's Equity Jurisprudence and of course, the latest statutes.

Nothing had changed since his last visitation some weeks before. Then too McMicken sat in the same position, wearing, as far as he could tell, the same sombre suit, concentrating on a neat pile of papers before him. He'd make an excellent undertaker, Lynch decided.

"Mr. Lynch," McMicken half rose from his chair and they shook hands. "So glad to see you. Do sit down." He motioned to a stately leather chair. "Thank you for your promptness."

Lynch took his seat, careful to sidestep the porcelain spittoon directly in front of the massive desk.

"Now then," McMicken carefully set aside a piece of correspondence and placed his pen delicately into the holder. "I must apologize for my abrupt summons. I hope it hasn't disrupted unduly your activities in Detroit?"

"Not at all," said Lynch. "I have pretty well completed my assignment there."

In fact, his assignment had proved a rather tedious affair and he was glad it was at an end. As an undercover agent for the British Consul he was to win the confidence of a certain wealthy dry goods merchant who purportedly was in the inner circle of Detroit's Fenian organization. The merchant, Lynch soon ascertained, partook in more bravado than action and he learned all he needed to know and then some about the impetuous but generally harmless fellow from his amorous but decidedly plain wife. Having just barely fended off her advances, Lynch welcomed the opportunity to escape back into Canada.

"Anything of significance to report?" McMicken asked, leaning back in his chair.

"A bit of a dead end sir. Our Fenian, Mr. Murphy, proved more a talker than a doer and the stories about his acquiring two thousand Mississippi rifles for the cause were a figment of his imagination – verbal bluster that amounted to nothing."

"And you are certain of this?"

"Yes sir, my information came from a highly placed… intimate source," Lynch replied sombrely, shuddering inwardly at the thought of Mrs. Murphy's earnest toils at seduction.

"Well, then, never mind writing a full report. I have another, undoubtedly more challenging matter that requires an agent of your talent and experience." McMicken gave the younger man a purposeful stare.

"I'm at the disposal of Her Majesty's service." Lynch said, a note of curiosity in his voice.

Lynch had not started out as a professional spy but it sort of grew on him. With the outbreak of civil war in the Republic, the provincial authorities needed men to collect intelligence on both Union and Confederate agents who were hatching plots and counter plots against each other with reckless abandon using Canada as their base. Lynch's experience with the Toronto constabulary held him in good stead when he offered his services.

Indeed, prior to the establishment of Mr. McMicken's network of secret agents, it was the Toronto constabulary that essentially performed the task. With the Civil War approaching its zenith it became a more onerous task with multiple dimensions, from keeping track of U. S. army recruiting agents' nefarious efforts to entice British Army soldiers stationed in the provinces to desert and join the Union Army to monitoring the increasing activities of Confederate and Union spies and their operations in the Canadas, especially as the fortunes of the South started to wane.

Nor was it limited to Canadian soil. Toronto police agents, under cover of occupations that required travel across the border, were sent on missions to northern American cities – mostly Buffalo, Chicago, Detroit and New York – where they engaged in their own clandestine work, meeting with informers and gathering intelligence on various schemes and activities as they pertained to the British Colonies. Invariably, these reports landed on the desk of the Chief Constable in Toronto. As one of the charter constables within the force with a license to spy, Lynch was among the most experienced by the time he was 'reassigned' to McMicken's ensemble of secret operatives.

For a couple of years he had led a far from dull life, frequenting all the better class of hotels in both Upper and Lower Canada, eavesdropping on Northerners and Southerners alike in order to keep abreast of their schemes. In accordance with his instructions he was to use his 'utmost diligence and judgement to find out any attempt to disturb the public peace, the existence of any plot, conspiracy or organization, whereby the peace would be endangered, the Queen's Majesty insulted or her proclamation of neutrality infringed.' More often than not, the trick was to separate the kernel from the chaff and mistakes were made.

On one occasion in one of Montreal's finer hotels, he struck up a friendly game of billiards with a mildly deranged American who claimed to be an actor. During the course of the evening the man, John Wilkes Booth, avowed that he would 'cook President Lincoln's goose.' Lynch thought nothing of it at the time – merely the ramblings of an unbalanced and quite intoxicated individual. Nevertheless, he made a brief register of it in his report. Three weeks later John Wilkes Booth fatally shot the President at Ford's Theatre in Washington. Lynch could hardly blame himself or McMicken for that matter – such threats were common enough to be sure.

No doubt Union spies, who no less than Confederate agents frequented these hotels, had written similar reports. In fact, Lynch read shortly after Lincoln's assassination that a particularly industrious reporter for the *New York Tribune* dispatched a chilling story from Montreal outlining a plot to murder Lincoln articulated by Booth to his Confederate followers (or anyone who cared to eavesdrop apparently) in the bar room of the St. Lawrence Hall Hotel. Booth even bragged that he had opened an 'operational account' at the Ontario Bank of Montreal for such a purpose just down the street from the hotel! The story was never printed because the *Tribune*'s editor believed that respectable papers did not publish unsubstantiated and sensationalist journalism.

Not that it really mattered. Reports, Lynch knew, had come in from other McMicken agents of Booth's assassination boasts in the Queen's Hotel in Toronto and at a Confederate sympathizers meeting in Niagara Falls. He rightly did not know if McMicken took any action or even noted it and he never asked.

Such then was the nature of his work. The advent of the Fenian menace ensured that his unusual occupation would continue to thrive. Despite its hazards, Lynch found he savoured his job although a constable's monthly pay plus expenses was hardly an extravagant salary.

McMicken's chair squeaked as he shifted his weight. "Your Irish lilt is still intact I hope?"

Lynch straightened in his seat. "My Irish lilt?"

McMicken smiled. "It won't be necessary to dip too low in your vocabulary – just enough to be convincing."

Perhaps the older man has a sense of humour after all, mused Lynch. "That I can manage."

The Chief of Detectives nodded. "Fair enough then. I shall get to the point. Now then, as you are aware, for some time we have been watching the Fenian Brotherhood. Of late, a fierce debate has raged among their ranks on how to proceed to liberating their homeland, with one faction preaching the original gospel of revolution in Ireland and another faction led by Messrs. Roberts and Sweeny advocating an invasion of Her Majesty's North American Colonies. The logic of such a scheme escapes me but there it is." McMicken shrugged.

"But it is this latter group in particular that has been the object of our surveillance. They're a dangerous lot to be sure – equipped with arms and in some cases encouraged by certain Yankee politicians who have malicious designs on our land and who depend upon the Irish vote. We have reason to believe that the Roberts/Sweeny faction is preparing an attack along our borders come the seventeenth. For that we will be on the alert. However, prior to such an invasion in all probability sabotage or assassination is planned."

"An act of extremism?"

"We think so – perhaps even a key element on which the larger attack depends. To explain further, one of our agents, Mr. John Rourke – ah, you by chance didn't know him?"

"No, sir."

"Yes, well, Mr. Rourke," McMicken repeated, "had infiltrated an extremely active wing of the Brotherhood in Buffalo. We don't know how well he became acquainted with the leader, a William O'Halloran – an undertaker who is suspected of using coffins to smuggle arms and other military accoutrements and store them on his premises. But, our man apparently did discover that an action of extremism, as you aptly put it, was afoot. Precisely by whom, where or who the intended victim or victims are is still a mystery. You see, Mr. Lynch, Mr. Rourke was murdered – gunned down on a public street," McMicken emphasized with a quiver of vehemence, "before he could gather that information or if he did before he could relay it here."

"I see," Lynch said suddenly feeling chilled. What was it with Americans and guns, he mused darkly, Irish or otherwise. Although no stranger to the occasional violence, he much preferred to play the spy game with polite words and clever deception rather than guns. McMicken's detectives were not allowed to bear arms but Lynch was willing to make an exception if the circumstances warranted it.

"You said Buffalo?"

"Yes, you are not well known in Buffalo, are you?"

"No, no. I've only been there once or twice."

"Good." McMicken seemed relieved. "Because that is your next destination."

"Mr. Rourke, he was betrayed then?"

McMicken stroked his beard and frowned. "That's a possibility although I don't see how. Any intelligence he obtained was sent directly to me. No, more likely Mr. Rourke, a careful enough man mind you, may have slipped and let his guard down and they got on to him in some way."

"Easy enough to do, I suppose." Lynch did not sound entirely convinced.

"It's a nasty business all right. Your assignment is to pick up from Mr. Rourke and find out the exact nature of the Fenian plot."

"A tall order, sir," Lynch grimaced.

"I realize that, Mr. Lynch. But I have received instructions from the Attorney General that I put my most competent agent on it. You are the best available at the moment."

"Thank you for the confidence." Lynch was not at all sure he deserved or necessarily wanted such a distinction.

"Yes, well sorry to place you in such a spot. The time is too short to provide you with adequate backup in Buffalo, I'm afraid. But you may not be entirely alone."

"Oh?"

"On your arrival you will proceed directly to a house on Washington Street where a Miss Molly Mahone resides."

"Molly Mahone?"

"Yes. She ... er ... lived with Mr. Rourke. It was she who telegraphed me about Mr. Rourke's death. She may have shared his confidence and perhaps is in a position to provide you with useful information on his activities or at least point you in the right direction.

"Oh and one other matter concerning Miss Mahone," McMicken stroked his beard before clearing his throat, "Mr. Rourke had wanted some assurance that we would provide for her should he meet some ... misadventure in our employ. He intended to marry her or so he led me to believe. While our budget is tight," McMicken's face soured in expression, "I am inclined to bend the rules to a degree in this case and award some kind of settlement or stipend ..." The spy master trailed off giving Lynch a sombre look as if to underline the seriousness of his statement. "I said that I would endeavour to make such suitable arrangements and wish to be fair but not, well I do not wish to be a spendthrift," he added.

Lynch nodded.

"In any case," McMicken continued "could you possibly make an assessment as best you can in regards to her present circumstance and future prospects?"

"I will make discreet enquires and ascertain her situation," Lynch said matter-of-factly. The request seemed straight forward enough.

"Good! Meanwhile, you'll be needing this." McMicken pulled out a drawer and took out a substantive file. "In here you will find the background material on O'Halloran and some other notable Fenian rascals in Buffalo, along with the reports Mr. Rourke supplied me. Miss Mahone's address is also contained therein. Read it thoroughly and make haste to Buffalo. You have a little over ten days or so."

Lynch took the file gingerly. "I shall return this within two hours."

"Very well. We'll discuss it further then but keep any notes you wish to make in a safe place."

"I shall commit what I need to memory."

"Excellent. You can use the Jury Chamber next to this office as your reading room if you like. I'll see that Mr. Spense serves some tea."

CHAPTER FOUR
New York City

Benjamin Matthews saw his quarry turn the corner and disappear into the mid-afternoon crowd. "Damn!" he cursed, flipping his half-smoked cheroot into the gutter. Tailing this hombre wasn't easy; for about the tenth time he wished he were back in Texas riding the range instead of soaking his boots in the slush and snow following some Irish arsehole.

Pushing down firmly on his brown, weather-worn Stetson, Matthews increased his stride. It just wouldn't do to lose the man now; his employer would be most upset and the U. S. government could be an ornery critter.

Even as Matthews acted through his "Texan" persona, he knew that it was a misnomer. This included his figure of speech and the Stetson planted on top of his handsome, square-jawed head. Not that he was a fake or postulant. The Stetson and his cultivated image had genuine meaning; he thought himself as a Texan. At the same time, like so many other fervent Texans, he was born and bred elsewhere – in his case Tennessee.

Mathew's father, an ambitious, enterprising man owned a lumber mill in eastern Tennessee. After the sudden death of his wife, he sought to take care of his two sons in a fair and equitable manner, especially since his own health was failing. He managed to get the youngest, Benjamin – the one who preferred horses and adventure over the lumber business – into West Point. It took some doing and the recommendation of the local congressman but it was only reasonable compensation since his oldest, Joshua, a "chip off the old block," would inherit the mill.

The old man died while Benjamin was in his second year at West Point and his brother saw the family business destroyed in the Civil War. As far as Matthews knew, Joshua simply disappeared into the mass of countless ex-Confederates struggling for a place during the so-called 'reconstruction period." Matthews did not rightly know where Joshua had gotten to or if he was still alive. If he was, Matthews hoped that someday soon, they would meet and reconcile for like so many other siblings, the conflict had left them on opposing sides. Matthews was certain that his hard-nosed, 'patriotic' father would have totally disowned him had he lived to see his son on the side of the Union.

Matthews wasn't the brightest student who had entered the hallowed halls of the military academy but he showed leadership promise and impressed his instructors – one in particular as it turned out. As it was, he graduated twenty-eighth in his class of thirty-nine a few days after his twenty-second birthday. That was 1854, the same year he was commissioned brevet second lieutenant and stationed at Jefferson Barracks, near St. Louis, Missouri. It was also the year he had to leave town over an 'affair of the heart' resulting in a reassignment (to put it charitably) to the Western frontier.

Tall and muscular, forming a fine figure in uniform, Matthews had an enviable reputation at West Point as a bit of a dandy among the fairer sex – a reputation he found no compelling reason to ameliorate. His short courtship of one Annabelle Dixon almost proved career, if not life, ending. During their torrid trysts she failed to mention that she was married!

The husband in question was quite prominent with means and influence; he was also suspicious of his wife's sudden disappearances and had her followed. One night in a dark alley, Matthews was beset by three burley rogues who proceeded to give him a proper beating. He would have acquitted himself better had he not been full of bourbon. At the end, while he lay retching out sour mash, the message was delivered. Leave town or be dead.

The message was fully received; by the end of the year he was out in Texas, a second lieutenant in the Mounted Rifles fighting the Comanche. A few skirmishes and close calls later where his horsemanship and shrewd sense of survival prevailed, he was promoted to first lieutenant.

After three years or so, Matthews considered himself a true Texan and when the Indian Wars were over, thought that he might settle down – once he found the right lady. In the meantime, he met none other than the famed general himself turned politician – Sam Houston. The man who had outwitted Antonio Lopez de Santa Anna thus creating the Republic of Texas, was well past his prime but still, if no longer quite the womanizer, liked his drink. On occasion, Matthews delivered dispatches to Governor Houston and idly chatted with the hero of the Republic. Houston, Matthews discovered, was also from eastern Tennessee originally and judging from their conversations might have met his father while campaigning for office there.

"So here you are," he said, "a fine West Point officer doing your daddy proud."

Matthews had not mentioned that his old man had died many years before.

"Yes, sir."

"Tell you what, every once in a while I need to disappear from all this," he waved his arms around his cluttered office. "You know what I mean," he gave Matthews a conspiratorial wink. "There's a particular establishment I visit – stocks the best whiskey in Texas – works wonders for the ole leg here that acts up sometimes."

Matthews nodded. Houston had his ankle shattered during the defeat of Santa Anna in the Battle of San Jacinto.

"Well, I take a small entourage with me to protect my backside while I'm on my back," he laughed. "And it so happens I'm a man short – poor bastard went and got his self shot. I should look into that ..." he trailed off. "I'm inviting you to take his place. The whiskey is the best in the territory and the ladies almost as good. You're not married are you?"

"No, sir."

"Good." Houston grinned. "There'll be time for both. You're not a gambler are you?"

"Try not to."

"Never mind, that's your business. Just don't want you to lose your shirt as well as your breeches. What'd you say, every couple of weeks or so. Call it extra duty detail!"

"It would be an honour, sir."

The young lieutenant didn't know it at the time but his acquaintance with Houston profoundly influenced his future course of action. When the Civil War erupted in April, 1861, he struggled with which side he should support. The debate came down to a matter of conscience on the one hand and history on the other. For Matthews, slavery, on the occasions when he thought about it, didn't strike him as particularly moral or just as practiced by the ebony hearted slave holders. To argue otherwise, one had to be willfully blind. However, he was born and raised in a Confederate state and nurtured sentiments that compelled him to look the other way and put away his conscience. In either case, it hardly seemed a reason to be marching off to war.

What swung him over to the Union position was Sam Houston. Not that the Governor endorsed the North, far from it. He argued for slave property rights and had a dislike for Lincoln, likening his administration to a bad batch of whiskey. Nevertheless, he considered secession a rash course of action that would lead to the ruin of the South.

"If you want to get sticky about it," he explained while on one of his 'medicinal sojourns', "it's just plain unconstitutional and even if it were somehow legal, let me tell you what's coming," he took a large gulp of what he called the 'good stuff' from his glass and leaned forward in his chair. "Hundreds of thousands will die, land and properties will lay in ruins, countless millions of the treasury will be spent and the Confederacy, even if it wins independence, will be devastated. More likely though, it will lose. The North is determined to preserve this Union and I fear, like a mighty avalanche will overwhelm the South."

So said Houston and paid the price. The vast majority of Texans were pro-Confederate and when he refused to take the oath of allegiance and join the Confederate states, a special secession council deposed him as Governor of Texas in the first days of March, '61.

Matthews thought that horribly wrong but did not give way to his feelings. To openly admit that one supported the Union became dangerous after the secession vote with reports of summary executions and lynching in some counties for those who objected to Texas joining the Confederacy. Despite grave reservations and an overpowering feeling of foreboding, he marched off with over seventy thousand other Texans to serve in the Confederate Army. In his case as an officer in the Texas Brigade lead by a wily and experienced old West Point graduate, John Bell Hood.

In all probability, Matthews would have served in 'Hood's Brigade' to the bitter end come what may; he had, after all, the rank of lieutenant in the cavalry, was respected by those under him and felt duty bound not to let them down. Fate, however, intervened in June, '62 in what was dubbed the Seven Days Campaign. Hood's Brigade fought their way to Virginia where, integrated into Robert E. Lee's Army, they found themselves defending Richmond. On June 25, at a place named Oak Ridge in what proved one of a number of bloody engagements, Matthews' horse was either shot or stumbled and fell; he was thrown clear and rendered unconscious when he hit the ground. He woke up hours later battered, bruised, his ears ringing and a prisoner – lucky, in fact, not to have been executed on the spot he was found.

He might have still suffered that fate after interrogation had not his former instructor at West Point been the interrogator, James "Bird Eye" Saunders – Bird Eye because he had that unblinking direct look when he lectured (or interrogated as it turned out) – quite intimidating and unnerving at the same time.

While at West Point, Saunders not normally prone to praise, once confided to Matthews that he had a future with the U. S. Army. This occurred after a particular field exercise where Matthews drew the short straw as team leader for a group of cadets who managed to outflank a similar group of more senior classmates by means of bluff and subterfuge rather than an actual mock attack. Saunders thought that "clever" and despite Matthews' middle of the class academic record, saw in the young cadet command qualities – at least the potential. For Saunders, leadership was all about audacity tempered with prudence and rational thought.

Saunders listened with a measure of sympathy to Matthews' evolving chain of events since West Point including his reluctant journey with the Hood Brigade across the Mississippi River. He understood when Matthews explained that despite his reservations about the Confederate cause, he was duty bound not to betray and desert those with whom he marched.

"And what about now?" Saunders asked, staring fiercely at him.

"Sir?"

"I'm asking you that given your present circumstances do you still feel duty bound. Answer carefully," he intoned in a lower voice. "If you found yourself released from any further obligations to your fellow Confederates there may be an opportunity to rescue you from your circumstances and make use of your training and talents for the unity of the country."

For his part, Matthews indicated quite truthfully that he had no desire to return to his unit or any Confederate army and that he believed that Sam Houston's predictions were indeed prophetic. It all depended, it seemed, on whether Saunders believed him or not and how well he was disposed to give Matthews a chance at proving himself trustworthy. In his heart of hearts, Matthews thought that he would end up a prisoner in some hell hole for the rest of the conflict fighting for survival.

It wasn't until the third 'interrogation' session that Matthews got an indication of his fate. "If we get out of here alive," the West Point professor informed him while they sat huddled in a large tent, the sounds of creaking supply wagons and snorting horses drowning out the more distant rumbles of war, "you will be transported to Washington. There, you will give Major General Joseph Hooker a letter of introduction that I will write. You possess, I will tell him, useful talents that the Union can use but make no mistake, I will leave your dispossession to his discretion."

Thus, a couple of harrowing months later, having escaped both the Confederate offensive and looming 'prisoner of war' status, Matthews appeared in front of "Fighting Joe" Hooker, who, he learned had a reputation mirroring Sam Houston's when it came to barrooms and brothels. Unlike Houston, though, Hooker was known to be more "reckless" in his military tactics. Matthews expected to be demoted and put out in the field to serve in whatever cannon fodder capacity Hooker thought fit. The tough Major General surprised him.

"According to General Saunders, you are just the sort I'm supposed to be looking for. Since you prefer not to shoot Confederates," he said with a heavy dose of sarcasm bordering on malice, "then this job should suit you perfectly. If you're good and bring results you'll survive; if you fool with me or are not up to the task, you will, no doubt, be found out and executed either by the Confederates or by me." Hooker smiled exposing his yellowed teeth. "Do you understand?"

"Yes, sir."

"Right." Hooker got up from his makeshift desk, which was camped under yet another army tent. He gazed down, shuffled some papers around and found the sheet he was seeking. Picking it up, he continued without preamble: "A Bureau of Military Information has been established – an intelligence gathering unit that apparently you would be suited for. About one hundred agents are needed whose job it will be to ferret out the enemy's plans, fortifications, troop and equipment movements and the like. I'm assigning you to a small group in this Bureau that would spy on their spies and report to the federal government – more precisely to the Secretary of State. It's sixty dollars per month plus expenses with a re-evaluation of your worth at the end of the year and," Hooker added, "you better be worth it!"

"Yes, sir."

"Report to Colonel Sharpe, he'll get you started."

Officially Matthews began his career as a spy in early '63 and here he was three years later, still with his Texan persona far from the Lone Star State and still spying, not on Confederates but on oddities, entrails of the war like McQuealy and his Fenian associates.

"How the hell did I get into this?" he muttered to himself, reaching the point he last saw the elusive Mr. McQuealy. Squinting, he again surveyed the plethora of bundled up humanity about the streets. Although the sun had a blinding brilliance, it was a bitterly cold day that pricked the toes, stunned the cheeks and numbed his hands, which he periodically stuffed into the pockets of his over-sized coat. *No wonder no one loitered,* he thought, *a panhandler could freeze his nuts off.*

Chagrined, Matthews was almost ready to concede that McQuealy had given him the slip (inadvertently of course, since McQuealy, Matthews was positive, didn't know that he had been followed). Then, as if providence had once more adopted him, he spotted a rather bulky madame with an unbecoming fedora rushing by an equally bulky little man as he passed under a lamp post at the intersection of Broadway and Canol Street. McQuealy tipped his hat and continued walking briskly down Broadway. Matthews ran up a few yards, aligned himself with the back of McQuealy's head and kept pace.

Another close call. Shit and amen in that order; that's the third time in two days that he almost lost him. The first was in Washington. With amazing agility the Irishman had disappeared behind a 4-4-0 locomotive and Matthews had to make a frantic coach-to-coach search to be sure that he had indeed gotten on the New York bound train. Then, at the train station in New York, Matthews had difficulty procuring a cabbie while McQuealy's carriage trotted away. He was forced to order a gentleman and his lady off another, produce his credentials and threaten the driver with official reprisals before the dour Scotsman would spurn his horse to give chase. And now here, not more than five minutes after the Irishman had alighted from his cab! Matthews promised himself to be less cautious and follow more closely.

Federal agent Matthews did not relish this part of his job. Pursuing extravagant crazy men to unravel what they were up to while remaining incognito was proving an uphill task. He wondered if the other agents were having as much fun keeping tabs on their charges as he had on this McQuealy character. It figured that McQuealy was in New York though. Matthews recalled from his briefing that Robert's Fenian headquarters was here, somewhere on Broadway in fact.

Suddenly, the Irishman stopped as if to get his bearings and cast a glance backwards. Matthews lowered his head and pulled up his coat collar shortening his stride a bit. An icy blast of wind speared the agent as he crossed an alley between two brick edifices. *Should have stayed with the Confederates*, he thought, shivering, *it was warmer down there.* He slowed his pace to a shuffle and let his eyes settle momentarily on a double-spring skirt hoop prominently displayed in a shop window.

McQuealy, meanwhile, seemed to reorient himself to his surroundings and hurriedly crossed the wide thoroughfare. He entered a substantial grey stone building with a piazza to three storeys. Matthews followed suit, pausing long enough to read the sign above the door: Forbes Hall.

Oh hell! Matthew cursed silently. Before him was seated a motley collection of three hundred or so men listening to a diminutive man giving some sort of animated lecture. He nervously tried to locate his quarry.

"To the friends of Irish independence," boomed the voice from a raised platform, "the Fenian Brotherhood of America, which for the last seven years has been preparing to strike a blow for Ireland's freedom, is now gathering up its energies for the conflict."

There was clapping and cheers from the assembled. The speaker raised his arms obviously delighted that his discourse was arousing the audience.

"I've wandered into a bloody Fenian meeting!" muttered the startled agent still attempting to locate McQuealy.

"A veteran Irish officer of unsullied honour and a brilliant military reputation who has spent eighteen years in the military service of these United States has volunteered his services to lead our brave men who are now about to be marshalled under the green flag of Ireland."

More clapping and cheers. *That'd be General Thomas Sweeny,* thought Matthews again recalling the briefing he had received in drawing McQuealy as his assignment. He moved forward skirting the periphery of the assemblage. Out of the corner of his eye he spied McQuealy, angling his way toward the stage.

Not much was known about McQuealy, Matthews realized. He appeared to be the Fenian money man and travelling ambassador, hobnobbing with the politicians. Indeed, Matthews reckoned that's why he was shadowing him. The government was interested in the doings of a mysterious man who seemed to know his way along the corridors of power.

"The time for action has arrived." The speaker seemed to be reaching a full crescendo. "The plans of action are perfected and all that is now required are arms to place in the hands of the thousands of brave men who are today ready to take to the field and fight for their country's liberation. Men of Ireland!" The voice lifted yet another degree. "The eyes of the world are upon you. The story of your wrongs has long furnished an eloquent theme for your orators and your poets and the suffering and denigration to which a despotic power has subjected your country have elicited the sympathy of all people who love liberty—"

More cheers erupted and hats were thrown in the air. *Whoever he is he knows how to talk,* decided the agent, edging up to a wooden support while keeping his eyes glued to the back of McQuealy's head. His vision was now unobstructed taking in the full measure of the Irishman who had sedately seated himself in the front row.

"An opportunity is now yours of showing that your professed love of country is sincere and that you are ready to offer every aid consistent within your means for the salvation of your native land." It was a recruiting and solicitation of funds meeting, Matthews surmised. Similar meetings had been held throughout the Northern states where the Irish were predominant.

"The men who are engaged in this movement are determined to fight. The Irish name and race will be redeemed from the humiliation which for centuries rested upon them." The silver tongue was becoming a little hoarse;

he paused and fortified himself from a glass of water set beside the podium, or more likely gin, speculated Matthews.

"Our American fellow citizens we feel assured, will not be deaf to the call which the Fenian Brotherhood of America now make on them to aid the work of winning Irish independence. The Irishmen of America have manifested the most loyal devotion to this Republic and died for the preservation of American liberties. All we await is the implements of warfare: to procure those, money is required."

The feverish appeal continued for a few moments longer and then another orator was announced. In the interval, McQuealy rose from his seat and conferred with two men briefly before proceeding behind the raised stage and through a back door.

"Now what?" Matthews mouthed softly to himself instinctively feeling for the slight bulge his trusted Smith and Wesson made under the heavy winter coat. "Looks like I'm about to find out."

As inconspicuously as possible, Matthews meandered his way around the stage, hoping that McQuealy had gone to meet someone or relieve himself and not out an exit. Taking a rapid sweep of those around him it appeared that he had not attracted any undue attention. Again, all eyes were riveted to the podium; a well-known (judging from the thunderous applause) city politician had just been introduced.

Cautiously, Matthews tried the door through which McQuealy had disappeared; it opened with a gentle click. Gritting his teeth, he peeked in. A short hall came into view with doors on either side. On as light a foot as possible he crept to the first door on the right. A crooked, faded sign above read CHESS. The door opposite signified the same as did the last door on the far right; the far left indicated STAIRS. Chess tournament room! But not those of the New York Chess Club bet Matthews inspecting the dingy hallway that was haphazardly whitewashed, no doubt to cover up the evident graffiti and urine stains, the faint smell of which assaulted the nostrils.

Hoping that McQuealy had not left the premises via the STAIRS door, Matthews put his ear to the first door on the right. Nothing. But further down – at the next 'chess room' – he heard muffled voices. So McQuealy did meet someone. The American agent was pleased. Here, finally, was a chance to do some eavesdropping.

As he tiptoed along the wall to the second door he heard, "All in place then." It was a high-pitched voice.

"Better than we'd hoped," came the reply. Matthews couldn't quite catch what followed.

"Good, I will make the arrangements with Kemp and Shannon for the transfer of funds."

"I know the firm—" A chair suddenly moved, scraping the floor, making the rest unintelligible. He caught part of the last line "… take care of your end in Montreal."

Surmising that the walls were thin, Matthews had just decided to vacate the hallway and escape into the adjoining chess room for more private eaves-dropping when the door to the main hall swung open. The two men that McQuealy had briefly spoken to now made their way toward him. On closer inspection they had the look and gait of wharf ruffians rather than gentlemen of leisure.

One was big even by Matthews' standards who at six feet was hardly a midget. He wore a green corduroy suit that was badly in need of pressing and possessed a full black beard which, reckoned the agent, was an attempt to at least partially cover the lengthy scar running from just below his left eye into the growth. The egg-shaped head was crowned by a green derby.

The other wore denim and a loose flannel shirt. Although much smaller in stature, he didn't exactly strike Matthews as being overly friendly either. He had a long face protruding to aggressive points where the nose and chin ter-minated, sunken cheeks seeded sparsely with red whiskers, and button eyes a shade too close together – 'snake eyes' they called them in Texas. If Matthews had to judge character he'd venture that here was a man who'd love to watch someone get pulped and get a few licks in himself when it was safe to do so. But then, maybe he was jumping to hasty conclusions.

Physically, Matthews could hold his own with most men and on occasion, when provoked, had exhibited a mean streak of his own. However, just past his thirty-fourth birthday (and figuring that he wasn't getting any younger and wanting to maintain what more than one gal thought was a handsome face) he resolved to settle unpleasant situations without resorting to violence, if possible. That was six months ago. He had a feeling that he was about to undergo his first serious test of that resolve.

Initially startled, Matthews recovered quickly, giving both men his best smile. "Howdy, gents."

Green derby spoke first. "Who might you be?"

"Pardon me, partner?"

"State your business."

"Chess… these are chess rooms?"

"Soun's like a trouble snooper to me," said the smaller man sourly.

"Methinks you're right, Riley."

"Now rest easy, gents. I ain't looking for trouble." Matthews tried to sound convincing and placating at the same time.

"Don't talk like anyone from these parts, do he?" growled green derby now at arms-length away.

"No, he don't. Soun's southern. You be southern?"

"Texas," replied Matthews lightly struggling to maintain his smile.

"Did ya hear that Riley!" guffawed green derby, "he's from Texas."

"Two things I hate," sneered Riley, showing his snarled yellow teeth, "Englishmen and Confederates."

"Hey! Hold on there, Jaspers. I fought in the Union Army. And besides, in case you haven't heard, the war is over."

Green derby and Riley gave him an acerbic stare.

Just then the door to the chess room on which Matthews had been eaves-dropping swung open and out stepped a slight, well-tailored man. McQuealy was nowhere to be seen.

"Did I hear someone say trouble?" he asked closing the door behind him and turning to the two men whom he obviously knew.

"We thinks we got ourselves a snooper," stated Riley.

"These fellas are mistaken. Is this not where the chess rooms are?" Matthews managed to produce another weak smile.

The dapper, clean-shaven man put his hands in the pockets of his pearl grey trousers and appraised Matthews shrewdly. At length he spoke, "Friend you don't look like a chess player." He turned to green derby. "Take him to the cellar." He jerked his head toward the door on the far left. "Find out who he is. I'll join you shortly."

"Now just hold your horses here," Matthews protested.

Green derby took that as a sign of belligerence and pushed the agent roughly against the wall. Matthews was taken by surprise but managed to grab his Stetson before it went flying off and secured it more tightly around his head.

"Best go along peacefully," warned the man. "That way you won't get hurt. Show him to our private chess parlour." With that he opened the door and disappeared back into the room.

"You heard'im." Riley, not to be outdone by his partner in manhandling, grabbed Matthews by the lapels of his coat and shoved him down the hall. *Strong little cuss*, thought Matthews as he stumbled a couple of steps.

"Yeah," chortled green derby. "We're going to play chess."

Then they both laughed.

"Mind you," added green derby with a menacing curled lip. "No ideas … see these?" From his rumpled pocket he fished out a pair of brass knuckles. "I have a mind to knock you insensible – just for sport."

Aw shit! lamented Matthews. It looked like he'd have to break his no violence promise. Fortunately, the dupes hadn't bothered to search his person and his revolver was still comfortably lodged high on his hip. No doubt, they would soon realize their omission, especially if he were forced to shed his coat. *Nearer to the stairs,* he thought, *would be the best time.*

Rivulets of sweat rolled down the Texan's back as they moved closer to the door marked STAIRS. He gauged their swagger carefully and… *Now!* Matthews swung around on the balls of his feet and with his right fist neatly clipped the chin of green derby. He knew that his knuckles would be bruised but no less so than the brute's chin. Green derby, now minus his catapulting head wear, caught totally off guard, reeled against Riley who in turn fell to his knees.

"What the—" yelped the smaller man as his companion's heavy bulk collapsed against him.

Matthews leaped across the path of the two ruffians at the same time liberating his Smith and Wesson. It was no easy feat. He feared his thick coat would trap his weapon.

"Stay where you are, hombres," he ordered, taking a quick glance down the hall to see if the brief tussle had brought any unwanted company. All seemed quiet.

"You bloody Tommy Atkins," cursed green derby, spittle spewing from his mouth, "you'll pay for this you will."

What to do now? wondered Matthews. Before he could marshal any coherent thoughts, Riley with more gall than brains pulled out a very long dirk knife from beneath his loose flannel shirt and made a lung at the agent's midsection. Matthews twisted his body while parrying the thrust. The end result was a slashed sleeve but no bodily harm.

Fortunately, green derby was very slow to react to his partner's initiative thus enabling Matthews to dislodge the knife with a rapid rap on the wrist with the gun barrel followed by a right toe to the groin that sent the man shuddering back into his cohort. Both ended on the floor in a pile. Riley lay hunched over green derby clutching his vitals and attempting to get his wind.

Matthews wished that his long, cumbersome outer garment hadn't prevented him from obtaining a truer swing on his kick. However, it seemed to get the job done. As green derby struggled to extract himself from the grimacing Riley, Matthews thought it advisable to depart before they alerted the whole hall.

As luck would have it, the door opened on his left and out popped fancy pants just as Matthews rushed by. "You—" was all he managed before the agent's revolver barrel hit the bridge of his nose. The Texan heard the distinct crack of bone on contact.

Opening the door to the main hall, Matthews glanced back to see the man crumple against the doorframe. Further beyond were green derby and Riley shakily staggering to their feet, the latter with a noticeable list.

"Stop that man! Stop that man!" was all Matthews heard behind him as he ran by the sea of astonished faces and out the entrance of Forbes Hall.

Later, over a bitter beer in a saloon some distance from his confrontation, Matthews nursed his swollen knuckles and contemplated his next move. He had lost McQuealy and certainly couldn't show his face again at Forbes Hall. It appeared that this particular assignment had come to an abrupt end. Wait! There was still a chance, Matthews realized. Didn't McQuealy say something about the transfer of funds – Kemp and Shannon. That was it – a banking house! Slim perhaps, but still a chance. Matthews quickly downed his beer and set out to find a directory.

CHAPTER FIVE
Ottawa

As usual, John A. Macdonald instructed Patrick Buckley, his cabman, to take him to his lodgings on Daly Avenue. On disembarking from his carriage, however, the politician did not proceed into his domicile. Instead, he walked briskly two blocks further up the street to an impressive two-storey dwelling. He had followed this routine one, sometimes two nights a week for over three weeks now. It wasn't that he thought he needed the exercise or that he had a craving for the subarctic fresh air. Both, in fact, he could do without. He simply wished to avoid any untoward gossip that could impute the reputation of a certain lady he had recently met.

This evening was reserved for his 'secret' French lessons. He wasn't sure whether his French or his appreciation of Molière or Balzac improved over the course of his visits but that scarcely seemed to matter since Mademoiselle Beaudoir had been remarkably beneficial in other ways.

Macdonald's public successes had been blighted by his private misfortunes. First, there had been the agonizing illness and wrenching death of his wife, Isabella. They met and fell in love in '43. But their happiness was oh so brief; within two years Isabella was mortally sick. He didn't know exactly what malady had afflicted her – quite baffling really when he thought about it. It began with debilitating headaches that laid her up in bed for hours, nay days. Then she succumbed to some form of neuralgia or so the doctors diagnosed that affected her extremities. Within a couple of years of their marriage, she required constant care.

In the meantime, it was evident to Macdonald that her spirits dwindled – alarmingly so – into an increasingly darker mood. Often she seemed wandering on a fog-engulfed moor abetted by her ever present 'blister box of medicine' that included vials of liquid opium. He could not but shudder inwardly in despair on entering her room perfumed with the wretchedly sweet scent of flavoured opium. On her good days, she'd smile encouragingly and feebly extend her hand but those expansive eyes had lost their glow, dulled by endless intake of her "relief remedies".

Not that he was always at her side – even remotely so. If the truth be known, he was away weeks at a stretch leaving Isabella to be tended to by his sisters, Margaret and Louise. He wondered in those few occasional moments of unadulterated honesty whether his political duties were merely a pretext for staying away. More than once in Montreal or Toronto, after a night of drinking in the company of congenial cronies and/or women of questionable morals, he'd wake up the next morning to view a vainglorious rogue in the mirror who needed to do better for Isabella's sake. He could see it in her eyes on her more lucid periods – reproach, perhaps jealousy – she did not have the strength for rage. If only she got better in mind as well as body, he would change.

Such thoughts, genuine and sober enough, invariably found no purchase with the next social gathering or enticing tavern. He was sadly lacking in will, he realized, when it came to drink and the fairer sex. Try as he might, it was a want within him that defied restraint.

Still, there were bright spots. "Madame Isa," as he called her, rallied in between prolonged convalescing intervals to surprising heights. In '47 they were blessed with a son – John Alexander – a healthy birth with no complications (which seemed almost a miracle to those attending Isabella). Alas, barely a year later, inexplicably he lay dead in his cot – "convulsions" said the attending physician with little further explanation.

Thereafter, an understandably distraught Isabella increasingly retreated to her opium world and he slipped away to his domain of politics, drinking parlours and the odd stray lassie. But once again, Isabella proved resilient giving birth to a healthy baby boy two years after John Alexander's sudden death. A family, it appeared, had not totally eluded him. It was a precarious and protracted labour from which Isabella tenuously recovered even as the intensity of her ailments grew – the dreaded tuberculosis now added to the list. Isabella died in '57, a chronic invalid in her last few years. Hugh John, John A. rejoiced, was growing into a fine strapping lad although he didn't see that much of him, the boy having been raised by Margaret and her husband. Another gnawing regret.

Deprived of a normal family life even while Isabella was still alive, with her passing Macdonald buried his melancholy in politics and alcohol. His slide into indeterminate widowhood, however, appeared to have been arrested when in 1859 he met Agnes Bernard, a tall, tawny-haired lady almost twenty years his junior.

Agnes was of solid Huguenot stock whose ancestors left France in the latter half of the seventeenth century and via England migrated to Jamaica where they established a thriving sugar plantation. For over a century and one half the Bernards had been part of the well-to-do Jamaican aristocracy. Her father, James Bernard, a noted lawyer as well as plantation owner, was a prominent figure in the Island's upper crust, holding a number of important public offices throughout the 1830s and 1840s. After his death in 1850, however, the plantation economy went sour and the remaining family members – his wife, Theodora, the two surviving sons, Hewitt and Richard and of course Agnes – decided to sell the estates and move elsewhere. Hewitt and eventually Richard went to seek their fortunes in Canada while Theodora joined her daughter who was attending finishing school in Britain at the time.

After some 'adjustment' problems in England (which from what Agnes said Macdonald took to mean Mrs. Bernard abhorred their reduced circumstances what with the higher cost of living and the difficulty of finding servants who behaved like slaves!) mother and daughter joined the two fairly prosperous sons in Barrie, Canada West in 1854.

In the case of Hewitt, the younger of the Bernard brothers, appearances were deceiving and "prosperous" was not quite the proper term. A lawyer by profession like John A., he found himself in serious debt (a condition that Macdonald too had experienced on numerous occasions). In fact, Bernard's property was seized by the sheriff for unpaid taxes! Nor did his other brief venture as a municipal councilor in Barrie bring any relief, pecuniary or otherwise. Most of his fellow councilors regarded him as a "tea toadying, toffee nosed snob." Nonetheless, Macdonald offered him a position as his private secretary. Hewitt was grateful for the job and besides, Macdonald reasoned, what better way to keep, albeit from a respectable distance, a courting eye on Agnes.

Macdonald first took notice of Agnes in 1856 in a Toronto hotel dining room but only formally met her three years later in Quebec City where Parliament had reconvened. He took the initiative by calling on Mrs. Bernard and Agnes – a social courtesy, he explained – to meet Hewitt's relatives.

For his part he found the young spinster charming, knowledgeable and witty in conversation with a set of "fine eyes." Agnes, meanwhile, was struck by his distinctive features – "a mixture of strength and vivacity" she once remarked to Hewitt who passed it on to his employer. It was a promising beginning or so he thought.

Once again he felt the impulsive pleasures of courtship and love. Indeed, in a rush of youthful enthusiasm he proposed marriage, prematurely as it turned out, for Agnes refused, wanting more time to assess her feelings toward him. Yet, they continued to develop their relationship and Macdonald was hopeful. Then, inexplicably, Agnes and her mother left for London late in 1863 intent on not coming back. Shocked and dismayed the politician could only conclude that Agnes had rather decisively rejected him.

Why he had been so firmly discarded remained a mystery. Was it their age difference? Macdonald wondered. Was it her strict religious upbringing that more than once exhibited itself in less than sympathetic terms when it came to his drinking a wee bit more than he should have on occasion. (She called it an 'evil demon' which would end in ruined health). Or had Mrs. Bernard (whom Macdonald thought a rather pretentious bitch) decided to return to 'civilization' with daughter in tow despite her 'difficulties' in the past? His awkward conversation with Hewitt shed little light on the subject; he too seemed genuinely saddened by the turn of events.

Thus, once more Macdonald found himself beset by oppressive loneliness that was only partially muted by the smoking room comradeship of his political cronies and by drinking a trifle too much. It appeared that he was destined to lead a solitary life. But quite remarkably, while wrestling with mounting personal depression, he met Luce Beaudoir.

As he approached the steps of her abode, his mind flicked back to the night at the British Hotel when he unpardonably spilt some brandy on her white tulle dress while hurriedly making his way to the billiard room. Out of nowhere she had just crossed his path and the deed was done. It might have been just his happy inebriated state but she took charge of him in a manner that he could not quite comprehend. Like a vernal goddess amid a dreary Ottawa winter, she lit him up. He felt something akin to a huge gas chandelier spinning at that … Certainly, her tall, fair form, taut high-cheeked face, mysterious ebony eyes and black locks of curly hair made a favourable impression. But more immediate, in that moment of encounter, it was her smile – somewhere between demurring and saucy – that truly had smitten him.

Aware, even in his slightly tipsy condition that he had ruined the lady's dress, he tried to make amends by profuse apologizes. Much to his relief no unpleasantness ensued; the lady maintained a cordial disposition and with an understanding mind frame remarked, "Accidents do happen." Throughout she maintained that enigmatic, enticing smile, which in retro-spect reminded him of another Luce – George-Étienne Cartier's mistress in fact, Luce Cuvillier. This Luce had the same 'joie de vivre' spirit but was more refined and discreet – not prone to wearing trousers or smoking cheroots. He couldn't recall the exact substance of their ensuing conversation except that he attempted to assuage his appalling clumsiness by offering to reimburse her for her soiled garment. She would hear none of it. He persisted in making some sort of amends, suggesting that perhaps he could escort her to dinner the following evening. And she accepted!

Macdonald quickly discovered an intriguing woman in her early thirties, he judged, full of Gallic charm who had somehow eluded marriage. Luce was originally from Quebec City, the only daughter of Gaston Beaudoir and his Irish wife Sarah. Monsieur Beaudoir, whose family roots dated back to the early fur trade of New France, apparently was a rather successful merchant – at least successful enough to provide Luce with a thoroughly bilingual edu-cation and leisure time for travel. She had lived in London for a number of years where she lost any traces of her native accent.

That Luce ended up in the backwoods capital was a providential bless-ing, thought Macdonald. It started, she told him on their third evening together, with her forlorn condition after a love affair gone awry. She didn't elaborate but he could well appreciate the circumstances given his own troubles. Distraught and miserable, living with her parents at the time, she felt a desperate need to flee Quebec City, at least for a while, to sort out her thoughts. As luck would have it her Uncle Jacques provided the solution. He was off on a six month trip to France and not wanting to rent or board up his home in Ottawa he wrote to his brother wondering if Luce would be interested in moving to the new capital to 'keep' the house while he was gone. He could even obtain a position for his niece suitable to her talents if she so wished... "And voilà, that's why I am here and how I have come to perform English-French translations for a publishing firm," she related to the captivated politician.

"And how long was that before I vandalized your dress?" he asked. The incident had become somewhat of a joke between them.

"Hardly a week."

Macdonald in a very short period indeed found that he had become quite infatuated not only with her intelligence and broad range of interests but also those other womanly qualities that Luce seemed to intrinsically exude, although to date in a platonic sense since he did not want to in any way compromise the mademoiselle without a clear and proper invitation. It had not been forthcoming (at least not in a direct enough manner that he could ascertain) but that did not disturb him. Whatever her motives in allowing him to call, he had come to enjoy immensely his nocturnal visits for the social company.

Uncle Jacques' house possessed a symmetrical façade – an imposing white door in the centre flanked on either side by evenly spaced cased windows, which now emitted a welcoming soft, yellow light. The building had character, Macdonald decided, particularly the bell cast hipped roof, an architectural feature one normally found in Canada East but rarely on the British side of the Ottawa River. The other feature that Macdonald recognized as unique was the elliptical arch crowning the main entrance. *Just as well that it has unusual lines,* he mused, giving the brass knocker three firm raps and stomping the snow of his half-Wellingtons. *That way I'd be sure to spy it no matter how much I've drunk.*

"John, come in, come in. You must be frightfully cold on a night like this."

"I'm too well fortified to freeze but aye, 'tis a night when even the hardiest of horses would appreciate a warm stable." The Attorney General rubbed his hands as he stepped into the centre hall. While Luce secured the door he removed his hat and coat and deposited them on the heavy oak rack located beside a flight of stairs leading up to the bedchambers.

"You are a lovely sight tonight, Luce" he commented. "The dress is most becoming."

Macdonald took full measure of the blue satin tunic cut in the points, the tasteful white skirt with the silver crescents interspersed among the puffings, the bandeau of blue velvet studded with bright silvery stars and the crescents in her silky raven hair. The dress was decorous to the utmost; moreover, it did not prevent him from admiring the nicely formed bosom and haunches. *A very fashionable female*, Macdonald thought approvingly, someone who was accustomed to finery as her boudoir closet would undoubtedly attest. For a brief moment he contemplated the earthly delights that lay hidden beneath the bustles, stays and multi-layered petticoats. He quickly dismissed his impolite thoughts as improper and unbecoming. Only a scoundrel would succumb to such scandalous thoughts!

"Why thank you, John," Luce chirped demurely as she swished by him. "I just bought it yesterday. I couldn't resist … just arrived from Paris. You are the first to see it. I'm glad you approve."

The parlour was impressively paneled in dark, rich walnut with the imposing fireplace, located on the north wall, now alive with crackling logs. The room was remarkably devoid of curios except perhaps for an intricately patterned oriental rug that partially covered a stained hardwood floor. Two Cherrywood armchairs with scroll-curved arms and a similarly fashioned sofa, upholstered in elaborately decorated plush cloth were the only pieces of furniture aside from an elegant side table and brass stemmed kerosene lamps on either side of the armchairs. By contemporary standards the chamber was fairly stark for such a large floor area, yet, ascetically pleasing, thought Macdonald.

Uncle Jacques had taste – expensive taste – Macdonald surmised. Luce hadn't specified as to the exact source of his obvious wealth explaining that he had business interests in Europe that necessitated frequent prolonged voyages abroad. "He's a bit secretive about his affairs," she had commented to him on his first visit.

"Sounds like quite a character."

"That he is ... somewhat eccentric I suppose."

"Does he live here alone?"

"Yes – except for a maid that comes in twice a week to tidy up things. Uncle Jacques is a confirmed bachelor."

"Ah..."

The man aroused Macdonald's curiosity but he let the matter drop. Luce didn't seem to know much about him. Perhaps he would still have an opportunity to meet her mysterious uncle after he returned from his current sojourn.

"Would you care for some refreshment?"

"Some tea for now would be beneficial I think," he replied, settling himself into one of the fancy armchairs with a deep sigh.

"You look fatigued," she observed, going over to the hearth, where she poured some water from a pitcher into an ornate kettle with ivory hands, and hung it on an iron rod above the fire.

"Aye, that I am – a long day 'tis been."

"Troubles?"

"Yes, I suppose you could call it that." A measure of chagrin crept into his voice. "Despite the expense in erecting our magnificent Parliament buildings our highly-priced engineers have failed to weatherproof it! The Eastern Departmental Building, in particular, is either too hot or too cold for comfort. It's been like that for days. So irregular is the heat kept up I shouldn't be surprised that those who inhabit it will end up with pneumonia!"

"What is the problem?"

"An engineering fault in the heating pipes I suspect, 'tis hard to say. But just today one of the pipes burst in the office of the clerk of the Deputy Receiver General. It was a loud report that could be heard echoing down the halls. I thought a bomb had gone off!" Macdonald shook his head. "Scattered water in all directions."

"Oh dear!"

"Aye... Terrible mess and an irony at that because the supply of water in the public buildings is very limited at the moment."

"Oh? Why is that?"

"Owing to the low level of the Ottawa River – four feet lower than usual. Indeed, the boilers that generate the steam for heating have to be filled with water drawn in by carters. I do hope the weather improves soon," he lamented.

"So do I," agreed Luce, grabbing a pair of padded mitts and pouring the scalding water from the kettle into a fine white terra cotta teapot that had rested atop the fireplace mantle.

"Take care not to burn yourself," Macdonald warned.

"Haven't done it yet," she answered cheerfully.

Luce removed a healthy portion of tea leaves from a blue opal glass container and deposited them into the pot. "There that should do it." She brought the teapot to the side table beside Macdonald. "Would you care for some biscuits with your tea?"

"No, thank you. I have eaten amply."

"Very well then. Be back in a moment."

While Macdonald relaxed stretching his lanky legs, Luce returned carrying a silver tray with two delicate cups and saucers of pearl ware, a little pitcher of cream, a sugar bowl and a decanter of brandy. "Should be steeped enough," she said setting the tray on the side table and pouring the steaming tea into the cups. "Brandy in your tea?"

"No thank you, Luce, just a little cream for now."

"A good choice – acquired fresh at the farmer's market today."

"Farmers still bringing their produce into the city even in weather like this?"

"Quite a number of wagons came in today. One overturned causing a ghastly spectacle – geese and turkeys spewed all over the road with feathers flying about – not to mention the piercing din of squawks and cackles!"

"I shouldn't wonder," Macdonald commented accepting the tea with a smile. "I've noticed the reckless speed with which horses are driven through the streets. Many drive without bells and I dare say some of these farmers are the most guilty."

"You may be right," said Luce sitting down on the sofa opposite the politician.

"Aye and it will only become more dangerous as we proceed with the sleighing season."

Later, over a glass of Luce's excellent French brandy and a game of steeple-chase regatta, Macdonald got on to one of his favourite subjects, books. An avid reader, he was particularly fond of French literature. He asked Luce's opinion of *Récit d'une soeur* by Mme. Augustus Cramer, one which recently had caught his interest. When Luce responded that she did not know the work he cheerfully offered to bring his copy on his next visit.

Then, inevitably, it seemed, their talk drifted to his political activities. He lazily prattled on about the idiosyncrasies of certain colleagues, the apparent standstill in the confederation movement and finally the topic that had begun to occupy more and more of his time. "Ever since the suspension of the writ of Habeas Corpus in Ireland, the Fenians across our borders have been in a frenzy," he explained.

"Is there no check on them?"

Macdonald took a sip from his glass and gazed solemnly at the blazing hearth. "Not on the American side," he said. "The journals of the United States are daily filled with the most inflammatory appeals to the Irish of the Republic to wage war on Canada – to strike a blow for Ireland. Large meetings are openly held to promote that end."

"What of the authorities in the United States?" she asked. "Cannot they be prevailed upon to take action?"

"Hah!" Macdonald chortled. "Public officials preside and speak at those meetings. Arms and ammunitions are purchased with the cash so raised. Aye, the American government should interfere and bring to an end the proceedings of the Fenian Society but alas…" He shrugged taking another sip of his drink. "It appears President Johnson and his cabinet look on placidly at it all."

"And our side? Is there action contemplated?"

"Aye. If these scoundrels think Canada is the shortest route to Ireland then they are sadly mistaken. A concentration not only of Imperial troops but our volunteer militia will be effected so that blasters like General Sweeny, if they do show themselves, will meet a warm reception. But enough!" Macdonald suddenly declared. "It seems that I forget myself and end up going on about politics, no doubt, boring you to tears with such recitals."

Luce straightened in her seat, a look of consternation spreading across her face.

"Luce?" he asked gently "Have I upset you with all this talk–"

"No, not at all," she responded rather tersely. "It's your presumption that because I am a female I would be disinterested in politics and other such manly pursuits—"

"I didn't mean to imply—"

"John," she cut him off, "you are not boring me. I am an educated woman who understands such matters perfectly. And it's only unenlightened men who think that women should be kept out of these kinds of discussions."

Surprised by Luce's spirited retort, Macdonald threw up his hands in surrender. "Forgive me, Luce, I meant no offence. Indeed, I welcome your succor in listening to an old political animal such as I."

"No offence taken," her tone softened, "I want to know what goes on in your public as well as your private life."

Macdonald nodded, feeling a little relieved. He had told her of Isabella (although judiciously excluding any reference to Agnes), her tragic illness, the devastating death in infancy of their firstborn, and of their second son, Hugh John, his pride and joy, who now at sixteen lived with Macdonald's sister Margaret in Kingston. Luce was a sympathetic and comforting listener and he naturally extended his conversation into the political arena. It had been careless of him to suddenly imply that perhaps politics and matters of state were above her. It obviously was interpreted as a slight although that was not his intention at all. Indeed, he had been quite frank as to the activities on Parliament Hill. Yet, in a way, she was correct. He did balk at informing her of certain distasteful subjects. Not wishing to assault a lady's sensibilities he avoided such topics as the murder in Buffalo and possible Fenian assassination schemes.

"Luce, your companionship means a great deal to me," he said. "It's been a long time since I have had such pleasurable female company. I only wish…" he let the thought drop.

"You wish what, John?" she leaned forward, hands clasped in her lap.

"Well, you are an astonishing woman," he ventured uneasily.

"Oh? In what way?"

"In every way. You're intelligent, beautiful…" he trailed off afraid to express his sentiments lest they lead him into dangerous waters. "You make me feel young again," he finally managed.

"Is that why you visit – to feel young again?" she asked raising an eyebrow.

A slight discomfort rippled through the politician. "My motives are more substantial than that Luce. The fact is I rather like …have become fond of you."

"I see," she said solemnly.

"But please don't misunderstand me," he added. "I don't wish to impose in anyway on your ... hospitality."

"I understand very well," she said.

There was an awkward silence during which Macdonald avoided her probing eyes. *Hell*, he thought, *I'm botching this up*. To forestall any further embarrassment for both of them he suddenly sat up and announced "Well, I've stayed a wee bit too long this evening (with too loose a tongue he was tempted to add) paying no heed to the hour – most ungentlemanly." He was suddenly reminded of the old adage that considered a man overly forward if visiting a woman alone.

"Please do not be concerned on my account. I too enjoy your company –immensely. And besides we've not finished our game."

"I'm afraid that I'm all played out," he chuckled nervously at his pun.

Luce regarded him with a coy expression. "Just like a man," she quipped. "First you draw my ire, then you flatter me and now you want to leave just when you have an opportunity to discover how astonishing I can be."

Macdonald started to laugh but ceased abruptly as their eyes met. "I'm twenty years your senior—" he began tentatively, desperately desiring her yet unaccountably hesitating.

"So," she challenged, "does that make a difference?"

"What I mean is—"

"I am a woman of some experience," she declared unabashedly.

Macdonald pursed his lips, his pulse racing, "And you find a rapidly wrinkling soul like me desirable."

"Oh John! What a thing to say. You're a mature man who would offer a woman much ... much more than most men I've known."

Macdonald suddenly felt lightheaded. "Kind words but my reputation as a *bon vivant* is greatly exaggerated, I'm afraid."

Laughing, Luce reached over and brought a soft hand to his lips. "As to your reputation I wouldn't know but you have a wide, generous mouth which pleases me when you smile. Besides, I suspect you underrate yourself."

Her hand lingered and he kissed it tenderly. "Luce," he began in a hoarse voice.

"Don't say another word," she whispered. "It's a bitter night and you are welcome to spend it here."

Macdonald clasped both of her hands tightly to his. Since he started calling on Luce he had yearned for such a forthright invitation yet daring not to hope. "I only imagined that you would—" he cleared his rapidly drying throat. "Are you sure that—"

"I am resolute," she cut him off.

They both rose in unison and embraced; their lips brushed gently.

"My bedchamber is upstairs to the right," she said. "Give me a few moments." With that she left the parlour.

CHAPTER SIX
New York

Kemp & Shannon
Bankers & Brokers
No. 8 New Street

Benjamin Matthews stared at the swinging shingle for what he reckoned was the hundredth time. *Shit,* he thought, *I've got to do something soon.* Since eight o'clock that morning he had patiently kept a stakeout on the banking/brokerage house hoping to spot McQuealy. It was now edging up to quarter to five and the Irishman was nowhere to be seen.

It had been a long, tedious day. From two different locations he had kept his vigil. It was too cold to loiter outdoors so he first entered the Osburn House, a first class three dollar a night hotel, which from the lobby provided a good vantage point. But after three hours of smoking cheroots and pretending to read *The Times,* he decided to move on. Hunger dictated that he should, if at all possible, find an eatery within sight of Kemp & Shannon. Madame's Café fulfilled the requirements admirably. From a cozy corner alongside a dirty window he continued his watch while indulging in a roast filet of beef and Yorkshire pudding. But now, many sugar cakes washed down with cupful of coffees later, he felt distinctly uncomfortable. His bladder was about to burst yet he hesitated to go and relieve himself. *It would be just my luck to miss the hombre while I'm taking a piss,* he thought miserably.

The U.S. agent was on the horns of a dilemma: either McQuealy had come and gone before him (in which case he had gone directly to the bank sometime after he left Forbes Hall the day before) or he hadn't as yet arrived

– assuming, of course, that he ever would! Matthews almost convinced himself that it would have been better if the fat Fenian had come and gone; that way perhaps with a little judicious arm twisting, information could be extracted from the bankers. However, if McQuealy had not put in an appearance and Matthews proceeded with his investigation then in all likelihood not only would he not know what McQuealy was up to but undoubtedly his visitation would be noted and McQuealy warned that a gentleman had made inquiries into his financial affairs.

Still, Matthews couldn't afford to wait any longer. Soon the establishment would close its doors and a full day would have been lost. And this was his only thread to the Irishman. Besides, his bladder would stretch no further. He rose stiffly, deposited some coinage on the table and made his way into the frigid air. En route to Kemp & Shannon he broke a little wind and made a hasty stop at the Osburn to take care of his urgent call of nature.

"Howdy, ma'am," Matthews tipped his Stetson and smiled as he approached a plump but agreeable looking lady at an empty wicket. "I'd sure appreciate it if you could get Mr. Kemp or Mr. Shannon for me. It concerns a substantial account," he added, lowering his voice to impart a note of importance.

"Whom shall I say is calling?" she asked officiously.

"Mr. Matthews – Benjamin Matthews."

She gave him an appraising look over and said, "Very well, Mr. Matthews. Would you be seated." She motioned to a large wooden bench against a wood panel wall. "I'll see who is available."

"Thank you kindly, ma'am." He again tipped his Stetson and she disappeared.

Presently, a tall man with a square face, dressed tidily in a blue serge suit came out from one of the inner chambers. Matthews, his hat in hand, rose and they shook hands.

"I'm Mr. Kemp – Mr. – ah…"

"Matthews."

"Mr. Matthews – yes. I was informed that I may be of some assistance?"

"I sure hope so." Matthews glanced around. Although there was only one other customer at the wicket, he did not want to conduct his business with the banker publicly. "I'd feel more at ease if we could talk privately – in your office perhaps?"

Kemp hesitated briefly. "Y-yes, of course. This way, Mr. Matthews."

The agent was led into a large imposing office dominated by a formidable writing desk.

"Now, what assistance can I render?"

Matthews cleared his throat. "I need information on a particular client of your establishment."

"Oh?" Kemp's eyebrows shot up.

"Yes, Mr. Michael McQuealy."

If the name meant anything to Kemp he didn't show it. Indeed, he became, not unexpectedly, quite indignant. "Sir, we cannot and would not discuss our clients – not without their permission—"

"Then he is a client?" Matthews asked forcefully.

"No! I mean I don't know. I am speaking on general principle here," Kemp admonished. "Now sir, if that is all you wish to discuss." The banker started to rise from his chair, hoping, no doubt, that Matthews would do the same.

"Not quite," Matthews said, crossing his legs.

Unsure of his next course of action Kemp eased himself back into his seat.

"My credentials." Matthews stuck his hand inside his coat and produced his U. S. government identification card.

Kemp scrutinized it closely before handing it back, his face perplexed. "I don't understand."

"Mr. McQuealy is – ah, under investigation. Nothing serious at present. Nevertheless, we have reason to believe that he did or shortly will engage in a financial transaction at your institution the consequences of which may be illegal."

"I assure you, Mr. Matthews, we are an honourable, law abiding firm."

"I'm sure you are and would wish to cooperate with the government. After I look at Mr. Quealy's file I'll trouble you no further.

Kemp rubbed his chin. "Well, as I said, I am not sure that this Mr. McQuealy deals with us. The name is not familiar to me"

"I'd be much obliged if you check your records."

"I think I better consult with Mr. Shannon first," Kemp said. "He may know more about the matter than I."

"I'll speak with Mr. Shannon then," Matthews said. "If you could fetch him?"

Kemp rather clumsily extracted himself from behind his desk and hurried off to locate his partner. Matthews was tempted, meanwhile, to light up a cheroot which he found relaxing as well as a good laxative but thought better of it. He had smoked too much already and his mouth felt as raw as a cowboy's arse after a long cattle drive.

A few minutes later a short man with a balding conical head burst into the room; he was sneezing ferociously into a red bandanna. Kemp performed the introductions.

"Excuse me, Mr. Matthews," Shannon let go another volley into his bandanna. "Blasted weather – must have caught a chill. Now, I am informed you are a government detective of some sort?"

"That's right – a federal agent."

"Well, we're a respectable banking and brokerage house, which has a reputation to maintain. Detective or not, we cannot disclose the financial affairs of our clients. It's a matter of trust."

"Now hold on there," Matthews drawled. It was time to get nasty. "I'm just doing my job. I aim to cause you no trouble but if I go away empty-handed you can rest assured there'll be hell to pay. I'd be obliged to come back with a goodly bunch of agents with all sorts of legal papers authorizing us to seize all your records. That would cause a commotion, disrupt business and other unnecessary unpleasantries. I don't want that. And I presume neither do you." Having made his bluff (Matthews had no idea if he could follow through on his threat) he shrugged. "It's up to you, gentlemen."

"May I see your identification?" Shannon requested sourly.

"Of course." Matthews produced his card again.

Like Kemp, Shannon carefully scrutinized it. "I don't know," he muttered to himself gingerly fingering the card before giving it back. "This is highly irregular you know—" Again he succumbed to a coughing spree.

"It will be kept strictly confidential," Matthews assured him. "You do know Mr. McQuealy?"

Shannon sighed "I do. Appears a respectable gentleman. Came in yesterday as a matter of fact."

Matthews' spirits rose. It seemed that his long shot might yet find its mark. "What transpired?"

Shannon glanced at Kemp and eyed Matthews malevolently, muttering once more that it was all highly irregular but evidently he did not want any further bother with the U.S. government. "Mr. McQuealy had some funds transferred as I recall."

The agent nodded. "I – the government would want to know the amount, where and to whom."

"I'd need to look that up."

Kemp, who had up to this point said nothing, chirped, "Mr. Matthews is this strictly legal?"

"I assure you it is and to not comply would constitute an obstruction of justice."

Matthews was talking through his proverbial Stetson but he could see Kemp cringe.

Shannon produced another mournful sigh. "I'll get the file but in the strictest of confidence you understand."

"It could not be any other way," Matthews said. "I won't tell if you don't," he added smiling.

"Uhm…" Shannon snorted before leaving the office.

Michael McQuealy was a wealthy man judging from his account. Funds had been deposited on a monthly basis, two to three thousand usually. Matthews had no doubt that it represented donations from various patriotic dupes who took the Fenians at their word. He quickly found the last transaction. Two thousand five hundred had been transferred from the New York firm to W.T. Cross and Co. brokers and general commission merchants. He stared at the address – corner of St. Francois Xavier and St. Sucrement Street, Montreal, Canada East. Ah yes, he recalled Montreal mentioned at Forbes Hall …

"Mr. McQuealy left no further instructions?" Matthews asked Shannon who barked a monstrous cough into his bandanna.

"No, not at this end."

"Did you personally speak to Mr. McQuealy?"

"Yes, as a matter of fact we did exchange some pleasantries. What is this all about?"

"I'm not at liberty to say. Did he mention this transaction?"

Shannon thought for a moment. "All Mr. McQuealy told me was this was the first instalment of two such transfers. Later he would leave word for another similar sum to be sent to Cross and Company."

Matthews properly thanked Messrs. Kemp and Shannon for their cooperation and departed just as they were locking the doors. He was not authorized to go into a foreign country and Montreal was definitely in foreign territory. However, he reasoned, having lost McQuealy he would follow the money. Thus, his next step was to obtain permission to continue his investigation into Canada East.

CHAPTER SEVEN
Buffalo

"Miss Mahone?"

"Y-yes?"

"My name is Lynch – Oliver Lynch. I've come about Mr. Rourke."

The woman hesitated and for a moment he thought that she'd slam the door on him. "It's important" he quickly added, noting the apprehension on her face.

"Were you a friend of John – Mr. Rourke?" she asked nervously, her eyes searching the street behind him.

"I've never had the pleasure of his acquaintance but he did work for my employer." Lynch extracted a card from his coat pocket and handed it to her. It read: 'Oliver Marshall Lynch, Her Majesty's Canadian Detective Service' signed Gilbert McMicken. "You sent a telegram to Mr. McMicken advising of Mr. Rourke's death," he prompted.

"Yes, yes," she said giving back the card.

When she offered no further comment but remained rooted to her place directly in front of him, Lynch gently asked, "May I come in? I do need to talk to you about Mr. Rourke."

"Sorry, of course." She stepped aside as he entered, locking the door behind her. "Forgive me," she continued, "the last few days have been very trying and I feel – well, at my wit's end."

"That's quite understandable given the circumstances."

Despite her grave, unsmiling mouth and pale complexion, Molly Mahone was a striking woman, gifted with a well-proportioned, slightly upturned nose, large green eyes, and high cheekbones all capped with a shock of flaming red hair. She flattered her attire: a plain linen shirt and green skirt opened in the front, French style, to expose a pleated petticoat. *Be no more than thirty*, judged Lynch, discreetly appraising her.

"Please," she pointed to a simple rush-bottomed chair near the fireplace as they entered a multipurpose parlour-kitchen area.

"Thank you."

Miss Mahone had not offered to take his hat and coat so he unbuttoned the latter and held the former in his lap when he sat down.

"I wasn't sure anyone would come," she said in a small voice with a hint of asperity in her tone.

"We are grateful that you informed us," Lynch said, his eyes making a quick sweep of the utilitarian room as she also took a seat on a matching chair beside an unpretentious pine top table.

"It seemed proper since John was in Mr. McMicken's employ."

"Yes, quite, Miss Mahone, I—"

"Why?" she blurted out, wringing her hands, "Why was John killed?"

"Actually," Lynch rubbed his brow, wondering how to proceed with the disconsolate lady, "any information that you could provide would be appreciated."

"You don't know?" she asked. "God knows he wrote enough reports to Mr. McMicken. That's why he died, wasn't it?"

"Miss Mahone ..." he paused, reflecting on how much he should tell her. He decided to be frank. "We believe that Mr. Rourke was killed because he had obtained some specific information regarding a Fenian plot against Canada. Unfortunately, he was not able to relate this information before his death. I am here to ascertain what he discovered; other lives may be at stake. Forgive me for my indelicate inquiries at this most tragic and stressful moment but time is of the essence. I need to know – Did Mr. Rourke convey or leave any information with you? It is vitally important."

She didn't respond immediately. Lips quivering, she gazed directly into the fire, transfixed on some imaginary point beyond. Finally, she whispered, "His funeral was a few days ago. Hardly anyone came."

"Miss Mahone, my condolences. This must be difficult for you," he said lamely, the words ringing hollow even to his ears.

"We were to be married come spring," she said, her hands now pressed into a tight ball on her skirt.

"I'm truly sorry—" Lynch faltered as she turned toward him her eyes glistening with tears. Fishing around in his pocket, he produced a handkerchief that she gladly accepted.

Lynch gave Miss Mahone a few moments to collect herself before returning apologetically to the task at hand. She was the only solid starting point he had in this grim assignment.

"Please forgive me, Miss Mahone, but I must ask some questions. Time is of the essence," he repeated. "And—"

"I can tell you very little Mr. Lynch," she said wiping her eyes. "I knew of Mr. McMicken, of course, and that John worked on his behalf to spy on the Fenians. He wrote reports to him in Windsor although I never read any of them. You see, John did not confide in me. He believed that the less I knew about his clandestine activities the better. He only told me this much because… well, because," she sniffled, "I was getting suspicious about his going out frequently at night. I even accused him of having a lady friend on the side. Oh John." She stopped to dab the corners of her eyes with the hanky. "He got a certain satisfaction in playing his undercover game as he called it. He saw no harm in it and it did provide extra income. I had no idea that … that it would get him killed."

"Nor did we, Miss Mahone—"

"Will you find the person responsible?" she asked, her voice barely audible.

"If at all possible," although as far as he was concerned that was his secondary objective, one with little likelihood of success.

"That someone should do such a vile thing." She shook her head.

"Did you witness it?"

"No, it was late – quite late. John was out on one of his 'fraternizing forays' as he called them. I stayed up, made some tea and was reading here by the fire. I heard the jangle of a key announcing his arrival, then it stopped. There was a moment of silence followed by two gunshots. I was petrified – numb. It took some moments for me to act."

"Yes, I understand."

"I – I peered out the window and saw John's crumpled body. That's when I rushed to the door. He was lying there in an unnatural position, blood all around."

"And you saw no one else?"

"No, no one else."

"What about the police?"

"Oh, the police," she let out a sigh. "They, of course, came and investigated – carted off John's body and disappeared."

"Did they question you?"

"They did and some of our neighbours. No one saw anything. They judged it the work of a robber who panicked. Of course, I suspected different. That's why I telegraphed Mr. McMicken I suppose."

"Did you tell the police that Mr. Rourke was an agent for the Canadian government?"

"No. John had told me never to reveal that under any circumstances. I hope I acted properly?"

"Yes, it was best you didn't," he concurred gently.

In fact, he was greatly relieved that she didn't. It would have complicated matters. The nature of his trade precluded any official visit to the Buffalo constabulary. They tended to frown on spies working for a foreign government amidst the citizenry. Besides, judging from what Miss Mahone told him, to approach them would yield little useful information and probably cause much consternation.

"Miss Mahone, can you recall anything, anything at all about John's most recent activities? Something he may have mentioned in passing perhaps?"

"No, not much really. As I said, he thought the less I knew the better. He didn't want to frighten me unduly I know now." She stopped and shook her head. "Just what I told you. Although," she continued slowly, "the day before he died he was agitated, more excited than agitated really," she amended. "He said that he been meeting this man who informed him that the Fenian rascals – that's the term he used – had a surprise for the colonials—"

"Did he mention the man's name?" Lynch's hat dropped to the floor as he leaned forward.

"Y-yes, yes he did! I didn't think much of it at the time – Bannion. No. O'Bannion, Shawn O'Bannion. I'm sure that's what he said. Good merciful God, you don't think it was he who—" she gasped.

Lynch frowned. "Did he say anything else?"

"Only that this O'Bannion was a miserable wretch who had big ears and even a bigger thirst. He met with him after the meetings."

"What meetings?"

"Fenian meetings I suppose – that's all John ever said. He was out frequently because of these meetings."

"He didn't tell you where they were held?"

"No, he didn't and O'Bannion was the only name he mentioned – at least that I can remember."

"O'Bannion." Lynch let the name roll off his tongue, planting it firmly in his mind. It was a start. But such a slim thread for the time he had at hand. "If Mr. Rourke met regularly with this O'Bannion character," Lynch thought aloud, "then he might live nearby, possibly in this neighbourhood. Is there anything, anything else that comes to mind?"

Molly thought for a moment. "No, not that I can remember, Mr. Lynch."

"Well, thank you for you cooperation." The Canadian detective reluctantly concluded that no more information was to be garnered from the distraught lady. He started to rise but checked himself. "Just one more thing, Miss Mahone. With your permission of course, I would like to inspect Mr. Rourke's personal belongings. He may have left a clue … notes perhaps in regard to his activities."

"I suppose that's all right. His belongings are still here. I took only some of the more personal items he would have wanted me to have."

"I understand. Did the police make a search through his things?"

"They had a look but found nothing – at least they removed nothing."

Lynch nodded. "Well, if you could—"

"Mr. Lynch," Molly's voice had a desperate edge, "I'm frightened. I – I think I'm being watched!"

"Watched?"

"The last couple of times that I've gone to the market. I can't be sure but I had the sensation that someone was following me."

Lynch frowned. It hadn't occurred to him that Miss Mahone might be at risk. But the possibility existed if those who murdered Rourke suspected that he had passed on what he found out to her. After all, he worked on the same assumption. "I shouldn't worry," he tried to reassure her. "However, as a precaution, is there a place you can go for a while – to a relative perhaps?"

She bit her lower lip and shook her head. "I would leave this house but," tears formed in her eyes again, "I've really no place to go." She broke off making use of the handkerchief once more. Then, with some dignity she straightened her back and said, "The fact of the matter is, Mr. Lynch, I find myself in a constraining situation. I don't wish to be trapped here but the rent has been paid three months in advance and I have very little money saved. John was not a rich man and … Oh God," she covered her head with her hands, sobbing, "what is to become of me?"

Lynch pondered for a moment, very uncomfortable in the presence of a lady so deeply distressed. "Please Miss Mahone, perhaps I can help. It may be possible for you to move elsewhere and not worry about the finances. After all, Mr. Rourke died in the service of Her Majesty's government. Some arrangements – provisions ought to be in order."

"Is that possible?"

"I'm sure it is," he assured her. After all McMicken had all but promised a stipend when he requested him to "ascertain the lady's circumstances" as the spy master put it. Lynch didn't have the foggiest how much but resolved that she should receive whatever could be made allowable and was prepared to argue the point with McMicken if need be.

"Mr. Lynch I – I've been going out of my mind these few days – afraid of shadows, terrified to step out the door. I don't want to be alone."

"Well, that's understandable." He had registered at the Wadsworth Hotel on his arrival in Buffalo and for a moment he thought that she could spend the night there but quickly rejected the idea as somehow too forward.

"There is an extra cot here and it's almost the dinner hour," she offered.

"Well, I…" He was taken off guard by the request and rightly didn't know how to respond.

"Please, it would put me at ease," she urged, her green eyes staring intently at him.

"I suppose it is getting on into the evening," he said thoughtfully. "I could pick up my bags at the hotel tomorrow."

"Thank you, Mr. Lynch," she said as her face flushed.

Over a very palatable meal of stewed poultry and wheat bread Lynch inquired with as much tact as he could command about Miss Mahone's life. After some initial reluctance her reserve broke. It was as if the dam burst open and her story came tumbling out. He supposed it was a way of releasing tension and her pent up anxieties.

Her father, Charles Mahone, had been a young, struggling barrister, originally from Dublin, who after a number of bad investments decided to take his wife to America and start fresh. The Mahones settled in New York City where Charles re-established what proved to be a successful law practice. Molly was born there in 1836, two years after their arrival. She was a difficult birth with the result that her mother could bear no further children. She suspected that her father was extremely disappointed by this turn of events. He had desired a son but he seemed to reconcile himself to the fact that it was not to be.

Molly then recollected her childhood and in particular her fondness for books: "Father was a bit of a patron of literature and I still remember reading the likes of Sir Walter Scott and G.P.R. James, which he had in his library. I became somewhat of a romantic I suppose," she said wistfully. "Anyway, in due course I was sent to a fashionable boarding school just outside of New York and having been refined into a proper young lady," she laughed, "at eighteen I made my debut in New York society. I got carried away. At one point," she continued, "I ran up such a bill with the dressmakers that I was dreadfully afraid to tell Father."

Lynch smiled wanly, wondering, given her prosperous past, how she ended up in a rundown part of Buffalo living with Mr. Rourke who although a fine man (judging from what had been said) was not at all wealthy.

The pivotal point in her life came with the death of her mother: "It had a devastating effect on my father. He became deranged – absolutely mad," she related, "and succumbed to the curse of many an Irishman – began to drink. With constant intoxication came abuse. I started to loathe him – desperate to get away. And I did!" she said with a melancholy sigh. "I met this dashing military fellow or at least I thought he was at the time and we eloped. Father responded by disowning me."

"Have you seen your father since?" Lynch asked, helping himself to another portion of chicken stew. He was making up for lunch, which he decided to forego in his haste to interview Miss Mahone.

"No, I wrote a number of times but he never answered. He died two years ago in an asylum or so I was informed."

"He left you nothing?"

"He took me out of his will and never retracted on the decision. Besides, there was nothing left when he died; it all went to creditors."

Lynch shook his head. "Most lamentable."

Molly gave a bitter laugh. "More lamentable still was my dashing young soldier."

"What happened?"

She shrugged. "The short of it was that he refused to wed me and then one fine day abandoned me in a cheap hotel in Albany, almost penniless. That cured me of my childhood romanticism."

"I guess it would," Lynch said weakly.

Molly concluded her rather woeful personal story after dinner. As Lynch settled back in a ragged sofa contently puffing on a bent briar that he took out only in the evenings, she conversed while washing the eating utensils. She wouldn't hear of his offer to assist.

She stayed in Albany for a couple of years obtaining employment as a librarian. "I enjoyed the work," she informed him, "but the wages were a pittance – scarcely enough to pay the rent, let alone those other necessities of life. Finally, I gave up and on impulse moved here to Buffalo in the vain hope that I could secure a more promising position in a larger centre."

"What kind of position were you hoping for?" Lynch inquired admiring Miss Mahone's striking form from the rear as she stooped over the sink.

"I thought of teaching school at first. I did have an expensive education after all – not that the pecuniary rewards were much greater as I subsequently learned. After a couple of weeks in the city with my meagre resources running dangerously low I become desperate. Finally, I answered an advertisement in the *Buffalo Courier*. A lodging house needed a proprietor and I convinced the owner – an old businessman who had property scattered through the city – that I would make a satisfactory proprietress. God, what a mistake!"

"Oh?" Lynch rose and relit his pipe from a taper from the fireplace. A cloud of blue smoke curled forth and spread throughout the room as he settled into the sofa again.

"Mind you, I didn't object to the cleaning and cooking," she turned drying her hands with a coarse yellow towel. "But the lodging house was frequented by all manner of rowdy men who lacked the most rudimentary social graces." She flushed, folding the towel and placing it on the rack above the hand pump. "Still, I had my own quarters and it was warm and dry. And I met John…" Her voice choked a little.

"He came to the lodging house?"

"Yes. He was originally from Halifax, worked as a clerk for a shipping company when he was seized by the call of adventure so he told me. He went to Boston and joined the Union Army. Ended up fighting with the sixth regiment at Gettysburg – at least I think it was the sixth. He received a frightful sabre wound and after recovering – which took some months – was granted an honourable discharge. Said he had had enough of the war, this country and was going back to Nova Scotia."

"But instead he settled in Buffalo?"

"It wasn't to be permanent and I would have gladly gone with him. He was a kind man who…" she broke off struggling to regain her composure. "At any rate," she continued her eyes glistening, "John secured a clerk's position at a distillery not far from here. He insisted that I quit the lodging house and we rented this place." She waved her arms in an arc as if to engulf the small chamber. "It wasn't until sometime later that I learned he had been recruited by the Canadians in your war with the Fenians."

"No doubt that's why he prolonged his stay in Buffalo," Lynch observed more to himself than for Miss Mahone's benefit. That, and of course, Molly, Lynch surmised, a woman worth taking risks for.

Molly lapsed into silence while Lynch took out his tobacco pouch and refilled his pipe. *Yes, an interesting woman*, he thought, *with an interesting past*. He found her attractive and compelling even in her distraught state for which she had just cause. Certainly, she was refined but he had known other 'refined' ladies whose qualities proved ephemeral. He quickly dismissed any comparisons as premature deciding that Miss Mahone was someone he wanted to get to know better before passing any judgement. Best he kept his wandering thoughts in check and his mind on the task at hand.

"Mr. Lynch—" she broke the silence.

"Please, I'll dispense with the formalities and call you Molly if you call me Oliver," he said, still preoccupied with his half-formed impressions of the person before him.

"Oliver then…" she said primly, "what about you?"

"Me?"

"I've told you about myself," she said sitting down on the rush-bottomed chair he had occupied earlier. "I can't believe that I just prattled on so to a man I don't know. It wouldn't be fair if you didn't reciprocate, would it?"

"Oh … well." He removed himself from the comfort of the sofa to the fireplace to again light his briar. "There's not much to tell—"

"Come now, Mr. Lyn – Oliver. I don't believe that and fair is fair. In a moment of weakness I have related the essence of my life. I'm curious about yours." She regarded him with some degree of intensity.

Lynch gave her his best pained look of chagrin but to no effect; she waited unperturbed for him to collect his thoughts.

"Where to begin …" He puffed furiously. "I was born in Cahore, County of Wexford, Ireland. That was longer ago than I care to remember. Finished high school at fourteen and entered the service of the Hudson's Bay Company as an apprentice clerk. For me it was most opportune – my father died when I was four and I felt that I needed to make my own way in the world as it were. I was the youngest of five boys; the others had grown up and had established themselves in the county. My mother had a small but adequate pension and I had decided that I'd leave and seek my fortune in the world, which meant, as it turns out, that I was prepared to go wherever the company sent me." He shrugged.

Molly nodded, encouraging him to continue.

"Well, I shipped out to Canada. Ended up in Sault Ste. Marie – that's on the Upper Great Lakes between Lake Superior and Huron – wasn't much of a place but I didn't stay there long; the company sent me to Fort Garry – the British territories north of Minnesota. Had a bit of a problem there."

"I read somewhere that it is a most inhospitable country," ventured Molly.

"Oh, that's true enough, cold and barren but my problem was of the human variety. The fact of the matter is I inadvertently killed a man."

Molly's eyes widened and she opened her mouth as if to say something but then thought better of it.

"It was a stupid incident," he continued hastily, regretting his bluntness. "I was working in the old converted barracks office of the company, pouring over the stock ledger when this crazed Métis burst in yelling half in French and half in Cree that he had been cheated ... I wasn't sure what about—"

"Métis?"

"I guess you haven't heard of the Métis." *Why should she,* he thought. "They're half breeds, part Indian, part white – mostly French mixed with Cree that inhabited the Red River area. Many were employed by the company. By and large a rough but generally friendly people but not this particular Métis. A big brute he was. Before I could gain my wits about me, he had me pinned between my overturned chair and the wall. 'No one cheats Louis La Rouge' he spat – I could smell the liquor on his breath. I tried to tell him that I did not cheat him – I had never seen him before – and that if there had been some accounting mistake made — I assumed he worked for the company – I would certainly do my best to remedy the error. Well, he would have none of that. The mad man pulled a knife—"

"Good Lord!" exclaimed Molly in horror.

"Those were my sentiments exactly," Lynch concurred. "I suddenly got religious. Fortunately, he stumbled as he thrust the knife and I was able to disengage myself from an awkward position. A struggle ensued. I was bruised but that was all—"

"Is that how you lost your ear?" Molly glanced at the stumped appendage on the right side of his head.

Unexpectedly, Lynch laughed and Molly looked embarrassed.

"No – it wasn't anything so dramatic. An ill-tempered horse bit it off."

"Sorry, I—"

"Don't be. I'm not offended and most people are curious." He touched his partial ear. "It has taught me a lesson: to be wary of ill-tempered nags. But to get back to La Rouge. Somehow in the process of attempting to overpower me the fellow impaled himself. The wound didn't appear too deep but as fate would have it he died from an infection some weeks later."

"Surely that was self-defense," Molly offered. "The man died by his own hand."

"Yes, all charges against me were dismissed. Apparently, La Rouge had been violent on other occasions and was not altogether mentally sound. Still, I was regarded none too kindly by the locals. La Rouge left behind a wife and six young ones. A sad business that was."

"So what did you do?" she asked.

"I resigned from the company and went east – to Toronto. The truth was that I had become a liability to the company and besides, I was becoming bored of my accounting job. At any rate, I got hired eventually by the Toronto Constabulary."

"You were a policeman?"

"That's right – a number of years before I was recruited by McMicken when he needed detectives during the Civil War." Lynch tapped the ashes from his pipe into the fire and stifled a yawn. "But that's another story, which perhaps I can save for another time. I think I'll take you up on the offer of that cot for tonight."

"Yes, yes of course." Molly got up. "I'll get some bedding."

As Molly departed up a set of creaking stairs, Lynch rubbed his stubble chin and cheeks wishing he had taken his travelling bags with him and not left them at the hotel. But then he supposed he could borrow Mr. Rourke's straight razor in the morning. For that matter he could use a clean shirt and a pair of socks – even a different pair of gentleman's briefs would be welcomed. He wondered morbidly if the dead man's clothes fit him.

Molly reappeared with sheets and a couple of blankets. "It's that army cot," she pointed to an iron frame affair set against the wall in the far corner Lynch hadn't noticed before. "You can bring it closer to the fire if you like."

"Thank you, that's fine…" He paused "I almost forgot. I'd like to see Mr. Rourke's belongings if I could?"

"Oh yes, upstairs in his writing room."

Lynch followed her up the noisy stairs to the second floor. He noted, however, that the stairway continued up into the darkness. "Where does this lead to?" he asked puzzled since the building, he thought, had but two floors.

"Onto the roof," she replied. "There's nothing up there except an alcove and a door. All these row houses were built the same with flat roofs. On

summer nights when the heat became unbearable John and I would sometimes spend a pleasant evening observing the stars and the city horizon."
She said no more and Lynch followed her to a tiny study just off what he
presumed was their bedchamber.

"Most of his things are here," Molly said, lighting the wicket on a bull
lamp, which sat prominently on a battered writing desk.

Lynch nodded. "Well, I guess I'll start with the desk."

The Canadian detective searched diligently through the drawers but
found nothing of note. He then proceeded to flip through the pages of a
number of slim volumes stacked on top of the desk; no pieces of paper fell
out. Nor was rummaging through a large chest productive. Lynch had hoped
for a notebook or some such record detailing some of Rourke's activities but
like Lynch, it appeared that the deceased, too, thought it wise not to write
anything down.

"Well, that's that," Lynch grumbled, hands on hips surveying the room.
"Where's Mr. Rourke's wardrobe?"

"In the bedroom," she said, hovering at the entrance to the study.

"If you don't mind – perhaps he may have left something useful in
his pockets."

"All right," she said skeptically.

Molly led him to the clothes closet in the adjoining room. Lynch rifled
through Rourke's blue belly uniform and sorted trousers, coats and shirts,
noting that, if need be the shirts at least would fit him. There was not a scrap
of paper to be found until he searched a faded waistcoat. From its pocket he
extracted a crumpled cigar wrapper.

"The Gods are with us," he stated with a satisfied smile.

"What is it?" Molly came close to him touching his arm lightly.

He handed her the wrapper. Scribbled faintly across the crease was 'S.
O'Bannion 6 Washington.'

"That's up the street, only a few blocks away!" Molly exclaimed.

"Good."

Lynch had resolved to hunt down O'Bannion first thing next day.
Rourke had just lessened by a great measure the time to be spent on such
an endeavour.

CHAPTER EIGHT
Ottawa

John A. had difficulty concentrating on the billiard game; he was thinking of Luce, caught forever like an erotic painting on the canvass of his mind, standing naked but for a camisole, stockings and pumps in front of a huge bed with burnished posts.

Without saying a word she leisurely moved toward him and with delicate fingers unbuttoned and removed his shirt and then his trousers, neatly folding each over a chair. Macdonald's member stood tall against the fabric of his shorts; he could scarcely contain himself. "Ooh la la," Luce cooed. The little game of false modesty that they had played was over. She had taken the initiative and now he took charge.

With the exuberance of a man half his age, the politician swept Luce off her feet and carried her to the bed. With quickened anticipation both discarded the last of their attire and abandoned themselves to carnal pleasures. Macdonald strained his back but regained a great deal of confidence in his manhood that night. What was it that Robbie Burns said about the lasses ...

"You're off your game, John. That's the second time you've missed that side pocket. Normally, that would be an easy shot for you."

"Aye, D'Arcy, my mind is pre-occupied — has been these last few days. I canna shoot straight." Macdonald put up his cue stick. "I concede. You win – let's go celebrate. I have need of a wee drink."

Thomas D'Arcy McGee's puffy round face, perimetered with a thin beard that stretched to either end of his ample locks, produced a mock scowl. This 'scholar in politics' as John A. once called him would be the last man to object to such a proposition but he was wary of the Attorney General's 'wee drink'; he had seen the infectiously likeable Scotsman soaked on more than one occasion in private and in public. Indeed, if the truth be known, Macdonald gave the best speech McGee had ever heard in the legislature while under intoxication and that was no frivolous judgement since McGee had a well-deserved reputation for the gift of gab himself. Of course, John A. in that particular instance spoiled his impact when he bounded over the paneled rail, crossed the floor to the opposition benches and proceeded to manhandle a Grit who had just finished insulting him!

"Perhaps, a few drops of scotch then – but mind, don't tempt me further," McGee warned half seriously, "I'm reformed."

"Hah," snorted Macdonald. "Since when does an Irishman turn his back on a sociable bottle?"

"Since my wife decided that she might do without a foul and foolish drunkard for a husband."

Like Macdonald, McGee in the past had had an unfortunate propensity for alcohol. On more than one occasion he too had found himself in a senseless stupor much to the detriment of his health and career. But with the patient help of his wife he learned the benefits of moderation if not total abstinence.

"Touché my dear D'Arcy. Touché!" Macdonald said flippantly. "An unarguable point. I, however, have no such encumbrances."

As they stepped across the lobby of the British Hotel, a favourite rendezvous for politicians since it was but a five minute walk from the Parliament buildings, McGee gave his friend a curious glance. "I heard that that may soon change," he said lightheartedly.

"What?" Macdonald stopped and looked at the diminutive Irishman, his face expressing bewilderment.

"You've been holding out on me, you old rascal."

Macdonald could have sworn that McGee winked.

"That's why you've been distracted these last couple of days. Am I right? Come on fess up!"

"D'Arcy, I canna think what you are talking about -"

"Tch, tch," McGee shook his head. "I spoke with Hewitt the other day. He informs me that you do not come home as regularly as you used to. He misses your company – thinks you might have found a lady."

Macdonald frowned. Hewitt, with whom he shared lodgings, evidently had noticed his altered routine. "My private secretary has a loose tongue and an active imagination."

"Oh, don't blame poor Hewitt. He mentioned your absences on the chance that I knew the reason … Who is she?" McGee's eyes had a twinkle in them.

As he was about to reply, Macdonald spied the portly figure of James Cockburn, the Solicitor General of Canada West, ambling toward them. McGee met and followed Macdonald's eyes, nodded his head in a gesture of understanding and the subject was summarily dropped.

"Ah, James!" Macdonald greeted him amicably "I've not seen you of late."

"John … D'Arcy," Cockburn acknowledged, shaking hands with both. He was one of those less than brilliant members of the government whose virtues consisted of an even tempered personality and loyalty. "I just come in – been attending to affairs in Cobourg."

"And how are things in the fair town of Cobourg?" McGee asked.

"Bloody cold – although, I dare say the weather is not exactly balmy here."

"Enough to shrivel the balls of an Angus bull," agreed McGee.

"Well, as the Minister of Agriculture you should know," quipped Macdonald.

The three men had a hearty laugh.

"We're off for a wee dram of scotch," declared Macdonald. "Care to join us?"

"Well, perhaps, just for a pint of bitter brew."

"Good man."

As they continued into the dining saloon, Cockburn, in fact, did talk about Cobourg – more specifically he related in some detail the financial difficulties of the Cobourg-Peterborough Railway of which he was the solicitor. "… There was no more to be raised on the money markets," he explained "and amalgamation is the only way out. I had an interview with the President and Vice-President of the Marmora Iron Works and we agreed to terms. The deed for the Cobourg-Peterborough and Marmora Railway and Mining Company was accepted by the stockholders – and a good thing too! Cobourg was on the verge of ruin."

Macdonald nodded gravely. Less than a week had passed since he listened to Cartier's involved tale of woes concerning the Grand Trunk. And here was another. He could sympathize. The good citizens of Cobourg had spent over one million dollars to build their iron band, including a three-mile trestle bridge across Rice Lake – the longest in North America – with little return to the community.

"As I recall," he said, "the construction of the original railway was a rather shoddy affair with the bridge proving quite unstable?"

"It was," affirmed Cockburn. "So much so that when the Prince of Wales visited the region on his royal tour in '60, he was dissuaded from traversing across the structure for fear it might collapse!"

"Wouldn't have wanted the 'boy prince' in the train when it tumbled into the lake," chortled McGee with a smirk' "What would the queen have thought!"

"Indeed," said Cockburn, "there was a spot of gambling done in the local taverns on whether the prince dared take the ride and if he did whether he would have survived. In any case, he would have been fine – the bridge didn't collapse 'til the following winter."

The thought of the prince's Canadian tour brought a sudden colic knot to Macdonald's gut even now six years later. The perils of politics ...

It began so splendidly. Queen Victoria had picked Bytown as the new capital to be and what better way to cement Her Majesty's choice than to have her eldest son, Albert Edward, make a grand tour of the North American Colonies. The prince was only eighteen years old but had the appropriate attributes for such an occasion, representing royalty with engaging pomp and circumstance. Nattily attired, slim framed and not quite having outgrown his round boyish face, which eschewed any noticeable stubble for fine curled locks on top extending to the neck, he was a most presentable royal poster boy, not to mention giving socialite women a flutter.

Macdonald met him on the Gaspé after his well-received Maritime Colonies tour. They steamed up the St. Lawrence River to visit selected venues in Canada East. Again, he was most graciously greeted by both the English and French, especially in Montreal where he christened the Victoria Bridge that connected Montreal to St. Lambert on the south shore.

The highlight – at least for Macdonald and his fellow conservatives who had lobbied vigorously for this royal visit – was Albert Edward's arrival in Ottawa. With a great sense of occasion and to enormous applause from a large, dignified audience, the prince laid what the local press described as "an exquisite piece of white Canadian marble" (crystallized limestone) as the cornerstone of the Centre Block that would "receive the legislation of Canada." This symbolized in a formal way (and we "Victorians" were anything if not formal Macdonald mused at the time) the transformation of Barrack Hill from simply a rocky outcrop of cleared brush and cut beech and hemlock where an old military base stood, to the site of Canada's parliament buildings. As the Prince's host/chaperone Macdonald was immensely pleased.

And yet, anxious and uneasy as they continued their tour down the St. Lawrence toward his hometown – Kingston. What worried him was his Orange Order supporters who were loyal to a fault and eager to demonstrate that loyalty – much too eagerly for the realities of royal politics, Macdonald knew. Orangemen would flaunt their protestant colours alienating both the Irish Catholics of Kingston and the prince who was duty bound to tolerate no manifestations of such religious feuding. Indeed, the English Parliament had just passed a bill suppressing the Orange Order in Ireland as a subversive political party. Thus, under no circumstances was the Prince going to recognize the Order or their fanatical anti-Catholic campaigns. Orange Order banners and other displays along with Orangemen marching in full regalia would be interpreted as a direct affront to Macdonald's young royal charge and he did the best he could at beseeching his Orangemen supporters to put way their flags and colours. But to no avail. As the royal steamer (ironically enough named the *Kingston)* put into the harbour, thousands of costumed and boisterous Orangemen waving their standards awaited his arrival on the wharf.

A standoff ensued. Despite Macdonald's last desperate pleas to their "good senses" they refused to take down their pennants and concomitant paraphernalia. The Prince was not amused. Appearing on deck, he noted with distain the excited crowd and their objectionable advertisements and declared that he had seen enough! He retired for the night and the next morning the *Kingston* weighted anchor and steamed toward Belleville and Cobourg.

Macdonald was forced to stay behind with the Orangemen whom he could not afford to alienate. The 'Siege of Kingston', as his political opponents called it, was a sad, sordid business that rendered him stupefied and he spent the summer of 1860 on a provincial speaking tour of his own to win back loyalties.

"It seems many a community has been cursed by the scourge of ruinous railway building," commented McGee who, although a staunch advocate of the Intercolonial Railway project to unite the Canadas with the Maritimes as a practical step toward a union of the British North American colonies, was skeptical when it came to the railway construction fever that ran rampant in the smaller centres throughout the provinces.

"True, so true," Cockburn shook his head. "The price of progress. Now with this agreement I have upset the citizens of Belleville."

"How's that?" Macdonald asked as they settled themselves comfortably in plush chairs in a quiet corner of the dining saloon. It was early yet for the more fashionable of Ottawa to partake in the hotel's dinner bill of fare; thus, there were few people about.

"Well, it appears that the Belleville folk believe it will siphon off mineral resources, which might be transported when the Belleville and North Hastings Railway is complete."

Macdonald pulled his mouth into a moue of distaste. "We can ill afford to antagonize a constituency that has steadfastly given us their vote. Perhaps you should have a word with the local member, smooth some ruffled feathers."

"Indeed, I will."

The 'railway discussion' ended only after the first round of drinks had been consumed. As they waited for refills, McGee produced three corpulent cigars and amid a rising, dense cloud of combusted tobacco, they engaged in a lively deliberation over the prospects of confederation.

All had been part of the Canadian delegation that had attended the Quebec Conference. Macdonald and McGee had been among the chief participants in the debates while no one could remember what Cockburn had said, if anything at all. Privately, Macdonald acknowledged that Cockburn was a minor actor in the advancement of the grand scheme. Still, he was the official host when the Maritime delegation visited Cobourg on their tour of

Canada West and could be counted on to further the cause of confederation in his own small way.

McGee raged passionately about the stupidity of the New Brunswick anti-unionists and the calamity that could befall the colonies if they were not soon defeated. Cockburn wholeheartedly agreed while Macdonald, as he had with the equally passionate Cartier, assured them both that the anti-confederates' days were numbered.

Then, the discussion turned to the machinations of the Fenians. Macdonald and McGee had agreed in a meeting a couple days before to keep the substance of McMicken's alarming report confidential, at least until the Chief of the Canadian Secret Service could produce concrete details of the suspected plot. That, however, did not prevent McGee from roundly denouncing the fanatical Irishmen. "Fenianism is a foolish and wicked conspiracy," he snorted, "against the existing civil authorities and I may add still more against the divinely constituted authority of the Church of God... Besides," he added, "it gives an excuse for the Orange Lodges to arm all their members to the great risk of the peace and poor Catholics who have no connection with the Fenians or their follies."

"I dare say you're right," Cockburn concurred, taking a swig of his bitter. "And they appear to be gaining strength. I read recently that just in New York alone they have enlisted some twenty-five thousand able-bodied men to march on Canada – that they are well equipped with cartridge boxes and knapsacks—"

"Gross exaggeration!" bellowed McGee. "Empty words for political gain. But no doubt they are being spurred on and easily gulled by American politicians in want of Irish votes. Their gullibility in that respect is only exceeded by them paying good money to Roberts and O'Mahoney!"

"Whatever their numbers and resources," interjected Macdonald, "the Fenians will see a strong arm put forth at the first sign of hostilities."

"In what state of preparedness are we?" asked Cockburn, draining the last of his glass.

"There are ten companies at Windsor, six at Sarnia, ten at Prescott, a regiment of artillery at Stanstead and about sixty men and artillery at Brockville. And that is only a start," emphasized the Minister of Militia. "The balance of the troops are held in reserve in Toronto, Hamilton, London, Kingston,

Montreal and Quebec." Macdonald counted off the cities on his fingers. "And volunteers are pouring into all the interior towns."

"Then I have no doubt that the situation is well in hand," remarked Cockburn pulling out his pocket watch and giving it a quick glance. "Oh, bloody hell, I've dallied too long in your splendid company, I really must be off." He took up his coat and hat. "I have enjoyed our conversation."

"Remember to smooth those ruffled feathers in Belleville," Macdonald reminded the Solicitor General.

"Count on me to do my best. See you both shortly."

"Aye, we'll be meeting officially soon enough," Macdonald responded good naturedly.

"A congenial sort, the honourable gentleman," said McGee, his eyes on Cockburn's receding back.

"A good man – but of limited capacity," retorted Macdonald candidly while picking up the bill of fare from the white clothed table. "I'm not sure he's the best man to fill his position in the ministry but," Macdonald shrugged "loyal supporters must be rewarded – that's in the nature of politics."

"Hmm," McGee pursed his lips. "A charitable view."

"Not at all." Macdonald's mouth curved in a shrewd smile. "Just being realistic. Now what do you say to sampling some of this establishment's culinary delights?"

McGee thought a moment. "Oh, why not! Our wee drink has run longer than I anticipated and I could use some sustenance."

"Splendid! Roast lamb is their special of the day."

"That will do nicely." McGee then leaned over conspiratorially. "But I'll not let you off lightly. I return to the subject at hand before Mr. Cockburn intervened."

"Which was?" Macdonald asked innocently.

"Your new lady friend of course! Come, come John, you cannot hold out on me."

Macdonald sighed. There was no getting around McGee's curiosity. "A fine woman, I can tell you that D'Arcy. Enough to make one a regular church goer."

What is the fair maiden's name?"

"Luce, Luce Beaudoir," Macdonald said almost wistfully.

"A foreigner?"

"Hold your tongue McGee! She's no more a foreigner than you or I. Indeed, her roots go further back into this land than both of ours. She's from a respectable French-Irish Canadian family."

"No prejudice intended John, it's just the name caught me by surprise. Are you seriously thinking of giving up your single gentleman's status?"

"Good heavens, man, I haven't even gotten around to serious courting." *Although I've made a penetrating beginning,* he mused to himself. "She's some years younger. She may not have an old scoundrel like me... past his prime."

"Nonsense! You'll never be too old, John," McGee remarked. "You've got too much joie de vivre."

Macdonald slid back into his chair. "If only it were true, D'Arcy. These last few years since Isabella's passing and Agnes's departure," the politician's face darkened, "I've wondered from time to time what it would be like to have someone waiting when the day is done, to share problems, failures and triumphs with, to raise young ones again. Understand my meaning?"

McGee suddenly felt compassion for the lonely man collapsed in his seat across from him. "Of course I do. You deserve a special woman. Here's to the best for you and your lady – together." He raised his glass.

Macdonald gave a faint smile, raising his glass also. "To Luce," he said.

CHAPTER NINE
Washington

Secretary of State Seward looked up from the report he had been reading in annoyance. Baxter had just made another officious entrance into his office. "Mr. Secretary—"

"My God, Baxter," Seward growled, "I'll have to put in an appropriation for contingent expenses to replace the carpeting the way you regularly come marching in. You are carving out a trench to my desk!"

"Sorry, sir—"

Seward cut him off. "I've just been reading the War Department's computations of the number of deaths in the Union Armies since the commencement of the rebellion."

"Yes, sir?"

"Ghastly, Baxter, absolutely ghastly – two hundred and fifty thousand men – that's just our side. Southern soldiers amount to at least two hundred and twenty-five thousand – perhaps as high as five hundred and seventy-five thousand lives lost. My God, what a high price to pay for a nation's life!"

"Yes, sir."

"At Gettysburg alone twenty-three thousand Union boys were killed or wounded. And Lee's losses," Seward turned over a page in the report. "From the time he crossed the Rapidan River until his surrender ninety thousand Confederates died."

"Appalling, sir. Mr. Secretary, a dispatch has just arrived from one of our agents assigned to the Fenian Brotherhood."

Seward motioned Baxter to sit down.

"Thank you, sir, it's from agent Benjamin Matthews – the one assigned to Mr. McQuealy."

"Ah, yes, Mr. McQuealy." Seward vividly recalled the interview he endured with the cocky Irishman a few days ago. "And?"

"It appears that Mr. McQuealy is quite elusive. Matthews lost him in New York."

"New York, eh?" The Secretary of State rubbed his chin. "The Fenians are making a notable stir up there."

"It appears so, sir. Agent Matthews is making an official request to cross the border into Canada ... Montreal."

"Montreal?"

"Yes, sir. As I mentioned he lost Mr. McQuealy's trail in New York but discovered that he transferred a substantial sum of money from New York to Montreal."

"How did Matthews find that out?"

"He didn't say, sir."

"Hmm..."

"Matthews – with our permission of course – thinks he can trace the flow of this money to its final destination. He also believes that Mr. McQuealy may show up in Montreal."

"Does he have any idea what the money is to be used for?"

"He speculates it is a payment of some sort – thinks the Fenians are up to something in Montreal, a disruption of some kind, possibly even an assassination."

"Oh? On what basis does he make such a deduction?"

"Apparently, the funds sent – two thousand five hundred dollars to be exact – is but the first instalment. The bankers – Kemp & Shannon of New York – on further authorization from Mr. McQuealy are to forward to Montreal an additional twenty-five hundred."

"Matthews must be a pretty persuasive man." Seward shoved his chair back and got up smiling wryly.

"Sir?"

"To get the bank to divulge such information. Wouldn't you say so, Baxter?"

"I suppose so, sir. I have Matthews' report right here."

"Leave it on the desk when you go." Clasping his hands behind his back Seward slowly paced to the window, staring at the gently falling snow and in the distance the half erected dome of the Congress Building. He seemed lost in thought. "You know, Baxter," he finally said, "I have always thought that Canada was incapable of sustaining itself and thus easily detachable from its parent state."

"Yes, sir. About agent Matthews' request?"

"Yes, agent Matthews. Inform me."

"Sir?"

"Tell me about him. He has piqued my interest."

Baxter furrowed his brow, recalling the file. "He's from Texas—"

"Texas! I thought they were all Confederates?"

"Conscripted into the Confederate Army, sir. Had no choice as I understand it, sir."

"So how did we get him?"

"Captured – apparently didn't need much converting. His instructor at West Point interrogated him, recommended him to Major General Hooker for the Bureau of Information. By all accounts proven to be a valuable asset to our 'secret service.' I don't know the details of his other assignments."

"A West Point graduate?" Seward seemed pleased at this discovery as if this made all the difference to this mission.

"Yes, sir."

"Cable Matthews and tell him to proceed to Montreal. He is, however, to remain in the background and not to interfere in anyway with the Fenians or their plans until he discovers what they are. Then, a decision will be made as to what he will do – if anything."

"I understand, sir. There is one more item." Seward turned from the window toward his able assistant. Baxter hurriedly carried on. "Agent Matthews requests Canadian identity papers … er, false ones with the appropriate governmental authority. These are indispensable in gaining access to information that the bank in Montreal has concerning the transfer of McQuealy's funds, to whom and for what purpose."

"Yes, I see. A resourceful agent our man Matthews. Make those arrangements but try to keep within budget."

"Yes, Mr. Secretary."

As Baxter left the office Seward returned to his desk. "Whatever those Fenians are up to, it better be worth the expense and resources I'm putting in," he muttered as he once again began reading the shocking statistics supplied by the War Department.

***

A diminutive black man was playing some 'Negro' songs on a battered accordion as Baxter entered the 'Potomac Hideaway', a seedy establishment in the heart of Washington. He entered just in time to hear someone yell, "Enough of that, play Yankee Doodle."

It was dark, smoky and reeking of beer and other indeterminate odours, definitely not the kind of place frequented by the capital's respectable citizenry. Baxter found this most comforting because the last thing he wanted was a chance encounter with a politician he knew or his colleagues from work. The trick for him was to be anonymous – just another nondescript sojourner in for a quick nip before moving on. He need not have worried, he supposed, given the nature of Washington. Once removed from the white-washed edifices of the Congress Building (even if not quite completed), the Supreme Court and the White House, one found a raw, coarse town inhabited by a motley population of lesser notables, from the recently-arrived to all manner of social outcasts. The solid citizens and the finer hotels were across the river in Arlington, Virginia.

His collar up, the hat pulled down, Baxter allowed a few moments for his eyes to adjust to the surroundings. It wasn't overly busy but there was enough of a clientele to serve his purpose. He placed some coinage on the bar, ordered a whiskey and made his way to an empty corner table with a good view of the entrance. He had come early to stake out the ground and to acclimatize to an unfamiliar environment. Now he waited, listening to the reedy sounds of the accordion.

The gentleman was right on time. They nodded to each other ever so slightly as the tall and exceedingly erect newcomer in a Napoleon overcoat strolled to the bar and procured his drink. Slowly, the man surveyed the room bringing the glass of mashed bourbon to his lips; distaste registered on his long aristocratic face. Evidently, his patrician nose took umbrage and he sniffed again, swirling the liquid in the glass as if to judge its colour and texture. Tentatively, he took a sip. Baxter could tell it went down unpleasantly.

The man remained at the bar for a few more minutes, shifting his attention from his drink to the hapless musician who was enduring mild harassment.

"Hey, darkie – do you know any Dixie war songs?" someone shouted.

"If he does, he better not play them here," came the retort from the far end of the bar. This was followed by a howl of laughter.

Amid this exchange, the man discreetly made his way to where Seward's chief aid sat. "Congratulations, Mr. Baxter," he said in a nicely clipped English accent as he eased himself into a creaky chair across from Baxter. "You have picked a thoroughly philistine water hole that could rival London's worst. Indeed, if I didn't know any better I'd swear someone urinated in my drink!"

"Do I detect a note of disdain, Mr. Trench?" Baxter quipped, rising to the levity of the comment.

"Absolutely!" Trench grimaced, carefully setting the glass in front of him and crossing his hands on the table. "Certainly a far cry from our usual social circles."

"That it is," Baxter acknowledged. "But, it's safer here."

"I presume we have some business of a delicate nature to discuss then."

"We do, Mr. Trench. Business that is of special interest to your ambassador," Baxter replied evenly.

Trench nodded. "Very well."

Baxter cleared his throat but said nothing. After a brief contemplative pause, Trench reached inside his coat and produced a white envelope, sliding it smoothly across the table. With hardly a glance, Baxter thrust it directly into his pocket.

"Partial payment as agreed," Trench said, "to show good faith. I trust that it will meet with your approval."

"I'm sure it will," Baxter replied taking a glance around him.

"Now then, the floor is yours, Mr. Baxter."

Baxter's Adam's apple bobbed a couple of times before he proceeded. "As suspected, the Fenians are plotting. It appears that Montreal is to be their striking point."

Trench leaned forward and toyed with his drink. "Go on, Mr. Baxter."

In precise monotones Baxter relayed the essence of Matthews' report that he had earlier that day delivered to Seward. "As yet neither the perpetrator nor the nature of the act is known. However, our agent is confident that he can ascertain that information on his arrival in Montreal," Baxter concluded.

"Does your agent have a name?" Trench asked, venturing another tepid sip from his glass.

"I prefer not to give any names," Baxter replied.

"Very well. So the trail leads to Montreal, and there is nothing else you can add?"

"Not at the moment, no."

Trench frowned and regarded Baxter intently. "And we don't know who or what, when or where in Montreal?"

"That is correct," Baxter replied nonplussed.

"Hmm... The devil is in the details and you haven't given me much, Mr. Baxter. I am not sure what Her Majesty's ambassador will make of it considering your fee."

"I have given you a starting point and for the moment that is all that is available to me. As I said, the agent will trace the money to the source and more will be forthcoming."

"I hope so, Mr. Baxter," Trench said, sounding unconvinced.

"Mr. Trench," Baxter lowered his voice to a whisper, "let me be frank. Despite my ... shall I say prominent position, my pecuniary reward is less than extravagant. Sufficient perhaps if I didn't have a young son who needs rather expensive medical care. But circumstances are such that I am forced to become entrepreneurial. However, that does not make me a Judas to my employer or my country. I am an honourable man and I have wrestled with this ever since our first chat. I am taking an enormous risk – traitors are not well thought of here. Still, I can truthfully say that I can't abide with what the Fenians are conspiring to do. Think what you will of me, I pass this on in good conscience in the sincere belief that it is the right thing to do for both our governments' sake."

"I understand perfectly, Mr. Baxter, and so will my employer. I do appreciate your candour. I am sorry about your son."

"With God's help, he will overcome his ailment."

Trench nodded solemnly. "Our business then is concluded?"

"For now."

"I trust that we will meet again very soon?"

"Yes, as soon as more information is available."

"Well, you know where to reach me." Trench pushed his glass away "A nasty concoction! Good evening to you, sir." With that he got up and made a measured exit.

Baxter lingered a few moments longer, half listening to a melancholy tune drifting above the din of the patrons. For better or worse, Baxter had made his bed and now he had to lie in it. *It can't be helped,* he consoled himself. His only offspring was dying from a rare blood disease. He had to take the money.

The squeeze box was starting to sound tired. Baxter finished his drink and decided that he too was tired. Time to call it a night.

CHAPTER TEN
Buffalo

Lynch had no difficulty finding Shawn O'Bannion's abode, if that were the proper word. It was no more than a hole in the wall, the cellar actually of a dilapidated building. The Canadian agent descended four decrepit wooden steps and easily pried open the rickety door after repeated banging failed to elicit a response. He found himself in a damp, ill-smelling hovel with bare stone walls on all four sides.

One cursory glance around told Lynch much about O'Bannion's lifestyle: a filthy bed, haphazardly scattered personal effects and an odious pile of refuse simply dumped in one corner indicated, at the very least, poor house-keeping. It was a hideous habitat, no doubt infested by rats and other vermin but typical, Lynch knew, of ghetto living in industrial cities. Evidently, O'Bannion was a man of meagre means.

The detective loosened his collar. Despite the fact that outside it was chilling to the bone and he could see his expelled breath by the light that crept around the door, he felt nauseous. It was the lack of ventilation and the permeating smell he realized. Every article exhumed a sweetly sour odour somewhere between that of rotting flesh and halitosis of the feet. Swallowing hard to keep his breakfast down, he blinked about the tiny room until his eyes finally adjusted to the gloom.

For a brief moment Lynch thought that the place had been abandoned but then he saw the half bottle of whiskey sitting on a scarred chest beside the rumpled bed. The occupant would return, he was reasonably sure. The kind that dwelled in such surroundings would not leave their sustenance if they weren't planning to come back. He then rummaged gingerly through the man's worldly possessions discovering nothing of value and most certainly no journals or letters. From this Lynch deduced that O'Bannion in all likelihood couldn't read or write.

Not a promising start, he told himself, feeling slightly disappointed. Lynch really didn't know what to expect but surely more than this. What can a drunkard living in abject poverty know about Rourke's murder and the Fenians? Yet, there it was, the only lead provided by Molly to this sordid business. He would just have to wait for the Irishman's return – wait and hope that something useful would come of his patience.

As Lynch turned to survey the chamber one more time, the toe of his boot sent an empty bottle skittering across the slimy floor. Annoyed at the sudden noise, he reached down and picked it up ready to toss it into the garbage heap where presumably it belonged when he noticed that the label on the bottle was not that of a liquor manufacturer – Batchelor's Hair Dye.

"What's this?" he muttered, examining the rectangular glass container more closely. Perversely intrigued, in the bad light he deciphered the fine print on the back: 'the original and best in the world. Perfect hair dye, reliable and instantaneous. Produces immediately a splendid black or brown. Remedies the ill effects of poor eyes.'

Somehow Lynch didn't picture O'Bannion as the kind who'd worry about the colour of his hair. Suspiciously the detective brought the top of the bottle to his nose; a faint trace of alcohol washed over his nostrils. He couldn't help but chortle to himself. This confirmed that O'Bannion couldn't read. Poor devil, probably thought that it was liquor, albeit cheaper perhaps than his usual rot gut. As he deposited the bottle into the accumulated debris, he wondered what other ingredients besides alcohol went into Batchelor's Hair Dye. Hopefully it wouldn't kill O' Bannion, at least until Lynch was through with him.

After another tour of the man's premises Lynch decided he'd had enough. Better to await O'Bannion's arrival in a more congenial locale. He desperately needed some fresh air.

Upon ascending the last creaking step, which brought him to street level, Lynch spied across the snowbound avenue a well-bundled man leaning against a lamp post. The detective's brows knitted in a frown. Was the gent staring in his direction? Before he could acquire a better second view, a cab-riolet drawn by a snorting, ill-tempered horse obscured his line. When the traffic passed, the man had disappeared.

Lynch tried to quell his growing unease. Surely the Fenians would not be on to him? More than likely it was just his imagination and the figure he spotted was innocently going about his business. But then there was Molly's statement that she had been followed. She was very apprehensive when he left her home that morning, fearful of sinister visitors. He told her to keep the curtains drawn, the doors bolted and not venture out until he returned assuring her that she was safe. Was it possible that she indeed was under surveillance and that he had been observed the day before paying her a call? Not likely, but then he had not been overly cautious. Steadying himself he shook his head and inhaled a gulp of cold air. *Clear the cobwebs old man,* he admonished himself. *You're getting a trifle paranoid.* Just the same he was glad that he had brought with him his improved Smith and Wesson Model No. 3.

For the next hour or so, Lynch wove an erratic pattern through the drab neighbourhood, ducking in and out of alleys and doubling back on the lookout for a potential pursuer. No one was dogging his trail. He then thought of hailing a cabbie to go and retrieve his baggage at the Wadsworth but changed his mind. It'd take too long and he didn't want to leave O'Bannion's residence unattended for an extended period. He'd venture out later with Molly to repossess his belongings and have a quiet dinner with her at the hotel. She'd be glad to get away. His mind flicked back to the woman he had learned so much about the night before. That she attracted him there was no doubt but as things stood he'd better concentrate on his business with O'Bannion before entertaining any stray, wayward notions.

In due course, Lynch was at O'Bannion's door again. He was about to knock but thought better of it. If O'Bannion was in there, perhaps it would be wise to catch him off guard – surprise the bloke. The detective carefully tested the doorknob. It turned easily but then he had left it unlocked after forcing it on his first visit. He nudged the aging door open a crack. Standing in the shadows he saw a man beside the bed, his back turned to Lynch.

Taking no chances, the Canadian slowly liberated his revolver from beneath his coat and delicately moved forward. It took a few seconds for his eyes to adjust despite the flickering candle on the chest. Lynch could hardly believe the view before him. The man was slightly hunched over with his bare arse sticking out from under a shirttail, the trousers around his ankles. In one hand he gripped the half bottle of whiskey Lynch noted earlier. The liquid sloshed around violently as the man rocked back and forth. It didn't take long to ascertain what was in the other hand. Sucking in a deep breath, Lynch moved stealthily toward his presumed quarry. The man was oblivious to his unexpected guest chanting rhythmically, "O Lordee Lord, O Lordee Lord."

A pungent odour assaulted the detective as he got nearer. He recognized the smell. It could only come from someone who was in need of a bath. As the wretch brought the bottle to his mouth for another swig, Lynch decided on his course of action. Normally not a sadistic individual, in this case the temptation was too great. He allowed the diminutive man to continue vigorously agitating his genitals to an auspicious moment before inching the cold barrel of the gun to the base of the man's skull.

"Don't move!" the detective barked hoarsely.

It was an inane command and quite inappropriate under the circumstances but Lynch couldn't think of anything more profound at that conjuncture.

Instantly, the bottle fell to the floor, shattering and the startled fellow leaped forward, tripping over his trousers while at the same time letting out a loud fart. He collapsed to the floor. The stench was overpowering.

For a few seconds Lynch just stood there speechless while his victim gasped for breath, his eyes wide with terror.

"Phew," Lynch waved his hand about his face to dissipate the breaking wind. "If I thought you were going to do that I'd have tried a different approach!"

When there was no response from the crumpled form Lynch continued, "You're Shawn O'Bannion I take it?" *Might as well get that fact established straight away,* thought the Canadian, although he had no doubt that he had found his man.

"Arghh, O Lordee," croaked the human as he twisted around and propped himself against the wall into a sitting position. "D-don't shoot me. I's no trouble, I's no trouble," he yelped putting his hands up defensively.

Lynch relaxed a little. The advantage was all his. He lowered his weapon slightly.

"Are you O'Bannion?" he repeated.

"'Tis me," the man finally squeaked catching his breath. "What you want, breakin' into me 'ome with that thing?" He eyed the revolver.

"A chat, Mr. O'Bannion. I need some information, which you can provide."

O'Bannion continued to stare at the stranger, still fearful but now with a flicker of anger registering on his scared, stubbly face. "Sod off!" he volunteered.

Lynch couldn't help but smile at the man's defiance under the circumstances. "Come now, Mr. O'Bannion. You don't wish to meet your maker before your natural time, do you?"

"An' who'd be you?" Despite his humiliating disposition, the bony stick of a man was feisty enough to want some answers of his own.

Lynch, however, had no intention of verbally sparring with the lout. "It's now or never," he hissed ignoring O'Bannion's bold inquiry. "Answer my questions fast and truthfully and I'll leave, troubling you no further. Refuse and you've beaten your meat for the last time. I'd have no remorse in putting a bullet between your eyes. Do you understand?"

The prostrated man nodded, suddenly losing some of his courage, evidently deciding that the menacing figure in front of him would indeed carry out his threat.

"Good, now let's talk about John Rourke."

At the mention of Rourke's name O'Bannion visibly shrank into the wall. "I didn't kill 'im. I didn't. I swear on me mutter's grave!" He started to shake uncontrollably.

"Calm yourself and tell me who did."

"O Lordee Lord," O'Bannion again started his mournful chant.

Lynch raised the six shooter and cocked the hammer. "I'm rather pressed for time and patience is not one of my virtues, Mr. O'Bannion."

"Please, please, it'll go bad for me if I tattle."

Whatever faint spirit O'Bannion had to resist was ebbing away quickly. The detective could sense it in his voice and in his desperate eyes. Lynch hated to be so dramatic an actor but, "Have it your way then," Lynch said forcefully aiming the weapon directly between the man's eyes.

"No!" screamed O'Bannion covering his head with his arms. "Tis O'Dell – Cooper O'Dell –'e'd be the one."

"Cooper O'Dell?"

"I heard 'im talkin'," sobbed the distressed Irishman. "They thought Mr. Rourke a traitor. Not me, no sir, not me. A friend he was. Treated me right as rain he did. Gave me a little silver for ole jug of distill 'e did. I swear!"

"Who's O'Dell?"

"Mean sod – a high muckety-muck in the organization he'd be."

"What organization?"

"Liberators – liberators of the ole land."

"The Fenians?"

"That be 'em. Please, all I did was listen in."

Keeping at arms-length from O'Bannion, Lynch eased himself onto the dingy bed. The springs produced a sorrowful groan.

"All right Mr. O'Bannion, tell me everything you heard. Don't leave out a scrap."

"Please sir," O'Bannion began squirming pulling his trousers up over his privates. "O'Dell'd slit me throat for squealin' 'e would. Kill me dead, like Mr. Rourke 'e will."

"I won't tell him. On the other hand, I will shoot you dead now if you don't. If you value your life you best start talking." To emphasize his seriousness Lynch again lifted his revolver toward O'Bannion's head.

"O Lordee Lord, O Lordee Lord," the man began wringing his hands.

"Mr. O'Bannion, the end of my patience is rapidly approaching," warned the detective.

"They's plannin' murder an' mayhem they is."

"The Fenians?"

"Them Fenians," O'Bannion's voice quivered.

"Where?"

"Up north, red coat country … Canada."

Lynch nodded. "Where exactly? The place?" He was becoming excited. Could it really be true that this poor excuse for a man had stumbled upon the Fenian plot?

"O Lordee," O'Bannion whimpered, "I needs a drink."

"Where, Mr. O'Bannion or you'll never live to touch a bottle again."

"The capital – 'tis what I 'eard. The capital built up some river."

"Ottawa?" Lynch prodded.

"That be it! Ottawa!"

"What are they planning to do exactly in Ottawa?"

"Like I said, a killin'"

"Who? Who is the target?" Lynch tried to keep his voice even.

"O Lordee – I 'eard no name. A high muckety-muck is all I 'eard. One of them politicians."

"A name? Give me a name!" Lynch rose from the bed and planted himself squarely in front of O'Bannion.

"On me mutter's grave I swear I heard no name." The Irishman curled closer to the wall, fear again gripping his eyes. "I heard O'Dell talk of snatchin' this important politician and killin' 'im. I sure heard no name, though."

"Snatching?" Lynch frowned. "You mean they're going to kidnap a politician and kill him?"

"That's what I 'eard."

"Is O'Dell to do the kid – snatching?"

"I couldn't say. All I heard 'im say was that it was all cleverly planned like an' all they – them Fenians – 'ad to do was wait for the word from the higher ups."

"Who might the higher ups be?"

"I heard no names. I know just O'Dell an' his boyos, I swear."

"When then? Give me a date for this snatching and murder?"

"The day before St. Patrick's Day, they'd said."

"The sixteenth?"

"If that be the day before St. Pattys."

"How did you learn all this?"

"I told you. I 'ave ears. An' they'd pay me no mind. I clean up after the meetin's, sometimes even run messages for the boyos. That be all I did. Killin's not in me nature."

"How did you meet Mr. Rourke?"

"Mr. Rourke talked to me after – after them meetin's. Said listen close an' he'd give me a little ole pocket change for what I heard. Enough to wet me whistle... I meant 'im no harm. I didn't know they were goin' to kill 'im, I swear."

"Yes, I know. On your mother's grave." Lynch said, pursing his lips in thought. All was quiet except for O'Bannion's belaboured breathing. Finally, the detective said, "Get up and get your pants on. We're going for a walk."

The Irishman eyed the unwelcome guest warily but pulled his trousers up to his waist and with his hands groping the back of the wall rose unsteadily to his feet.

"You promised to leave me be if I talked," he whined.

"I changed my mind," Lynch retorted, his revolver now levelled at O'Bannion's chest.

"Where you takin' me?" O'Bannion asked.

"We're going hunting. You'll show me the Fenian meeting place and point out O'Dell and his friends if they're about."

"O Lordee, O Lordee Lord." O'Bannion's knees buckled. "E'll kill me for sure – please I'd not—"

"You'll be all right. I won't give you away," Lynch cut off the pleading man. "You just point him out to me and disappear. I'll replace that broken bottle of whiskey for your troubles," Lynch added with a hint of a smile. What the detective proposed was risky but he wanted to know where these Fenian meetings took place and to identify O'Dell on the chance he was lurking about.

O'Bannion hesitated and stared at the shattered glass around him. "That's mighty Christian of you."

Lynch sensed it before he heard the door violently swing open. Instinctively, he hurled himself across the bed as two shots rang out. O'Bannion screamed while Lynch blindly returned fire with a couple of quick bursts from the other side of the bed.

The candle on the chest flickered out but daylight flooded the room as the door remained open. Lynch shivered in the silence that followed; a blast of cold air and snow rushed into the room. He shifted his position and felt a sharp stinging pain above his left elbow. A bullet had shredded his coat and grazed his arm. Blood seeped through the material.

"O'Bannion?" he whispered, trying to steady his breathing, "O'Bannion, do you hear me?"

Keeping his eyes fixed on the entrance, with some effort, he shoved the bed forward and crawled toward the slumped figure against the wall. O'Bannion stared into infinity, a hole clearly visible in the middle of his chest, blood and spittle trickling from the corner of his slack mouth.

"Damn," Lynch expelled his breath.

The detective waited for what seemed an interminable length of time before turning the stained and tattered mattress on its side. Using it as a shield, he inched his way toward the open door. Cautiously, he peered up the stairs. There was no one there. The assailant probably didn't loiter around; no doubt the shots had been heard and the police summoned. Buffalo Bobbies at this conjuncture Lynch could do without.

Grimacing, he made his way up the stairs, carefully scanned the surroundings and finding no gunman, he half sprinted, half trotted toward Molly's house. There was no time to lose. He had to get Molly and himself out of Buffalo and into Canada as fast as possible. He now had become a hunted man.

CHAPTER ELEVEN
Buffalo

"Pack what essentials you need. Tonight we'll be doing some hard travelling," Lynch said, grimacing as Molly swabbed and bandaged his arm.

"There, that should do it. Fortunately, the bullet just grazed you."

"Hurts worse than my ear the day the horse had it for lunch!" declared the detective, gritting his teeth and flexing the sore limb.

"That's not too tight?" She carefully inspected her handiwork.

"Fine, thank you. I'm indebted to your nursing abilities." He gave her a wan smile.

"Where do you propose we go?" she asked removing the wash basin and a bloodstained towel from the kitchen table.

"Actually..." Lynch thought for a moment. "I ... we should make our way to Windsor but I need to be in Ottawa—"

"Ottawa? Why Ottawa? What happened? What did Mr. O'Bannion tell you? Who shot you?"

"I'll explain later. Right now hurry and pack. We may have unwanted company at any moment. Oh and throw in a couple of Mr. Rourke's shirts and such for me," he added as a practical afterthought. There was no way he was going to take the time to stop at the Wadsworth for his belongings, not after the events that had transpired earlier in the day.

As Molly retreated upstairs to her bedroom, Lynch tried to marshal his thoughts. Given the time of year, rail would be the fastest mode of travel. Indeed, the only sane method to reach their destination. They'd have to get to the Canadian side of the Niagara River and catch the Great Western that connected Niagara Falls and Hamilton to Toronto. Once in Toronto he would worry about schedules and other logistics of reaching the capital. He really didn't know when he would arrive in Ottawa but figured he'd get there in plenty of time to help foil the Fenian plot. It sounded like a tortuous route but he couldn't think of any shorter alternatives.

For a brief moment he reconsidered going to Windsor. It was much shorter by rail and familiar (he had just taken that branch of the Great Western from Windsor to Fort Erie, which was just across the Niagara River from Buffalo). It had taken him only about eight hours to make the journey and he could certainly retrace this route but in the end he decided against it. Since O'Bannion's demise and his own near miss, it had become a personal matter. Besides, he rationalized, McMicken in all probability would send him to Ottawa anyway to complete his mission. Meanwhile, once he got to the Canadian side he would inform McMicken of the situation by telegraph. Having settled on a plan of action he became increasingly impatient.

"Are you almost ready?" he called upstairs somewhat irritably. He could hear Molly's footsteps overhead. They sounded a trifle loud for such a graceful woman. He realized, however, that a contributing factor was the dull pain emanating not only from his arm but increasingly from the region near the base of his skull that had escalated to a sudden pounding in his head.

"Yes, almost … but I hardly know what to take."

"Just what you need. We're travelling lightly. No more than one valise," he added under his breath.

A short while later Molly came down the stairs struggling with a large suitcase in either hand, appearing slightly disheveled.

"I was thinking more of a small valise," he said with a trace of exasperation.

"These are my essentials," she countered. "Besides, I packed a number of items for you as well."

Lynch sighed. No point in arguing.

Molly had changed her attire, he noted, from the bleached cotton skirt she had on to a longer green dress complete with a similarly coloured velvet hat from which wispy tendrils of red hair curled out. Although not entirely suitable for a potentially hazardous getaway, thought the detective, it did complement her large green eyes and accentuated her full figure. *An enticing woman,* he concluded as he rose from the kitchen table, buttoned up his shirt and grabbed his corduroy jacket from the chair.

There was an awkward pause in which he caught himself staring at the stylish woman. Recovering belatedly, he said, "Better get your coat and boots."

Molly nodded, set the suitcases down with a thud and went over to the closet near the entrance. "I didn't pack much really," she remarked removing her winter garments from the rack.

Lynch eyed the two rather substantial double-strapped cases dubiously. Aloud he said, "Well, don't worry. Arrangements can be made to procure the rest of your wardrobe and chattels when this sorry affair is over."

She sighed, her eyes giving the room a wide sweep. "I suppose so."

Taking care with his sore arm Lynch slipped his own coat on. It was a little worse for wear; just above the left elbow the ragged gash with dark stains of blood remained. There was no time for needle and thread. He felt his right pocket instinctively to make sure his revolver was where he had put it after his departure from O'Bannion's hovel.

"Right," he said, his mouth drawn tight around the corners. "It's off to the train depot." He quickly explained the travel itinerary. "We need to get the train that will get us to Niagara Falls, then it's across the suspension bridge to Canada. Should be simple enough," he reassured her.

"That would be the New York Central, I think," she said. "But I don't know the schedule."

"We'll sort all that out at the depot," he said, grunting as he lifted the two pieces of baggage.

"Here, do you need help with that?" she asked, looking at his injured arm.

"No, thank you… I can manage," he responded wondering what weighty objects she had stuffed into the cases.

At the door he set his burden down and moved to the window. Slowly, he drew the curtain back and carefully scanned the street. At first, he saw nothing unusual. Darkness had descended although the lamplighter as yet had not been around to the gas lamps. Washington Street appeared cold and quiet with no traffic of any kind, pedestrian or vehicle. Then, from the corner of his eye he saw a flame flicker. Someone had lit a cigarette or cigar at the edge of the alley directly across the street.

"Damn!"

"What is it?" Molly came up behind him, alarmed.

"We're being watched." He ushered her back toward the kitchen/parlour area.

"What are we to do now?" she asked.

Lynch started pacing; he suddenly felt a cold chill down his spine. "Let me think. We can't readily walk out the front – or the back for that matter. Certainly there's someone stationed there as well. That leaves only one other route – the roof."

"The roof?" Molly looked at him doubtfully.

"Why not? You said yesterday the stairs lead onto to the roof."

"Yes, but—"

"These houses are adjoined, right? We'll make our escape across the rooftops."

"How will we get down?"

"A fire ladder. I'm sure we'll find one. It's our only chance to leave unobserved," he added when Molly still retained her skeptical expression.

Molly led the way up the stairs as Lynch followed awkwardly with the two suitcases. *Might have to dump these if the going gets too rough,* he thought, although for now, he could handle them. At the top there was a small dais and a four foot door.

"Our salvation – I hope," he intoned while struggling with the rusty hook that kept the wooden door shut. Once the hook was off it took another few minutes to pry the door open because of the ice and snow that had accumulated on the other side. Finally, with the full force of his shoulder put into action, they were on the roof.

"Stay down," he ordered, catching his breath against the chilly wind that seemed to spring from nowhere. In the intermittent glow of the moon that darted in and out from behind the clouds, he surveyed his surroundings. "Remain here for a moment."

Molly didn't say anything but crouched against the splintered door shivering. Lynch quickly skirted the perimeter of the building returning winded, his breath forming irregular curls in the night air.

"We'll go across to the other dwelling yonder, put some distance between ourselves and our pursuers. Stay crouched and follow me. Be careful – the footing is treacherous."

With the baggage in either hand the detective and his charge slipped and slid their way to the north end of the row house. There they discovered that the buildings were not attached to each other as they had assumed.

"It's only a two or so foot jump over to the other side," he informed Molly in a placating tone.

Molly stared at the gaping black crevice.

"Don't worry," he assured her, "you'll make it."

He tossed the suitcases across the gap and followed after, making the leap effortlessly. "Come now," he beckoned.

"Mr. Lynch," she said in her best formal tone, "I don't think I can do this!"

"You have to, Molly," he whispered across the dark void between them. "Now, hitch up your skirt, take a little run at it and lean forward. Watch your footing."

She nodded, petrified at the prospect of what she was about to attempt. Her adrenalin pumping, the agitated woman took three steps backward, then vaulted forward like an unleashed colt. With her eyes tightly shut she executed a formidable leap that carried her with considerable force into Lynch's waiting arms. He fell hard on his sternum with her landing cushioned by his body. On the ice and snow she clutched him fervently as an infant her mother.

"Well done!" he said with bravo, trying not to grimace.

"When I informed you that John and I use to venture out on the roof," she gasped, her breathing erratic, "I neglected to state that I kept well away from the edges. I'm dreadfully afraid of heights, you know."

"I would never have guessed!"

"Are you mocking me?"

"Of course not!" he smiled as they disentangled. The Canadian would have cheerfully held her in his arms longer if under more conducive circumstances.

They repeated the process one more time to get onto the next relatively flat roof. Molly performed much better on her second jump. She landed softly against the detective and both retained their balance.

"Well, this is where we climb down," he pronounced matter-of-factly, his eyes scanning the steep slant of the roof they would need to conquer should they wish to continue their present course.

"Oh God!" Molly stopped abruptly as she saw the peak loom before her.

"Here, sit on the suitcase while I look around. There should be a ladder here somewhere." Lynch then hurried off to inspect the edges of the edifice. Eureka! He found what he was searching for: weather-beaten, rather fragile-looking but it would have to do. The ladder provided an exit to a back alley.

Timidly, Molly came closer to the edge, saw the top of the ladder perpendicularly fastened to the wall of the structure and let out a mournful cry: "I can't climb down that!"

Lynch ignored her comment. "I'll go first to make sure it's sturdy enough."

"This is not going to work!"

"Shh… Noise carries a long way in the night. We don't want to alert our friends," he admonished her.

· Taking a suitcase in hand, he eased himself backwards onto the ladder. With one foot he cautiously tested the slippery rungs step by step before putting his full weight on them. It was a slow descent but uneventful until about three or four feet from the ground. Abruptly, the ladder ended and for a few seconds he found himself dangling in mid-air as one boot groped in vain for the next perch. He let go of the suitcase and heard it thud in the darkness below. *Hope Molly didn't pack any delicate heirlooms,* he mused, as he scrambled back up the ladder.

"Oliver?" came an anxious voice from the top.

"I'm fine." His head popped into view. "It's sturdy enough, Molly. Now hand me the other suitcase and follow me down. There's a drop at the bottom of a few feet but don't worry, I'll catch you."

The Irish woman sighed, resigning herself to another ordeal. "I'm not properly attired for this sort of activity," she complained as her rear end backed into Lynch's face.

The climb down, however, was accomplished without any further drama; the baggage too survived intact. Once on solid ground, they made their way to a main street and in a relatively short space of time miraculously hailed a horse-drawn tram. The craggy-faced driver informed them that indeed it went right by the train station.

Quite fatigued by their exertions, they gathered close on the wooden bench for support and warmth. There were three other passengers on the tram in the seats ahead of them bundled against the cold. Two more got on before they reached their destination. Lynch felt relatively certain that they had eluded their pursuers.

As the tram trotted along, Molly again repeated her fear of heights. "I once saw," she explained, "a young man slip off and fall while sweeping the snow from the roof. Hit a woodpile. He remained insensible for the longest time. Gives me the shivers just thinking about it. My knees wobbled all the way down that wretched ladder."

"I can appreciate that," Lynch remarked dryly. "I'm now wary of hungry horses."

He laughed although his cold, sensitive, partial ear reminded him that it was a lamentable experience, which drew no humour at the time. He could barely restrain himself from shooting the animal afterwards.

Ten minutes after boarding, the tram turned onto Exchange Street and there loomed the rather imposing towers of the train station composed of brick core walls faced with ashlar masonry of freestone and Cleveland stone. Although the crowds were sparse it took some time for the haggard couple to establish their bearings, make the necessary inquiries and locate the proper wicket. Since they were embarking together on what ultimately would be a long journey, Lynch suggested that for appearances sake they travel as Mr. and Mrs. Lynch. Molly offered no objections.

"Well, we could've done worse!" Lynch exclaimed holding up two tickets.

Molly, who had been standing beside the suitcases off to one side of a small queue while the Canadian conferred and then procured their passage, smiled weakly. She appeared totally exhausted.

"We're in luck," he continued, "the New York Central for Niagara Falls leaves within the hour. Certainly, we don't want to be hanging around here for too long." He picked up the suitcases and started toward the platforms.

Catching up to his stride Molly said, "I'm glad … glad to be leaving."

"So am I and not a moment too soon. Our Fenian friends will, no doubt, before long realize that we have eluded them and quite likely come here looking for us. But, with any luck, we'll be well on our way."

"I hope so," Molly said wearily.

"Once across the border," Lynch pondered aloud, "I must at the earliest opportunity telegraph a message to McMicken, and also to the authorities in Ottawa. Warn them."

"You haven't told me exactly what this is about," Molly reminded the detective. "Mr. O'Bannion must have said something important to have someone shoot you and those men wanting to—" she broke off, letting the thought drop.

"I'll explain the details," Lynch promised, "as soon as we're comfortably settled on the coach." He suddenly became aware of the dull pain in his arm. He would also get the bandage changed then.

***

He saw them the moment they emerged from the alley. A wolfish grin cracked his skeletal face. *I guess I'll 'ave to take care of this m'self after all,* he mused, keeping in step some distance behind them. It was a lucky thing that after a couple of pints he decided to double back and check up on Timothy and Thomas – not the brightest lads – *Stupid sods,* he amended. Their job was to make sure that Rourke's fancy woman and the noisy detective did not leave the house, at least not alive. But as he half expected, they bungled it. He should have known from their dumb questions.

"What if they's not comin' out durin' the evenin'?" asked Thomas, scratching at his russet foliage nervously.

"Then wait 'til the lights go out. They'd be in bed. Slit their throats," he instructed them.

"It's too fockin' cold ta be in the street waitin' for them ta decide to sleep," grumbled Timothy. "'Sides, what if they's fockin' in bed?"

"Then they'll be distracted when you take'm, won't they?"

"Why aren't you comin' with us?" Thomas persisted.

"'Cause I got me some business to take care of. Can't be 'specting me ta hold your hand all the time. Now, off wit you – take care of that red coat spy and Rourke's slut."

"Shit 'eads," he muttered under his breath as he surreptitiously kept pace with the fleeing pair. Probably lost their nerve and are now in some pig of a pub drunk and swonking the first ugly wench that let them. The Fenian army was in trouble if it consisted of blokes the likes of Timothy and Thomas.

Well, he supposed, it was partly his fault. He got on to Rourke quickly enough and did his duty. He should have tidied up the loose ends right after. Instead, he dallied, especially with that Mahone wench, thinking he'd like to sample her wares before disposing of her. The time and place never seemed to his liking although he followed her about. And with the police snooping around the neighbourhood he didn't dare risk inviting himself into her living quarters. He'd thought he'd wait a while.

Then he was informed that another Canadian agent was coming to investigate. Another bloody spy to worry about. And how the bastard got on to O'Bannion so soon. At least that runt had been attended to. Damn shame he missed the agent though. He didn't figure much information could be obtained from O'Bannion. What would that liquor soaked sod know? Half the time the man couldn't remember his own name! Still, maybe he should have rubbed him out the same night he did in Rourke. No matter now. He promised his superiors that he'd wipe the slate clean – no leaks, no potential for a miscarriage of well-laid plans. He'd been paid amply to do what any true patriot would do.

Shooting them in the street would be tricky, however. There were witnesses about. Best follow them and pick a more congenial local. He slowed his pace when he saw the man set down his suitcases and hail a passing tram. Oh, oh, wouldn't do to let them get away on him. He quickened his pursuit, instinctively reaching for his weapon. *Might have to chance it,* he thought. As he got closer he heard the Canadian ask the driver if the tram went by the train depot. When assured it did; they got on. He briskly walked by. He'd get on a half block down and accompany them to the station.

I'll get them on the train, he decided. It been a while since he took an excursion.

119

CHAPTER TWELVE
En Route to Niagara Falls

Oliver Lynch studied the timetable and then glanced at his gold hunter. The train was scheduled to depart at 11:50; however, it was now a quarter after midnight and it still hadn't begun its journey to the Falls. He supposed it really didn't matter that so long as it got moving without too much further delay. The important thing was that he had obtained berths in the sleeping car. Otherwise, they would have had to do with a day coach. Although the trip on the New York Central would be relatively brief, after what both he and Molly had been through, a couple hours repose was in order.

He rubbed his eyes and folded the timetable, stuffing it into his pocket. The flat-wick coal oil lamps hanging from the clerestory roof were acceptable as general illumination but not ideal for reading. He glanced up the carpeted aisle flanked by triple-tiered berths and partitions of black walnut, taking special note of the location of the cast iron pot belly stove. Both he and Molly had been chilled to the bone and he didn't want them to spend the night shivering under their blankets. From past experience he knew that those passengers too close to the stove baked while those on the extremities of the heat source froze. This particular stove, however, was enclosed in a sheet metal circular casing designed to circulate hot air through scoops in the roof throughout the entire length of the car. He hoped that the system worked properly since their berths were near the end of the coach. It was functioning well, he concluded, as he was comfortable without his winter coat, which he had tucked away in his berth.

With a great hiss of steam the 4-4-0 locomotive had finally begun moving off from the station when Molly returned from the ladies' lavatory, carrying her small reticule of toiletries.

"Yours is the upper berth unless you prefer the lower," he said with a subdued smile.

"The upper will do nicely," she answered, stifling a yawn. "I'm totally fatigued. It's been an eventful evening."

"Indeed it has, too eventful. Are you still disposed to hear about it?"

"If I can keep my eyes open." Molly sounded less than enthusiastic.

"That settles that then," he said decisively, taking note of her weariness. "I'm not altogether inclined at the moment to recite my sordid adventure. It can wait. Say over breakfast tomorrow?"

"I can wait 'til breakfast," she readily agreed.

For a moment their eyes met, each probing the other in that anticipatory yet uncertain communication that passes between a man and a woman when mere acquaintance threatens to develop into something more intimate. Lynch noticed that she had applied a touch of rouge to her cheeks while in the lavatory. As well, a faint scent of perfume washed over his nose. Molly blushed (*or was it the rouge,* he wondered), then broke their visual embrace.

"Well ..." she said, "I shall retire then."

Lynch helped her up the three-step ladder to the second berth where she pulled back the blanket, smoothed out the sheet on the horse hair mattress and fluffed up the pillow.

"Satisfactory?"

"First class – complete with bedsprings!" To illustrate the fact she proceeded to give the mattress a little bounce with her rump.

"Good." Lynch restrained the impish urge to climb up after her, wondering how she'd respond to such forward conduct.

"Are you also about to retire?" Molly had propped her head up with her elbow, a long strand of hair had fallen over her green eyes, which again focused on his face, inches away.

"Not just yet. Think I'll wash up, tend to my arm and indulge in a smoke."

"Before you do..." she leaned over and with the back of her hand gently stroked his rough cheek. "Thank you, Mr. Lynch."

"Not at all, Mrs. Lynch," he responded pleasantly surprised.

Before he could fully appreciate Molly's unexpected gesture she demurely said good night and drew her damask curtains.

Whistling softly to himself, the detective made his way down the aisle maintaining a swaying gait in balance with the gently rocking coach. He heard the clickity-clack of the driving wheels increase steadily as the sixty-ton engine now surged ahead on its iron coaster. They'd be in Niagara Falls in the early hours of the morning but when exactly, Lynch supposed, depended on the number of stops it made and if the engineer would increase speed to make up for the tardy departure.

In the course of his activities as a McMicken detective, Lynch had travelled by rail often but rarely in cars equipped with such luxurious accommodations. He marveled at the beautifully appointed interior replete with solid, polished walnut lavishly adorned with velvet and brocade hangings. Even the oil lamps were set in silver plates while the windows were curtained with canary silk complete with matching tassels. *Fit for a vice regal,* he thought as he sat down heavily on one of the cross seats at the end of the coach provided for day use. But then it cost a pretty penny that undoubtedly will cause McMicken's whiskers to stiffen when he receives the expense account.

The first order of business was a long, leisurely smoke. For Lynch an evening would not be complete without one. As he took out his briar and slug of tobacco, which he cut with a juice-stained knife, he was reminded of a certain sergeant major of the Toronto constabulary who was always fond of saying, "A woman is just a woman but a pipe is a good smoke!" *Perhaps,* Lynch mused, *but there is a certain lady, comfortably settled in her berth who shows promise of challenging such a confidently aired notion.*

While immersed in thought, Lynch cast around for signs of other human activity. Except for an undernourished looking gent who appeared to be solicitously reading a newspaper – or at least making a valiant attempt given the poor lighting and swaying car – two seats in back of him, Lynch had the area to himself. Most of the passengers, Lynch surmised, had bid good night much earlier on since the majority had boarded the train either in New York where the train originated some fifteen hours before, or at the various stops en route to Buffalo.

Puffing contentedly, the tired detective sank back into the cushions and let the miles roll by. Once or twice he almost dozed off, nearly dropping the pipe into his lap. *Enough of this,* he finally concluded, *better go to bed before I make an ash of myself.* He emptied the smoldering contents of his bent briar into a windowsill tray and with a grunt heaved himself up. He felt as stiff and wrinkled as his clothes.

Lynch gave the briefest of nods to the figure huddled in the shadows behind him as he traipsed by toward the lavatory. The man did not look up from his paper. However, when the detective passed the man folded his paper, placed it on the seat and quickly got up. Scanning the car he followed after. As Lynch was about to enter the toilet, the man in two hurried strides was at his back. The detective felt the barrel of a gun nestled against his lower spine.

"Best we take a walk … the other way toward the day car," he instructed, making sure that Lynch felt the weapon.

Lynch released the handle of the lavatory door. "Can you wait until I heed the call of nature?"

The man let out a low, gravelly snort as he quickly frisked the detective for any weapons. "I likes a sod with levity. If you wish I'll shatter your spine here."

"In that case, nature can wait."

"What'd ya do with your pea shooter?"

"Left it in my coat … unfortunately."

"That's too bad. Have your hands where I can see 'em," ordered the assailant as Lynch turned slowly toward the front of the car. "And walk careful like."

As they proceeded up the aisle Lynch cursed himself silently, first for letting his guard down and secondly, for leaving his revolver in his berth under the pillow – not that it would have done him much good given how handily he had been surprised. His self-admonishment, however, was interrupted by an elderly gentleman getting out of his berth and proceeding toward them.

"One word an' I'll use me gun," whispered the man. "Got that?" He jabbed him with the barrel.

Lynch nodded.

"Good evenin', sir," the gunman said cheerfully as the other party approached.

"Good evening, gentlemen," came the perfunctory reply. The rather stout chap squeezed by without taking too much notice of his fellow passengers and continued without a glance to the lavatory. Lynch had no opportunity to disarm his adversary and at any rate he didn't want to chance it with the possibility of an innocent person getting in the line of fire.

"Now that we're quite alone keep movin'." Again the gun poked him in the back.

"Who are you? What do you want?" Lynch hissed, purporting total ignorance.

"Just keep walkin' mate – to the end of the car."

Lynch did as he was told, his body tense, his mind suddenly alert. All weariness had left him.

When they got to the end, Lynch was ordered to lean against the door and turn around slowly. For the first time the detective had a good look at his opponent. He was about three inches shorter than Lynch, of slight build with a long, thin, pockmarked face and rheumy eyes. He was dressed more shabbily than one would expect of first class travellers and the detective silently cursed himself for not picking up on that detail when he first saw him reading the newspaper. The Fenian (of that Lynch had no doubt) stepped to his right and with his nasty Whitney revolver pointed at the detective's mid-section cautiously peeked through the window. The moon was out and he was searching, Lynch could only speculate, for some landmark.

With a satisfied grunt he turned to the detective. "Now then, you gave me a spot o' trouble at O'Bannion's."

"Ah… so you're O'Bannion's killer," Lynch remarked, not at all surprised.

The man smiled malevolently. "Poor Shawn, a spot o' drink an' he'd be talkin' too much – to the wrong sort of folk, if you git me meanin'. Mind you, he weren't too reliable for passin' on what he heard." This the Irishman said with heavy jocularity. "But we couldn't take chances now, could we?"

"Whatever plans you have, you won't get away with it." To Lynch it seemed the standard thing to say under the circumstances.

"You won't know me friend. You'll be leavin' this train soon – unscheduled stop as it were."

Beads of perspiration settled on Lynch's brow. He would have to act expeditiously or be a dead man. "You proposing to throw me off?"

The Fenian shrugged. "You kin jump, volunteer like or I'll shoot you." He looked out the window again. "Don't want you to be found too soon, though. Out in the countryside …maybe o'er a bridge or gully. Yeah, not a nice prospect that – gittin off in mid-air an' fallin' straight down as you please. That is, if the wheels don't git you." He smiled ruefully.

125

Lynch forced himself to remain calm. Best keep the man talking while finding a way to distract him long enough to make a play for his weapon. The detective judged he could physically overpower the bastard if he could only disarm him. "Did you also murder Mr. Rourke?"

"Ah … Mr. Rourke," the Irishman said expansively. "O'er reached himself, he did. No harm in tellin'. Took care of 'im meself."

"How did you catch on to him?" Lynch probed.

"The same we knew about you. We have spies too. Your organization ought ta git more reliable help." He laughed lewdly. "We knew you wos comin' before you arrived in Buffalo. Now ain't that a kick in the ole head!"

"You planted an informer?" Lynch was stunned. No one knew he was coming except McMicken and … Spense?

"You might say that o'right."

"Who?"

"I don't rightly know," responded the Irishman with laudable honesty.

Lynch thought for a moment, recovering from the shocking revelation. He then countered with some information of his own, hoping to draw out the talkative Fenian further. "Kidnapping and killing a politician in Ottawa won't win Ireland her independence."

The Irishman in turn raised an eyebrow in surprise. "Oh, oh … O'Bannion's been talkin' hasn't he? I knew I shouldda takin' care o' him early on."

"Satisfy the curiosity of a doomed man. Just who are you planning to abduct and murder in Ottawa? O'Bannion didn't quite get around to telling me before you put a bullet in him."

The diminutive man screwed up his lips into a lopsided grin. "Wouldn't you like to know." His eyes narrowed. "That's privileged information."

"Come now, Mr. O'Dell." Lynch stated the name he had obtained from O'Bannion deliberately hoping to confirm his assumption as to the identity of the man before him. "As you said, what harm would it do?"

"Oh, oh but you 'ave been industrious. Know me name even. Not that it'll do you much good."

"Who are the Fenians conspiring to kill, Mr. O'Dell?" the detective repeated with more bravado than he felt.

Inexplicably, given O'Dell's talkative disposition, he balked at providing a straight answer. "You already know enough to take wit' you to your grave," he stated acidly. Then he chuckled. "Methinks I'll let St. Peter tell you if your goin' that way. Maybe you'll even meet O'Bannion – discuss ole times. It'll be blissful like. Speakin' of which, hows Rourke's doxy? Swonked 'er yet?"

"Miss Mahone? You leave her alone," Lynch retorted fiercely. "She's got no part in this and knows nothing—"

"Caught a nerve have I? Well, I'll be payin' her a call shortly. Taste me a bit of o' luscious Irish crumpet."

Lynch clenched his fists and took a step toward O'Dell. The Fenian backed away a foot and pointed his weapon directly at Lynch's head. "Standfast or I'll put a bullet between your eyes here an' now I will."

The Canadian relented feeling helpless and more desperate as the train chewed up the miles. His time was rapidly running out. "Look O'Dell—"

"Shuddup – no more of your bloody talk! An' git back against the door."

Lynch had no choice but to obey. He was simply too far away to make a successful lunge at the Fenian. He prayed that he would still get his opportunity. For now all he could do was stare belligerently at the despicable little man.

Taking a peek down the coach O'Dell suddenly motioned Lynch to move away from the door further to his right. At the far end, Lynch saw the same stout gentleman that they had met earlier making his way up the aisle toward his berth having concluded his business in the lavatory. O'Dell stepped two paces forward putting himself directly behind the bulky stove. Forlornly, Lynch realized that they were at least partially hidden. Not that it mattered. The man barely gave them a glance but climbed into a lower berth and closed the curtains.

A few more tense moments passed and O'Dell, after another quick reconnoiter out the window, gave a satisfied grunt. "You'll be takin' your leave soon. I'll be relievin' you of your wallet now."

"I left it in my berth," Lynch said truthfully.

O'Dell took a step toward him, then backed off, assessing the detective shrewdly. "I'll take your word for it. Git it at me leisure." Evidently, the Fenian thought it better to stay an arm's length away from the bigger man and not risk searching him. "Undo the latch," he ordered, motioning to the door.

This is it! thought Lynch, gulping in a deep breath. *Got to make my play now!* Without pausing to second guess himself he half turned toward the door and then whirled around and sprang at the Fenian. Better to die fighting than to be dumped from the car like a sack of potatoes onto the track or into a dark abyss below.

At that very moment the coach lurched as it rolled onto a bridge with wooden trestles, throwing O'Dell slightly off kilter. Lynch stumbled awkwardly against him, feeling a sharp pain in his injured arm, but managed to grab the wrist with the revolver just as the Irishman staggered sideways. The little Fenian was amazingly strong and almost wrenched his wrist free. Lynch used both hands to point the weapon away from himself as they both tumbled heavily into the corner. The revolver let off a loud pop and to Lynch's astonishment, O'Dell gasped and released his hold. Oozing blood appeared squarely on the Fenian's chest. Shaken, Lynch slipped the revolver from the man's lax fingers and placed it on the floor safely away from further discharge. He then scanned the aisle. Evidently, no one heard the shot. At least, no curious heads popped out from any of the berths.

Catching his wind, the detective knelt beside the prostrate figure. O'Dell's face was ashen, his mouth slack and his breathing irregular. Grimacing because of the throb in his injured limb, Lynch seized the man's collar and glared into the glazed eyes. He was not in a charitable mood. "Who are the Fenians to kidnap in Ottawa? Tell me," he shook him roughly, "and I'll get a doctor ….save your wretched life."

"Up your stinkin' arse," the Irishman managed to gurgle. And before Lynch could utter another word death overtook the Fenian. Lynch dropped the head with a thud.

Too bad, he thought, not that O'Dell had expired but that no further information was forthcoming before he did. Now the question was what to do with the body. He couldn't leave him for someone to discover. There was at least one witness who had seen them together. If he called the conductor, no doubt, he would be detained at the next stop while an investigation was undertaken by the authorities. That would be time consuming and awkward. At this point, he couldn't afford to cool his heels in some sheriff's office. He had to proceed to Ottawa with haste, especially now since he didn't dare telegraph McMicken directly what with a spy at the heart of the Chief of Detectives organization. He would have to think hard about that … although the prime suspect had to be Spense who had access to all the files. Meanwhile, the best course of action was for the corpse to disappear.

Quickly, Lynch rifled through the death man's clothing, literally ripping open the pockets. If he were spotted by a passenger, he would surely be taken for a murderous thief, he realized grimly. Hands trembling, fingers numb, Lynch extracted a tattered wallet and a small notebook from O'Dell's pockets. Perhaps, there was some useful information to be garnered from it. He stuffed the items into his trousers. Next, he picked up the revolver, scrambled to the door and undid the latch. A blast of cold air freshened his face as he forced the door open just enough to fling the weapon out. *The train must be crossing a bridge,* he judged, squinting into the darkness before letting the door swing back shut.

That accomplished, he stood over the supine O'Dell and placing his hands under the armpits dragged the corpse to the door. "Good thing you're not too heavy," he muttered as he struggled to hoist the Irishman against the door. Finally, after stumbling about, he had it nicely perched. With one supreme push O'Dell fell out the door. Lynch couldn't see well but it seemed that the Fenian had been sucked under the carriage of the car. So much the better because with O'Dell in pieces strewn all over the ice and snow for a couple of miles it would be that much harder to ascertain his identity or confirm foul play should the body be discovered shortly and the train stopped. There was little chance of that, Lynch reasoned. He'd explain it all to McMicken in due course.

It took Lynch some time to collect himself, to actually think about what had occurred and feel a tiny tinge of remorse for killing a man – even if in self-defence – and for disposing of his remains in such a grizzly fashion. While in the lavatory in the midst of a long overdue bowel movement, it suddenly dawned on the detective that it was the second time in his life that he had been involved in an incident where he, the intended victim, had managed to escape his fate. Not a particularly religious soul, Lynch, nevertheless, crossed himself in humble thanks while his mind momentarily flicked back to the struggle with the half-breed some years before.

Having assayed any lingering guilt feelings as well as emptying his guts, he tended to his throbbing arm and washed. He then again sat down in his smoking seat and took out O'Dell's chattels. After confirming that he had indeed avenged Rourke and O'Bannion's murders (Michael Cooper O'Dell was his full Christian name) the detective liberated a handsome wad of American bills from the Fenian's wallet and put them in his shirt pocket. The rest of the trip would be at O'Dell's expense. He also found a calling card of sorts. There was no signature but an illustration – two clenched fists grasping the handle of a double-edged sword over which appeared a shamrock. At the bottom was the inscription 'Green Above Red'. He supposed that the card represented O'Dell's Fenian credentials. The little notebook contained indecipherable scribbles, which overtaxed Lynch's power of concentration at that moment. He decided to tackle it later.

As the train shuddered to a stop at the Niagara Falls station in the wee hours of the morning Lynch lay fully awake in his berth staring into the darkness. Sleep had become impossible and now he had to gather his wits about him and get himself and Molly across the suspension bridge and onto another train. Hopefully, it would be a less eventful journey than the one he had just experienced.

CHAPTER THIRTEEN
Montreal

The fat bank manager blinked at Matthews as stupidly as a cow, then he produced a massive frown which wrinkled severely his protuberant forehead. Matthews had no doubt that the man was fervently wishing he'd disappear or at least desist from questioning him further.

This was going to be harder than he thought, realized the American agent, but then he had obtained satisfactory results using a similar approach in New York and he saw no reason why Canadian bankers should be any less obliging. He had to give it his best shot. If he failed to get the information from the blob before him, he might as well go back to the American House, pack his bags and go home.

Matthews tried again, careful to keep his distinctive accent in check and to pronounce his words in that clipped, brisk manner British Canadian officials seem to have developed when dealing with government business. Indeed, in his efforts to pass as a Canadian official he'd gone so far as to purchase a Billycock hat and a dark blue suit of broadcloth with a matching overcoat. His comfortable Stetson and regular travelling apparel he left bundled in the hotel room. "Look, Mr. Primboght, we already know that this firm received the funds in question from New York. All I ask is the name of the party or parties that are entitled to the money transferred by Kemp & Shannon."

"I can't do that!" snapped the officious manager his jowls quivering. "As I have explained," he continued with an evident effort to curb his annoyance, "I can give you no information without a letter of authorization from those concerned. It is a matter of trust, you know. Moreover, I would need Mr.

131

Cross's permission and he is in Toronto at the moment. Perhaps, if you came back in three days—"

"This matter can't wait that long."

"I can do nothing to assist you," Primboght reiterated in a tone meant to conclude their business.

"Mr. Primboght," Matthews adopted a placating note, "I fully understand your position and perhaps I can ease your mind. This is a matter of utmost importance to the government. I assure you that it will be treated with total confidentiality." Reaching inside his unfamiliar coat, the American produced a letter. "Here are my credentials, sir. You will notice that it has the government's official seal."

He handed the forged document to Primboght who quickly read it, pursing his lips and frowning again. He then placed it on top of his large mahogany desk and leaned back heavily into his chair as if totally exhausted by this unwarranted intrusion into his afternoon's peace.

"It states, sir," Matthews emphasized, "that as Her Majesty's duly appointed servant engaged in the United Province of Canada's security I am to receive full cooperation."

"Nevertheless," Primboght's voice produced a sudden squeak, "I still cannot divulge such information without Mr. Cross's concurrence. You will just have to take up the matter with him." As if to underline the finality of his decision, Primboght moved his gargantuan girth forward and shoved the letter toward the agent.

Matthews rose from his chair and loomed over the desk, taking the letter and stuffing it into his coat. "Very well," he said tartly. "It appears that I shall have to take a course of action I had hoped to avoid." He paused as if to find the proper wording. Primboght appeared nonplussed but his blinking increased.

"Refusal to render assistance," Matthews said ruefully, "assistance to the authorities," he added, "is taken seriously by my superiors. Thus, I must warn you sir that I shall file a report and return within the hour with an order from a magistrate compelling you to release the information I seek. Moreover, because of your intransigence in this official matter, the Attorney General of the Canada East shall hear of this. You deal with government securities, stocks, bonds and the like?"

"Yes-s." For the first time Primboght seemed hesitant, unsure of himself.

Ah, thought Matthews, *a kink in this stuffed armadillo's armour.* "Then take heed. This firm might not for much longer."

Primboght gasped involuntarily, then he set his jaws defiantly. Struggling with himself he made one last attempt to be resolute. "If this is a threat, I shall contact our solicitor—"

"Contact whoever you wish," Matthews bluffed. "Meanwhile, when I leave I will take the course of action I have just outlined. I don't suppose Mr. Cross will be too pleased. But you can explain it to him on his return. You may even retain your position here."

When Matthews left T.N. Cross and Co. he wore a satisfied smile, congratulating himself on his stellar performance. He had finally browbeaten Primboght to a most helpful bowl of jelly. Not only had he been provided with a name but also an address to go with it.

***

The old cabbie nodded vigorously when Matthews stated the address where presumably one Murdo McCloskey lived. "That be down by the waterfront guv. Can git yah there right quick."

True to his word the cabbie flicked the reins of the snorting horse and the well-used hansom sped down the wide thoroughfare known as St. James Street. Matthews had little opportunity to admire the impressive stone buildings and respectable looking shops as with apparent reckless abandon the hansom lurched sharply to the left and then to the right and finally left again at the corner of Common and rue De Calières. From St. James the streets narrowed dramatically and now on either side amid the piles of dirty snow peppered with yellow blotches and horse shit Matthews saw old tenements and shabby warehouses. Three blocks up Common Street the cabbie suddenly pulled in the reins and the hansom came to an abrupt halt.

"Here we are, guv," he shouted over his shoulder in a coarse English accent.

Matthews alighted from the hansom and paid his fare. "Much obliged," he said taking a whiff of pungent air coming from somewhere on the waterfront.

Except for a wagon hitched to two nervous horses the street was deserted, not like St. James Street, which was a panorama of activity.

"Straight across the road, guv," the cabbie gave him a toothless grin and winked.

Matthews nodded somewhat puzzled by the man's gesture.

McCloskey's abode was a seedy looking two-storey edifice sandwiched in between much larger buildings. It had a couple of faded white doors, which opened straight onto the narrow street. On either side of the doors were encased windows framed with limp curtains, tightly drawn. The door on his right bore the number he was looking for: ten with the zero hanging on its side, fastened precariously by a rusted nail. The other door had an arched fanlight on which the number twelve had been clumsily painted. It appeared that McCloskey inhabited only one half of the house.

The American agent pondered his next move for a few moments. His orders were only to ascertain what connection the recipient of the funds might have with McQuealy and the Fenians and to report back to Washington. Under no circumstances was he to interfere with any Fenian activities until he received further instructions, even if they were plotting mayhem and murder. Those guidelines, Matthews decided, did not preclude him from conducting a thorough search of McCloskey's residence at the earliest opportune time. He might uncover some useful information although in all probability he would still have to follow the man about for the next couple of days – a task he was beginning to heartily dislike.

Taking care that no one saw him, Matthews ducked into the alley beside the house and proceeded to inspect the structure from the rear. With some relief he noted that indeed McCloskey's half did possess a back entrance, which evidently hadn't been used in some time. (A number of boxes stuffed with refuse had been deposited against it.) He quickly moved some of the debris to the side and inspected the lock closely, satisfying himself that it could be easily forced.

Meanwhile, he had better make sure that no one was inside. Proceeding back to Common Street, he decided on an indirect approach. He would inquire of the adjacent neighbour if a gentleman by the name of McCloskey lived nearby. It might be of some use to know who dwelled in the other half and if the address Primboght had provided him was correct. There was always the possibility (especially if sinister motives were involved) that the bank manager may have been given a false address. He approached the door marked twelve and after a slight hesitation made use of the small brass knocker appended to the door.

"*Un moment, un moment,*" he heard a female voice clearly through the door. This was followed by a click of a latch as the door swung open. "*Oui?*" A very painted, very perfumed lady with fluffed up blonde hair and an aquiline nose, which bore a striking resemblance to her pointed chin, smiled at him. A cold wave of air rushed by. The woman, dressed in a rather skimpy red dress shivered. "*Entrez, entrez, vite!*" she ushered him in, closing the door firmly. Adjusting his eyes to the dim interior Matthews couldn't pick out many features but he heard the distinct babble of females coming from the hallway. "*Maintenant ... Puis-je vous aider?*" The Madame still had her frozen smile as she looked up at him expectantly.

Matthews stood speechless. He hadn't counted on a language barrier. Everyone he had encountered thus far in Montreal (which admittedly included only a couple of cabbies, a haberdasher, a hotel proprietor and a bank manager) spoke English to varying degrees.

"*Oh, maintenant!*" exclaimed the lady, hand on hips, eyeing him curiously. "*Qui désirez-vous?*" she inquired.

"Madame," he bowed awkwardly, putting his hand to the rim of his new hat. "I don't know any French—"

"*Anglais ... Américain?*" she shook her head. "*Un moment.*" With a flourish she turned and proceeded down the dimly lit hall. "Giselle," she shouted, "Giselle! *Où es-tu?*"

Shortly, a rather full-bosomed young lady attired in a silky blue dress came to where the perplexed agent was standing. The Madame who had answered the door was behind her. "*Américain, je pense ... Quel homme, eh!*" With that pronouncement she laughed, gave them both a wink and disappeared.

Giselle, for her part, gave Matthews an inviting smile. He suddenly felt very warm. "*M'sieur,* I speak English," she stated in a heavy accent.

"Yes, ma'am." Matthews' throat was unaccountably dry. "I guess I must have come to the wrong house."

"Wrong house?" Giselle's pretty, elfin face frowned.

"Yes," he cleared his throat. "I'm looking for Mr. McCloskey."

Her eyes lit up in recognition. "M'sieur McCloskey, he sent you here?"

"No, no. I want to know where he lives. I was told it was around here," he motioned vaguely with his hands.

"*Ah, oui M'sieur,* that house there," she jerked her head toward the other half, "but he never be there now. He's gone to work."

Matthews nodded sagely. He had the right address. "Do you know when he'd be home? I'm a friend of his…"

"Not 'til late, often very late … Sometimes he comes here first," she added smiling.

"Then there is no one next door at the moment?"

"No, I don't think so," she shook her head decisively.

"Well, much obliged ma'am."

Giselle put a small hand on his arm. "You have time before he comes home … Much time."

The full impact of what the maiden was suggesting finally filtered through to Matthews. No wonder the cabbie acted so strangely. He thought he was going to a brothel!

Matthews smiled weakly; it had been almost two weeks since he had enjoyed the pleasures of a female. Just before drawing this assignment he and Jeannette had locked themselves away in her father's study while the senator was entertaining some of his Washington cronies. Jeanette was a bit feckless but she knew what she wanted when it came to men. She homed in on Matthews like a trout to a mayfly. As he recalled, she sat him down in one of her daddy's fancy chairs, drew up her dress and petticoat, dropped her drawers and baldly informed him she was 'gonna ride his steed'. Matthews happily obliged.

Looking now at Giselle he was sorely tempted. Indeed, the thought of that evening with Jeannette and Giselle's inviting smile aroused a growing concern in the region of his groin. However, he decided that duty must prevail. He had a golden opportunity to search McCloskey's house if what Giselle said was true. But, on the other hand, that shouldn't take more than an hour.

"You're an attractive woman, Giselle, but I can't stay now. Later, I'll come back in one hour."

"One hour?"

"Yes," he raised his forefinger, "one hour." Then, as if to reassure himself that he indeed had the right idea, he asked, "this is a brothel house?"

"Brot'el house?"

"Yeah, you know, where a fella and gal," he pointed at her and himself. "Where we can—"

"*Oui, oui,*" Giselle laughed. "Dis is fock house."

Matthews nodded. He reached into his pocket and produced a number of British bills. "Advance payment for your services," he said, pressing the money into her hands.

Her eyebrows shot up "Advance payment?"

"For when I come back – in one hour."

Giselle brightened in comprehension. "*Oui, M'sieur...*"

Matthews emerged from number twelve feeling a little lightheaded from his encounter with Giselle and squinting as his eyes once again adjusted to the relative brightness of the mid-afternoon sun. *Well, ain't that a stroke of luck,* he mused as he lit up a cheroot. He'd definitely mix a bit of fun with business – and charge it to his employer.

Taking a couple of long, greedy drags from his cheroot, he turned his attention to number ten. Just to make sure that neither McCloskey nor anyone else was inside, he knocked loudly on the front door. As expected, he received no response. He then quickly made his way around back.

It took Matthews a little longer than he anticipated to penetrate the stubborn lock but finally it surrendered to the insistent assault of his short-bladed knife. (He needed to be careful and not obviously damage it since the last thing he wanted was to have McCloskey think there had been a break-in.) Inhaling one last draw from his cheroot before flicking it into the alley, he yanked the door open and stepped inside.

A central hall, which ran through to the front, greeted the agent. On one side lay the kitchen and dining room. On the other was a long, narrow parlour with a staircase leading to the second floor. The furnishings were sparse. A plain pine eating table, two wooden chairs and a storage cupboard flanked by a number of pots and pans attached to large hooks were the only items of note in the kitchen/dining area. Matthews gave this section a cursory inspection and moved on. The parlour, too, was utilitarian, containing one sad looking sofa, a balloon back side chair and a low cut Cherrywood table. Only the huge painting over the fireplace saved the chamber from being described as nondescript. It was a military scene of some sort; a man in a green sash stood out in the foreground, sword raised in defiance of the carnage around him. History was not one of Matthews' fortes, especially European, which this obviously depicted, so he didn't know the significance of the portrait.

As he stood before the canvass, it occurred to him that the parlour lacked a woman's touch. There were none of the niceties that would give warmth to the interior – laced curtains, memorabilia, and statuettes. Moreover, thick coats of dust had settled everywhere adding to the faded shabbiness of the living quarters. Matthews got the impression of benign neglect. *Certainly, the place could use the services of a good charwoman,* he thought.

Having satisfied himself that there was nothing to be learned from the lower portion of the dwelling, he proceeded up the creaking stairs. There he discovered two relatively spacious rooms – the bedchamber and the study. The former contained the usual articles: a clothes closet, a commode with three drawers, one wooden chair, a night table and a rumpled rope bed. As he suspected, the closet held no female garments. McCloskey's wardrobe, meanwhile, was far from that of a well-to-do gentleman. The dress shirts were scruffy around the neck and cuffs and the two serge suits were threadbare on the elbows. Although it was not always insightful to judge a man by what he wore, Matthews would have bet McCloskey earned his livelihood not by his brawn but by some other skills he possessed – perhaps as a clerk or salesman of some sort. Maybe Giselle knew. He would ask her when he finished his business here. At any rate, he resolved to be about early the next morning and follow McCloskey to his place of employment.

Before leaving the closet Matthews also noted the uniform of grey cloth, double breasted with horn buttons hanging tucked away in the corner. British, he thought, although he couldn't be sure. He then spotted the gun stock; it was resting against the wall directly behind the uniform. He took the weapon out and balanced it in his knowledgeable hands – a single shot, pillow block, breach-loading Enfield; a fine rifle in very workable order. Evidently, McCloskey had some experience in the military.

The study appeared a much more promising arena in which to conduct a search. It contained an enclosed writing desk, a scarred brown chest and a substantial bookcase on the north wall. The American didn't know exactly what he was looking for, only that he hoped to find something that would establish the purpose for McQuealy's handsome partial payment to McCloskey. What McCloskey had to do to earn the money had piqued Matthews' interest. His gut instinct suggested a sinister task.

The bookcase held no clues. The top shelf was lined with a number of volumes on general history, works on the history of Ireland and a recent publication, with a book mark midway through, entitled *The Catholic History of North America* by a Thomas D'Arcy McGee. Neither the title nor the author meant anything to Matthews. The remaining two shelves held sundry tomes, mostly, it appeared by Irish poets. *A bit of a learned man,* judged Matthews, who himself, although educated, wasn't much of a reader.

The chest yielded nothing but bundled letters in indecipherable scribble (which he quickly gave up trying to read) and copies of old newspapers from Ireland. After leafing through the newsprint Matthews returned them to their original resting positions (minus some dust) and gently closed the lid. That was that!

The last remaining fixture to be searched was the writing desk. Matthews tried the rippled lid that descended to the writing surface but it held fast. Extracting the knife with which he disabled the lock, the lanky agent, now sweating profusely in his fancy new coat, fiddled around for a few moments until the latch gave.

The cavity was full of notes on curled, yellowing paper and clippings from a journal – the *Montreal Gazette*. The notes, as with the letters, were virtually unreadable but the street map sketched in the same uneven hand proved extremely interesting. It marked an area called 'Place d'Armes' from which a dotted line followed St. James Street to the corner of St. François Street. Where the two intersected, a small box had been inked beside which was written St. Lawrence Hall.

Matthews' puzzled frown gave way to a knowing smile when he turned his attention to the newspaper clippings. There before him circled in ink was the name of the city's eminent guest of honour, who, on March 16, was to give a speech in the 'most salubrious and fashionable' St. Lawrence Hall.

Calmly, Matthews placed the materials back into the cavity and closed the lid, making sure the latch caught. As he made his way down the stairs and out the back entrance he had every reason to be pleased with his efforts.

He knew now why McCloskey had been paid, who the intended victim was, where and approximately when. The only mystery that remained was how, although that scarcely mattered. His next step would be to wire Washington his discovery and await further instructions.

But that can wait for an hour or so, he thought as he emerged from the alley and stepped sprightly to number twelve.

CHAPTER FOURTEEN

The whistle blew for brakes and the belching locomotive came to a grinding halt. Lynch awoke with a start and for a brief moment was seized by a great anxiety. Why had they stopped? Had O'Dell's body been found already? And were the authorities now coming aboard to question the passengers? Surely not this soon? Rubbing the sleep from his eyes, he realized that he had been dreaming – that Molly and he had safely crossed into Canada and now were on the Great Western en route to Toronto. Still, why were they stopping? *Have we reached Burlington, already?* he wondered, gazing out the window for any familiar landmarks. All he could vaguely make out was an undulating snow-covered countryside with a line of stands of wood in the hazy distance.

Molly remained asleep in the berth above him oblivious to the sudden lurching of the coach. For a moment or so the train remained stationary and then with a jerk it slowly moved backwards a few yards and stopped again. Lynch eased himself out of his seat, careful not to disturb his companion and made his way down the aisle to investigate. At that instant, the conductor, a large black man, attired smartly in regulation uniform, entered the car.

"What seems to be the trouble?" Lynch asked. By now some of the other passengers had poked their heads out into the aisle, curious about the unscheduled stop.

"We've hit something on the track," announced the man in a booming voice. "But there's no cause for concern."

"Hit something?"

"An animal, sir," clarified the conductor. "Happens occasionally, although rarely at this time of year. There'll be a short delay to clear the track."

Lynch breathed easier. "Just where are we?"

"Let's see …" the conductor's florid face screwed up in concentration. "I'd say just past Hamilton, not far from the Desjardins Canal in fact." With that pronouncement he continued briskly down the aisle, no doubt, to deliver the same message to perplexed travellers in the next car.

"Did he say Desjardins Canal?" A balding man with an enormous set of side whiskers emerged from a berth to the right of Lynch.

"That's what he said," the detective agreed.

"Betcha he knows," said the gentleman, his eyes wide as he glanced at the receding back of the conductor.

"Knows?" Lynch had no idea what this well attired, and respectable fellow was talking about, except that his demeanour betrayed an unsettling measure of concern.

"Happened in '57 almost to the day," the man continued, in a shaky voice. When Lynch gave him a look that was clearly puzzled, he added, "The Desjardins train wreck."

"Oh," was all Lynch could say. But now that the gent had mentioned it, Lynch did remember reading something about the accident some years back.

"On its way from Toronto it was … broke an axle approaching the trestle across the canal they figured. Plunged sixty feet into the canal."

"Yes, I do recall vaguely … tragic loss of life."

"Fifty-nine people died," the man confirmed. "Most horrific scene I ever witnessed."

"You were there?" Lynch asked, surprised. No wonder the traveller was discomforted by their sudden stop near this particular locale.

"Not on the train, thank God. But I was one of the hundreds that rushed along the line to the fatal spot when the news got out. Tried to save whom we could. No easy task that. It was in the evening. Large locomotive lamps were brought in so we could see … used ropes to descend the steep slopes of the canal. In the glare of those lamps all you could see was twisted metal, flames shooting out here and there and bodies – sometimes only parts of bodies." The man shivered. "The train crashed through the timbers you see and the whole bridge gave way. The engine, tender, baggage car and two first class passenger coaches went headlong into the canal. The ice was about two feet thick but the engine and tender broke through straight away – first passenger coach rushed after, landed on its roof and flew part. The next passenger coach fell end ways on the ice and I can still see it stuck in that same position. Strange ..."

"How many lives were saved?" Lynch asked not really knowing how to respond.

"Not many," the man shook his head sadly. "Thirty perhaps. I swore I'd never travel by train again. This is my first trip since and history could have very well repeated itself to the day," he emphasized again. "Had we been closer to the canal and the train derailed..." he let the thought drop.

"I see your point," Lynch said.

"Well, we were lucky," the man concluded, a sentiment with which Lynch could only agree. "Sorry to have related this experience," the man smiled weakly, "but I found the circumstances ... er ...harrowing. Certainly, not an endorsement for our modern mode of transportation."

Lynch silently concurred. His recent experience on the train, although of quite a different order, was no more reassuring.

As it turned out, the train's unscheduled halt was due to a stray horse. The unfortunate animal had been hit broadside and somehow its carcass had gotten under the 'cow catcher'. Lynch was informed of this when the conductor returned fifteen minutes later and asked for volunteers to help remove the debris. Figuring he hadn't much else to do, the detective, along with a number of other travellers, donned their coats and followed the conductor to the front of the locomotive.

When Lynch saw the mess, he realized that it was indeed sheer luck that the train had not been derailed. The agitated fellow had a point, Lynch decided. It took almost an hour to remove the well-wedged torso and another hour or so for the engineer and his crew to inspect the undercarriage for damage. Finally, they were satisfied that no immediate repairs were needed and the train could continue on to Toronto. Lynch, who stood huddled against a chilling wind while the engineer meticulously examined the various fittings that might have been affected, was relieved. He had visions of the train limping back to the Hamilton depot in reverse!

The upshot of this unexpected delay, as Lynch later discovered, was that he and Molly would have to spend a night in Toronto. They would arrive too late to catch the scheduled train for Montreal and the next eastbound train was not due to depart until the following morning. Getting to Ottawa, even by the province's fastest mode of transportation, was becoming a painfully slow process.

Back inside the coach, the Canadian found most of the passengers fully awake, including Molly. All had been informed of what had happened and resigned themselves to the fact that they would be arriving in Toronto at least four hours late.

"Damn," he cursed to himself. "That's what I get for volunteering. Whew, I stink!"

And indeed, he did – of warm entrails and feces – as Molly's wrinkled nose testified. He needed no further testimony. At the first available opportunity he rushed to the lavatory and made use of the pitcher of water and wash basin. It would have to do until he got a proper bath. Later, he sat down with Molly in the last row of cross seats away from curious ears and gave an account of his adventures at O'Bannion's (judiciously editing the more unsavoury parts) and of his frightening experience with Rourke's murderer.

"Well, I can't say I'm sorry about O'Dell," she remarked, flinching a little when Lynch told her of how he had disposed of the body.

"A nasty man he was," the detective said. "Still, I wished that I could have disabled him without the shooter going off."

"But how did he know we'd be on the train?" she asked wide-eyed. "I thought we eluded them."

Lynch shrugged. "So did I, but there it is."

Molly bit her lower lip and said nothing more after that. Indeed, it seemed to the detective that she was remarkably calm, probably numbed by the whole sordid affair, he concluded.

The only item of substance Lynch left out in his recounting of events was O'Dell's admission that there was a spy in McMicken's organization. He hadn't quite come to grips with this piece of information but the more he thought about it the more he became convinced that it had to be the Chief Spy's secretary, Mr. Spense.

The 4-4-0 puffed and snorted it way into Toronto without further incident. The first order of business for Lynch was to dispatch a telegraph to Ottawa. After some thought as to who should receive it and how to word it, he approached the telegraph office near the station. He fervently hoped that old Jimmy Nickelson still worked there. He had known the telegrapher from his days on the Toronto police force – a solid citizen who knew how to keep his mouth shut. And that was exactly the sort he needed to tap out the highly confidential message.

Luck was with him. He spotted the bony little man hunched over his desk jotting something down on his note pad.

"Jimmy!"

The telegrapher stopped writing and looked up from his battered desk. *He hasn't changed much,* thought Lynch. The face had a few more lines, perhaps the hairline had recessed a bit but there was still that sparkle of recognition lighting up the eyes behind the pair of steel-rimmed glasses he wore.

"Well, I'll be a son of a gun! Oliver – Oliver Lynch as I live and breathe." They shook hands. "I thought you'd died or something. How long has it been? Three ... four years?"

"'Bout that," said Lynch. "I see you're still converting dots and dashes to the Queen's English."

"Yup. I'm doin' the same ol' job. What about you? Heard you quit the force and left town for parts unknown."

"Well, it's a long story and I guess I did leave in a bit of a hurry."

"I'll say. What's you been doing with yourself? Even the Sarge didn't know."

Lynch saw his opening. "I still work for the authorities. Special assignment as it were. In part, that's why I'm here."

"Oh?"

"Need to send off a telegraph."

"Oh ..." Nickelson sounded a trifle disappointed. The old man probably wanted to chat, catch up on some news. But Lynch had Molly waiting outside the office and really he couldn't spare the time. He would have to make it up to Nickelson on his next visit through.

"Look Jimmy, something very important is brewing."

"Oh?" The telegrapher perked up.

"Got some writing material?"

Nickelson neatly tore off a clean sheet from his pad and handed it to Lynch along with a stubby pencil.

At the edge of the desk the detective quickly composed a wire to McMicken's superior in Ottawa, John A. Macdonald.

URGENT/ FENIANS TO ABDUCT AND KILL MEMBER OF THE GOVERNMENT/ DATE: ON OR ABOUT 16 OF THIS MONTH/ PLACE: OTTAWA/ INTENDED TARGET: UNKNOWN/ WILL BE ARRIVING IN OTTAWA BY RAIL ON OR ABOUT THE 14TH/ REQUEST MEETING/ MORE DETAILS FORTHCOMING/ DO NOT/ REPEAT/ DO NOT CONTACT MCMICKEN THROUGH USUAL MEANS/ BELIEVE THERE IS A FENIAN SPY IN MCMICKEN'S OFFICE/ SUSPECT: MR. SPENSE/ TAKE THE NECESSARY PRECAUTIONS/ MCMICKEN SHOULD RECEIVE THIS INFORMATION DIRECTLY AND CONFIDENTIALLY/ OLIVER LYNCH/ GOVERNMENT AGENT.

"There, that should do it for now." Lynch handed the note and pencil back to Nickelson who quickly scanned his scrawl.

"That's some message!" he exclaimed, whistling through his teeth. "You have been a busy boy."

"That's why I couldn't let just any telegrapher send it off."

Nickelson smiled. "You can count on me, but you'd better come back and tell me about it when it's over."

"I'll come back, I promise."

"Well, you'd better."

Lynch waited while Nickelson expertly tapped out the communication on his bulky transmitter. He then thanked the telegrapher and collected Molly outside the telegraph office. "There," he said satisfied. "That's done. At least they'll be warned in Ottawa. Was a bit short with Jimmy though ..."

"The man in the office?" she asked her eyes returning to the little man who smiled at them through the window.

"The one and only," Lynch replied, taking their suitcases in each hand.

"You know him well?"

"Well enough. Helped me out on a case I was involved in once."

"Oh, that's right. You mentioned you were a constable here. Toronto must feel like home." She followed him out of the building.

"Lived here about two years but been away almost four. I imagine it's changed some." He started walking up an incline away from Queen's Wharf.

"Where are we going?" she asked, trying to keep in step.

"The Grand Trunk doesn't leave until tomorrow morning. We need accommodations for the night and I know just the place."

The temperature had dropped considerably with the setting sun and a brisk northerly breeze had suddenly sprung up. "Sure a bite to the air," he gasped as he stopped and put down the suitcases at the corner of Yonge and Front Streets. Molly sniffled and wiped her stinging eyes.

"How far from here?" she asked.

"Not far," he assured her, noting the woman's wind-burned cheeks.

It took another five minutes before Lynch pointed out their destination – the Queen's Hotel. They continued walking toward the hotel along the east side where there was a vacant area. "This is the hotel's garden," he commented. "Not much to look at now but quite impressive in the summer, especially with the water running in the playing fountains yonder and the rows of flowers that surround it."

"Yes, I can see that it would be beautiful."

"And so is the hotel. It once was a group of four attached houses, then Knox College, I think, before becoming a hotel in the '50s … Best house west of New York some say."

"Won't it be expensive?" she asked hesitantly, obviously mindful of her modest resources.

"Five dollars will provide us with the best room they offer and a fine meal to boot, I should think. But that's the least of your concern. Her Majesty's Secret Service, courtesy of Mr. McMicken, shall foot the bill." Besides, Lynch realized, he still had a fat roll of O'Dell's money and American tender was as good as any (albeit at a discount!)

Molly brightened. "I certainly would treasure a long hot bath."

Lynch grinned. "Amen to that. I'll make arrangements for two hot baths!"

Only when they entered the plush lobby did it occur to Lynch to ask if Molly preferred a separate room.

"Well," she seemed to blush, although it was hard to tell with her reddened cheeks. "We have travelled thus far as man and wife. Perhaps we should keep up the pretense until this is over."

"I concur," Lynch said, pleased that she made the suggestion. "It would avoid any awkwardness."

After Lynch registered them as Mr. and Mrs. Lynch and made arrangements for the suitcases to be brought up to the room, they headed for the dining salon. Both discovered suddenly that they were famished.

"You said that the man in the telegraph office helped you in a case?" They were seated at a white-clothed table, enjoying their gilded surroundings, Molly contently sipping her tea. They ordered the roast beef and Yorkshire pudding followed by scones and pastry – a repast that seemed to invigorate them both.

"Yes, what happened was that a professional gambling ring had infiltrated the city – from St. Louis as it turned out," Lynch sampled his liqueur coffee. "Ah, it's been a while since I had this. Games of chance of all kinds are forbidden in Toronto you know but as in all cities of any size ... well, it's carried on. At any rate, we had difficulty in ferreting out this particular, highly organized operation. We then decided that perhaps we should attempt to get a man inside the operation. But who? The police force was small and there was always a chance any one of us would be recognized by one of the patrons if not by the perpetrators. That's where old Jimmy Nickelson fit in – the telegrapher."

Molly nodded.

"Yes, well, he knew Sergeant Major Dixon and, I would guess, got wind of our problem over a few beers with the good Sarge – which reminds me I was so preoccupied with getting that telegraph off I forgot to ask Jimmy about the Sarge. But, well, Jimmy, after talking with the Sarge, apparently went out on his own and got himself invited to one of these illegal games. Then he came to the Sarge saying that he could help crack this gang. Since I had been put in charge of the investigation, the Sarge came to me. And that's how I became acquainted with Jimmy Nickelson."

"So, what happened? With Jimmy and this gang I mean?" Molly asked impatiently, leaning her elbows over the table.

"The short of it was that for the next couple of weeks Jimmy was our informer, providing names, dates, places – enough evidence on these characters for us to put them out of business. It all ended one night when we raided a home up north of Bloor Street. Thanks to Jimmy we caught the whole ring. Twenty men were arrested and convicted as I recall."

Molly nodded, finishing her tea. "And Mr. Nickelson has been a keen friend of the constabulary ever since," she surmised, delicately applying her napkin to the corners of her mouth.

"You could say that. I think he enjoyed the excitement. He's a widower or was a widower at the time," Lynch amended. "Probably got him up and about in the evenings I dare say. Life can be lonely for a man like him."

"Yes, yes I suppose it can." Her eyes met his and held. Lynch's thoughts strayed back to their overnight sojourn on the train when a spark had passed between them.

Molly was the first to break contact. "Thank you for supper. I hadn't realized just how hungry I was." She fiddled with her napkin before placing it on the table.

"Me, too," he concurred. "Now, perhaps we should look in on our suite?"

"Actually, I was thinking I could use a change of wardrobe and—"

"Say no more," the detective held up his hand. "You'd like to do some shopping."

"Yes!"

"Good idea." Lynch pulled out his gold hunter and noted the time. "The shops will still be open. I could use a change of clothing myself. And I know where the best establishments are."

Forty-five minutes later they entered the premises of P.W. Smith & Company on Queen Street. While Lynch waited near the front of the store, absent-mindedly studying the complexities of Bradley's double hoop skirts (a diagram illustrated two finely tempered steel springs braided tightly and firmly forming one distinct hoop – apparently, according to the advertisement, guaranteeing strength, durability, elasticity and comfort to the wearer over all other skirts), Molly tried on a number of dresses and made her purchases.

"I bought a white satin and Brussels lace dress," she explained as they made their way back to the hotel. "High, fastened at the front – and a lace chemisette to wear under." She stopped herself. "Also, two skirts with narrow quilling of blue and satin and two deep flounces. Oh I love them.

Makes me feel like I'm back in society again. Second debut! But it was awfully extravagant."

The detective smiled, struggling with her boxes. He encouraged Molly to indulge, the expense be damned. And after seeing the selection of fancy ladies wear, she did. For his part, he made a quick foray into a respectable haberdashery and clothing store at Queen and King and emerged with two more parcels containing a waistcoat (to replace the one he left at the hotel in Buffalo), a pair of trousers, two shirts, socks and a number of flannel drawers. Once he took a bath, his new attire would take off the rough edge of his bearing and make him appear more a gentleman again.

"We might not be able to fit all this into our suitcases," Molly worried.

"Then we'll leave the old clothes behind," he suggested.

The hotel suite was spacious, complete with a huge trussed bed, a soft brocade sofa, twin armchairs on either side of a brick fireplace, a central table with silver tea service and a Queen Anne writing desk in the corner. Lynch took off his boots and waded through the thick Persian rug to the broad window overlooking the street. He drew the curtains. "I think we've got the bridal suite!" he exclaimed with exaggerated surprise. (Unknown to Molly, he had asked for the best the hotel had available when he registered – for his bride and himself.)

Molly literally danced her way around the chamber. "Gorgeous!"

For Lynch, the evening with Molly was developing perfectly, except for his own state of mind. He just couldn't let one matter drop. The presumption that Spense was a spy kept nagging at him; Spense, after all, had access to all information in McMicken's office and his telegraph to Ottawa not-withstanding, he would feel much more reassured if word could be gotten to McMicken directly. Thus, between stoking the fire and unpacking some of his own belongings, Lynch decided rather belatedly that he should pay a visit to the one man (besides Jimmy) whom he could fully trust to help him, Sergeant Major Dixon, his boss and mentor on the police force and the man who'd rather smoke his pipe than have a woman. He'd go and have a private chat with the policeman – convince him to take a couple of days off and travel to Windsor to inform McMicken of the situation personally. Who knows, if McMicken acted with dispatch Spense could be squeezed to reveal all he knew about the conspiracy.

"I'll be going out for a couple of hours," he told Molly, having made up his mind but still feeling very pensive about his decision. "Be back before it becomes too late."

"Something wrong?" she said, looking at him intently.

"No, not at all. I should have done this earlier and tomorrow there will be no opportunity. I'm going to see Sergeant Major Dixon in connection with this nasty business. I believe he can be of assistance."

"Oh, yes ... of course."

"The room is comfortably warm now. If there's anything you wish—"

"You've been most splendid, Oliver, thank you. I'm fine. Think I'll take a bath and rest a bit while you're gone."

"Good idea." He too would take his long awaited bath when he returned. *Pity though,* he mused, *I would have liked to have scrubbed her back!*

As the Canadian detective hurried down the stairs to the lobby he wondered how Molly would react to an amorous advance. Would she be receptive or was it too soon? Obviously, she had cared for Rourke. He knew, for his part, that he was coming dangerously close to falling for the lady. But how did she feel about him? Perhaps he would find out later that night. Certainly, there wouldn't be a better opportunity.

CHAPTER FIFTEEN
Montreal

Murdo McCloskey was a burly, heavyset man with straight black hair, dense eyebrows, a thick, drooping moustache and a handsomely chiseled chin. He looked to be in his late thirties to early forties, judged Matthews from his vantage point across Common Street.

As the Irishman marched briskly down the street with the stiffness of a soldier on parade, the American agent cautiously followed him. He was glad to be getting some circulation flowing after standing for almost an hour waiting for his charge to emerge. *What a damned profession,* thought Matthews as he lit up yet another cheroot, *freezing my balls off in the shadows of an alley in the small hours of the morning while everyone else sleeps!* But then he was especially annoyed because he had to crawl out of Giselle's very warm, very comfortable bed to make sure he would intercept the Irishman.

While keeping pace with McCloskey (albeit at a respectable distance) Matthews' thoughts wandered back to the petite French-Canadian prostitute. She had the most perfectly rounded breasts he'd ever set his eyes on. Ample yet firm, they were captivating; like a baker kneading dough he squeezed, shaped, caressed the delightful globes with enthusiastic aplomb for a good portion of the night. Not that the rest of Giselle lacked appeal. *Au Contraire!* She was the most uninhibited woman (with the possible exception of Jeanette) that he had ever had the pleasure with. His member still tingled from the vigorous exercise the nimble lady had administered to it. Although not at all sure he was up to Giselle's demands for a second night in a row, on his early departure he did promise to return very soon.

In another area, however, Giselle was somewhat of a disappointment. Other than confirming that McCloskey lived next door and that he visited the brothel periodically, she knew very little else about him. When Matthews casually inquired about his profession and place of employment she was vague. "We didn't talk much," she confided. She thought he owned a business but confessed ignorance as to what sort or where. She did point out that another girl, Josée, would probably know more since McCloskey had most of his liaisons with her but Matthews, not wanting to arouse suspicions by questioning other members of the brothel, quietly dropped the matter.

Focusing his attention fully on the bulky figure ahead of him, Matthews realized that he was being led very close to the waterfront. Instinctively, he patted the lump that his revolver made inside his coat; waterfront neighbourhoods in any port city were dangerous places. Hoodlums, thieves, pickpockets and other assorted 'wharf rats' were not hard to attract in this part of town, especially if one was well dressed and walking alone. However, all that Matthews saw emerge from the shadows into the fresh light of dawn were two bruised and haggard hombres, still reeling, it appeared, from a combination of alcohol and a late night brawl. They posed no threat.

McCloskey, meanwhile, concentrated on his forward progress. Not once did he stop or even glance around. Here was a man totally at ease with his surroundings, a man who knew exactly where his destination lay. Certainly he wasn't concerned for his physical safety, thought Matthews, but then he was big enough and looked mean enough to deter all but the most desperate (or foolhardy) attacker.

The agent suddenly slackened his strides when McCloskey crossed the narrow street and entered a large rectangular wooden structure sporting a plain sign over a single light fixture – The Traveller's Canteen. A drinking establishment? Could it be that his quarry was the proprietor of an ale house? Matthews would find out soon enough.

As he approached the building, Matthews debated whether it was wise to show his face inside at such an early hour. He didn't want McCloskey to take undue notice of him and probably there'd only be a few customers about – if that. On the other hand, how did he know that this represented McCloskey's final destination. Perhaps, he had just gone in for an early morning brew or breakfast?

To satisfy himself beyond any doubt, Matthews casually walked in front of the saloon window, paused long enough to pull out a cheroot and while striking and cupping his hands over the match, he took a quick survey of the interior. As he suspected, there was no one to be seen except the Irishman who was now taking off his coat and striding behind the bar where he proceeded to take stock and rearrange some liquor bottles. From a side door to the left of the bar there emerged a rather stout woman wiping her hands on a ragged towel. They acknowledged each other curtly, it seemed to the American, and each went about their business, the woman ambling from table to table giving each a perfunctory wipe. Matthews flicked the match away, took two drags from his cheroot and kept walking.

Well, that was one curiosity appeased. McCloskey was a bar man or/and the proprietor – it hardly mattered. And it was a good thing that he didn't step inside. He surely would have been singled out and locked away in his quarry's memory. What to do now? His orders were restricted to reconnoitering, nothing more. He was simply to find out as much as he could about what McQuealy and friends were up to in Canada and report back. For now, he had completed his task. What remained to be done was to send off a coded telegraph message to Washington delineating the particulars of the Fenian plot, which he had pieced together from the evidence he found in McCloskey's home and then await further instructions. Did they want him to interfere in some way or remain in the background? He rather hoped it was the former but who knew what his superiors had in mind. Meanwhile, he'd stay close to McCloskey who evidently wasn't going anywhere for a while. Later, when the canteen was filled with patrons he'd return and quaff a couple of beers.

At the moment, however, it was imperative to send off his communication. Time was quite short and the sooner they received it the sooner they'd instruct him further. After that was done he'd go to his hotel room for a shave, a wash-up and change of clothing. Then, perhaps, he should also take a scouting trip to St. Lawrence Hall where in about three days an assassination was due to take place.

***

Matthews was right. In the late afternoon the Traveller's Canteen did indeed become a lively place. Sitting with his back to the wall in the smoke-filled shadows, the agent took measure of the human menagerie around him. A motley lot they were – unkempt, unshaven, fierce-looking men who, no doubt, were ready at the drop of a hat to pulp the nearest to them whether for profit or for sport. Given their ragged appearance Matthews could almost berate himself for taking a shave and changing into a fresh suit of clothes. He was bound to attract attention.

The bar room was large if somewhat crudely furnished with simple wooden tables and chairs. The floor was liberally covered with sawdust. Treading heavily on the sawdust but with surprising dexterity among the tables and chairs was a husky maiden, well past her prime (but still more palatable than the madame he saw earlier with McCloskey). To the sneering, clamouring rabble she dispensed tankards of ale. McCloskey, meanwhile, worked the long, high bar filling the tankards and generally ruling over the pit of chaos below. Periodically, he'd glance to the cage suspended at the end of the bar where two bickering parrots were in the process of denuding each other. A domestic dispute judging from the loud screeching and flying feathers.

Matthews signaled the maiden for a refill and once again turned his attention to McCloskey. There was no question the Irishman was an imposing figure. His unmistakable military bearing marked him as a man who could deal with this boisterous crowd of toughs. The agent did not doubt that behind the bar he had easy access to a club or other such weapon and that anyone who disturbed the peace or challenged him verbally or physically would be unceremoniously disposed of – probably thrown out on the street. After taking delivery of his second tankard of ale and tipping the wench generously (she gave him a smile that could have curdled milk) Matthews continued to surreptitiously study the proprietor reflected in the large mirror behind the bar. A formidable hombre all right – someone that McQuealy and his associates could expect to fulfill his part of the bargain.

"May I join you for a spell?"

Matthews averted his eyes from the bar to view a tall man with fair, thinning hair and a wispy moustache, like himself very much overdressed for the company he was in.

The American shrugged. "Why not? The chair is free."

"Thank you, very kind." The man pulled out the chair and set his bitter on the table.

"Clancy's my name – John Clancy."

"Howdy," was all Matthews said sipping from his tankard.

"I've not seen you in here before." the man ventured settling himself down comfortably.

"No," Matthews responded guardedly. "My first time here."

"A stranger in town then?" he asked.

"Yup, that's right."

"On business?"

"You could say that."

"You don't seem to be the kind of fellow who would have business in this section of town or would frequent an establishment like this?"

Matthews said nothing for a few seconds but toyed with his tankard. In his profession one became suspicious quickly. He suddenly wondered why this prosperous looking gentleman, who he noted was assessing him shrewdly, should be plying him with questions. Maybe that was his nature but the agent decided that perhaps he should find out. "I may seem out of place here, Mr. Clancy, but I reckon so are you?"

Clancy smiled broadly exposing an even set of white teeth. "Touché … Good point, Mr. … ah, what is your name?"

"I didn't say but it's Jakes, Thomas Jakes," Matthews gave him the alias that his employers had supplied him with on his false documentation.

"Mr. Jakes," Clancy pronounced the name carefully. "I may seem out of place but I assure you such is not the case. You see this is my sector."

"Your sector?"

"Quite. I'm charged with maintaining public order – a trying duty at the best of times I'm afraid."

"You a lawman?" Surprised, Matthews appraised the man more critically.

"Deputy Chief Constable."

"I see …"

"And naturally finding a gentleman as yourself in and among the danger-ous classes as it were, attracted my curiosity."

"I've not broken any law I hope?"

"Oh no. No, nothing like that." Clancy raised his hand in a gesture of appeasement. "Quite the contrary. I'm concerned that no crime is to be committed – particularly against a visitor who might inadvertently stumble into some bad company."

"You're here officially – on patrol?"

Clancy let out a good natured laugh. "Yes, I suppose you could say that – after a fashion. This is a favourite hangout for all manner of depraved beings. The only reason the Canteen's not been closed down is because it makes it easier to have all the scoundrels in one place where I can keep an eye on them."

"So, you come here regularly?"

"Regular enough," replied the Deputy Chief Constable taking a healthy gulp of ale.

"And you picked me out of this crowd because I'm … conspicuous?"

"You, sir, stand out like a tart in a nunnery."

Matthews nodded. Was that all there was to this unexpected encounter with a Canadian policeman? Or did this dapper constable have something else on his mind?

"I thought it my duty to warn you," Clancy continued with a distinctive lilt to his voice. "A lone gentleman like yourself should take care around here, especially after dark. Neighbourhood is filled with footpads, cut throats and rowdy drunken sailors itching for a fight. I dare say you may have been marked for a tumble already. Best beware."

"I appreciate the advice, Deputy Chief Constable."

Having delivered his counsel, however, Clancy showed no inclination to depart. Instead, he stroked his stringy moustache contemplatively. "You seem preoccupied, Mr. Jakes, with Murdo McCloskey, the proprietor there." He inclined his head toward the bar and the Irishman.

Matthews shifted uneasily in his chair. Had he been that obvious or was Clancy that observant. "Not at all," he replied evenly. "Actually, I was more interested in the combative parrots."

Clancy shifted his eyes to the cage and laughed again. "A bird lover are you, Mr. Jakes? I must say they are a pitiful looking pair, though."

Matthews shrugged.

Clancy gave the agent a hard stare and asked matter-of-factly, "you don't per chance know Murdo?"

"No," Matthews replied. He was now certain that this was no chance meeting. But what did this man want? Surely he didn't know who he was or about his mission in Montreal? How could he?

The Deputy Chief Constable continued unperturbed. "Ah well, the locals know Murdo. He's an institution here. In his own way he runs Griffintown."

"Griffintown?"

"That's what they call the Irish community here. Largely working class. Twenty per cent of Montreal's population is Irish and most of them live in this area. The Canteen is a favourite rendezvous as the Frenchies would say – especially during the shipping season when there's an influx of transients and the like. Murdo has sleeping quarters – about thirty wooden benches, which serve as beds – upstairs. For ten cents you get a blanket and the use of one of those benches. But I wouldn't advise spending the night."

"That I wouldn't contemplate. I'll be gone before darkness sets in."

"Wise, very wise Mr. Jakes." Clancy stroked his moustache again.

"Doesn't McCloskey mind you dropping in? It could be bad for business." Matthews asked casually, downing the last of his ale.

"Oh, we've reached a mutual understanding about that. He keeps order inside his premises and I make my arrests when the occasion warrants outside. Murdo is a bit of a strange one. He was a military man you know – with the Royal Artillery. Fought in the Crimean War. Came to Quebec with the British forces. Got into some nasty trouble with his superiors, not exactly sure what about. Rumour has it he was dishonourably discharged – quite bitter about how he was treated—" Clancy abruptly cut himself short. "But, of course, that wouldn't be of interest to you now would it, Mr. Jakes?"

"No. None whatsoever," replied Matthews, shoving his tankard aside.

"Satisfy a policeman's curiosity, Mr. Jakes," the Deputy Chief Constable persisted. "How did you happen upon this particular canteen?"

The man is tenacious all right, thought Matthews, wondering if Clancy too was on to McCloskey. He, however, was in no position to reveal anything, at least not without further orders. "Just took a stroll and found myself in the warehouse district. Thought I'd warm up with a pint or two."

"Ah, there it is then," he said. After a pause he too finished his ale. "Well, I should continue with my patrol, as it were – have a few complaints to check on. You take care, Mr. Jakes."

"Yes, I'll do that. And thank you again for your advice."

"Oh, by the way." As he rose he reached into his pocket and produced a card. "If I can be of service to you during your stay in our fair city here's where I can be reached." He placed the card on the table. "One never knows."

Later, on his way to Giselle (he decided that his manhood was up to it after all) Matthews couldn't quite shake from his mind the encounter he had had with Clancy. The man was too brazen, too obvious in the way he sat down and started asking questions. Matthews had a feeling that he would meet the shrewd Deputy Chief Constable again.

CHAPTER SIXTEEN
Ottawa

"Gentlemen," John A. Macdonald addressed the rather perplexed group of politicians assembled in the sedate Privy Council Chamber at the end of the East Block. "I have called this meeting of ministers – those of you who are in Ottawa – because I have just received an important telegraph concerning the activities of the Fenians." He paused and cleared his throat as a murmur rippled through the coterie of men seated on either side of the enormous leather-topped table.

The more astute present at the table realized as Macdonald resumed speaking that he had something highly confidential to relate because the clerk of the Privy Council was not where he should have been, sitting at his small desk off to one side taking notes. This obviously was for their ears only and would explain why they were so hurriedly summoned.

Macdonald made a mental head count noting the ministers in their places and those absent. The opening of Parliament was a few weeks away yet although a good number were in Ottawa already, getting familiar with their new surroundings and with the intricacies of their particular portfolios. George-Étienne Cartier's chair was empty, of course, since he was still in Montreal. Jean-Charles Chapais, Commissioner of Public Works was missing too as were a number of others but the majority were in their places including Alexander Tilloch Galt, Minister of Finance; Alexander Campbell, Commissioner of Crown Lands; William McDougall, the Provincial Secretary; Hector-Louis Langevin, Solicitor General, Canada East; James Cockburn, Solicitor General, Canada West; and of course, the diminutive but redoubtable Thomas D'Arcy McGee, Minister of Agriculture and Statistics. Macdonald was satisfied; he had managed to round up most of the government's senior members available in very short order indeed.

"Before I proceed I must make it plain that what we discuss here this afternoon shall not leave this room nor will any notes be taken."

A silence prevailed. Some stirred uneasily wondering what extraordinary revelations the Attorney General for Canada West and Minister of Militia had to disclose.

"You all, no doubt," Macdonald continued "have read or heard rumours that the Fenians have designs on the province – indeed, there is strong evidence to suggest that they plan to invade Canada at selected points and seize her as a base of operations against the mother country—"

"Utter nonsense!" snorted McDougall. All eyes turned on him, some clearly annoyed. His interjection was not unexpected since he was known for his petulant outbursts by colleagues and foes alike. "Empty rhetoric from a vainglorious bunch of warped Irishman!"

"You're quite correct in the latter part of your observation," commented Macdonald suppressing his irritation. The man was already gearing himself for an argument even before he heard the substance of the matter. But one could expect no less from an old Clear Grit! "But I must trust Gilbert McMicken and his able detective force, which has been supplying me with an abundance of information to suggest otherwise. His informants report that this Saturday coming, while citizens of this fair land are celebrating the anniversary of St. Patrick, the Fenians will cross in force at Detroit, Buffalo, Ogdensburg and possibly some other points to do their mischief. We, of course, will be prepared. I have called out ten thousand of the Canadian Militia and volunteers to be strung out at strategic areas along the border. The police of Toronto, Montreal and other principal cities have been reinforced and are on the ready for infiltrators who might join in processions got up by Irish societies to do what they can to disturb the peace and distract the authorities."

"Do ya really think such measures are necessary or might we be overreacting a wee bit?"

Macdonald turned to Alexander Campbell, his former law partner. "Nay, Alexander, I wish I were exaggerating but these scoundrels are hell-bent on their course, mark my words."

"I too have heard the rumours," persisted the Commissioner of Crown Lands, "but there have been no deeds to match the words – and words are cheap."

"I wish that were true but a murder has been committed."

There followed gasps and shocked silence as all eyes refocused on Macdonald.

"Aye, a murder has been committed," he repeated "Mr. John Rourke, one of Mr. McMicken's detectives was shot down in cold blood in Buffalo. We are certain that the Fenians were responsible because it has become apparent that Mr. Rourke learned of a Fenian plot to kidnap and possibly harm a Canadian official. He died, alas, before he could ascertain who the intended party was to be."

"Lawless bastards!" muttered Campbell, shaking his head in disbelief.

"A murderous, piratical band they are," agreed Macdonald.

"When did this crime take place?" asked Galt, plucking nervously at his side whiskers.

"Beginning of this month, I believe—"

"My God! That's almost a fortnight ago. And the culprit has not been apprehended?"

"Nay," Macdonald told his finance minister. "The foul deed took place under cover of night. The perpetrator made good his escape without being seen."

"And we 'ave no further information?" The inquiry came from Hector Langevin, Macdonald's earnest colleague from Canada East.

"Indeed, we do. That is why I called this unusual meeting. Having discussed this with our honourable friend D'Arcy McGee – because of his expertise on the subject – I decided and he concurs, that all members of this ministry should be aware of the situation to date. Now, after Mr. Rourke was murdered, Mr. McMicken, with my approval, sent one of his best lads to Buffalo to pursue the matter further. What he has been able to discover is quite startling. The Fenian plot I have alluded to is to take place here in Ottawa."

An exclamation of incredulity echoed through the chamber. "It appears, honourable members," Macdonald continued after he got their attention again, "that the Fenians have picked a Canadian politician – in all likelihood a minister as the intended victim. The deed is to take place on or about Friday, the sixteenth. Unfortunately, as I indicated, we do not know who specifically or any other particulars. Mr. Lynch, the detective responsible for this information, is at this very moment on his way to the capital. When he arrives he may have more to relate. What I am telling you he dispatched to me directly from Toronto—"

"You mean to tell us," interjected the irrepressible McDougall, "that we are all in mortal danger?"

Macdonald ran his hand through his thick lock of hair. Leave it to a Grit to put things bluntly in their most crude manner. "Potentially, aye ... but," he quickly added, "that is precisely why we've gathered here – to prepare. I suggest and will so instruct, with your agreement of course, that each person present in this room be escorted for the next few days by a selected member from the Civil Service Rifles—"

"Good Heavens! I don't want to be fastened to a bloody militia man," McDougall interjected.

"They will be discreet," countered Macdonald, catching from the corner of his eye D'Arcy McGee screwing his eyes up to the magnificent gas chandelier, which hung low over the table. He was understandably becoming annoyed at McDougall's outbursts.

"The fact is – if I understand what is being said correctly – a politician is the intended target but not necessarily any one of us."

"True." Macdonald turned his attention once again to the finance minister. "It could be almost anyone in the assembly. Yet, it would seem that for maximum impact and disruption, the Fenians would concentrate on one or more of the senior members. That brings us back to those of us here in this chamber. Further, we canna provide escorts for all assembly members. Aside from rounding up those that have already come to the capital – which is an enormous undertaking for the time we have – there is the question of the availability of manpower to guard them. The Civil Service Rifles have other duties and the Ottawa police have but ten constables who are fully engaged keeping order in the town as it is. I have, however, informed Police Chief Thomas Langrell of the situation."

"We could always leave Ottawa – disperse for a few days until the danger is passed," suggested Campbell.

That brought a couple of chuckles from those seated around him. McGee, silent until now, spoke up. "I appreciate your sentiments, Alexander, but there is no guarantee the Fenians will not try to carry out their scheme no matter where their target happens to go."

"Or they might decide on a different target," added Galt.

"Leaving the capital would not be the manly thing to do – cowardly in fact," McDougall challenged.

That prompted an icy stare from Campbell. Unperturbed, McDougall continued, "I suggest we arm ourselves—"

"And do what?" exploded McGee, no longer able to contain himself, "Shoot up the town? Or a stray dog that may come out of the shadows?"

A guffaw of barely suppressed laughter broke out – this time at McDougall's expense. He turned slightly red. "I'll wager I'm a better shot than any Fenian and I'll be wearing a pistol in my trouser belt."

"And I'd say Mr. McDougall," replied McGee, "that if you do within two days you'll be missing your testicles."

This time the laughter could not be contained.

"Honourable gentlemen," Macdonald quickly interceded before the two ministers challenged each other to a duel thus saving a potential assassin the trouble. "Without prejudice, I believe the prudent course of action is as I outlined. We can go about our duties confident that we will be protected."

"I must agree," intoned Galt. "We'll be safe enough if we take some elementary precautions. Not indulge in solitary walks, for example, or make too many public appearances."

"What about those ministers who aren't here?" asked Campbell. "Surely they should be warned."

"Agreed," said Macdonald. "If at all possible I'll be contacting them to explain the situation and advising them to take the necessary measures to protect themselves for the next few days. Of course, that may not be possible since the time is short and I don't know where two or three are at the moment. If they should arrive in Ottawa before St. Patrick's Day then they too will be assigned a guard."

"The very notion that we should quiver before these lunatics is simply repulsive," persisted the still peeved Provincial Secretary.

"Your sentiments are well taken, Mr. McDougall," James Cockburn spoke for the first time. "Indeed, the feeling of this province's population I am sure would be one of intense indignation – that the peace of the country and the lives and property of its inhabitants should be threatened by a horde of miscreants. But I must also agree with Mr. Macdonald. Until we unravel the full extent of this plot and smash it, we have no choice but to protect the province and ourselves as best we can."

There was a lull in the discussion as the politicians seemed to ponder their alternatives. "I take it," Macdonald filled in the void, "that we are all then agreed that we go about our duties with a watchful Civil Service Rifle nearby?"

Everyone solemnly nodded their heads with the exception of McDougall who fixed his eyes on a stenciled gold flower on the wall opposite to where he rigidly sat.

"Good, now D'Arcy," Macdonald turned to the Minister of Agriculture, "you have had some experience with the Fenian Brotherhood. Is there anything you wish to add?"

"Only that from my association with the Young Ireland party and my idealistic journalistic days in Dublin and later in New York and Boston, the Fenians are not to be taken lightly. They are dangerously fanatical, prone to wild excitement and I have no doubt that they have amassed large stores of arms, munitions and the like with the money supplied by patriotic but misguided dupes. Some sort of dastardly demonstration against Britain and her provinces is in the wind and we would be foolish – nay – irresponsible if we did not prepare to counter them, although we ourselves cannot take the law unto ourselves by taking up arms."

McGee gave McDougall a pointed look but the latter didn't rise to the bait or meet his eyes. Instead, he found great interest in inspecting the pale powder blue cornicing above the gold flowers. "The proper authorities," continued the Minister of Agriculture, "should be alerted and this city blanketed with vigilant militia men to safeguard the citizens, including ourselves since we have solid reason to believe that at least one of us has the dubious distinction of being singled out as some sort of sacrifice to their hopeless cause."

McGee's comments curtailed further debate. Even McDougall sat mute. Macdonald surveying one last time the patchwork of beards, side whiskers and moustaches decided that indeed a consensus had been forged. "If there is no further discussion then tomorrow I will instruct Lieutenant Lawrence of the Rifles to assign his men – one to each of us. Be guarded in your activities for the next few days and don't take any unnecessary chances." With that the extraordinary meeting of ministers was adjourned.

Later, Macdonald and McGee had a private parley in the anteroom of the Privy Council Chamber. "Well, I find him contemptible, mean, miserable, driveling, a scoundrel, and a pitiful poltroon – not to mention the fact that he is utterly unworthy of the notice of anyone having the merest pretensions to the character of a gentleman!" McGee concluded in a fit of pique.

"Please, D'Arcy, don't hold back – tell it like it is," Macdonald smiled. "Granted, Willie McDougall has a number of repellant qualities about him," he continued in a placating tone, "still, he is competent enough in what he does and we're stuck with him. However, McDougall's shortcomings are the least of my worries. Two points – actually three – arise out of this. First, there is Lynch's allegation of a spy in McMicken's office – in fact he accuses McMicken's private secretary, a Mr. Spense by name! I, of course, did not dare mention it at the meeting. For one thing, I don't quite know what to make of it." He shook his head and frowned.

"Nor I," confessed McGee. "It seems highly improbable and yet …"

"Aye, but there it is. McMicken, of course, must be informed and get to the veracity of such a charge but I am inclined to do nothing until I have talked to this Oliver Lynch. That's why I want you and Captain Lawrence on hand to meet him, which leads me to point two. When in the hell is he to arrive and by what means?"

"By rail I presume," said McGee with a puzzled look on his face

"Ah yes, D'Arcy, but that is not as straightforward as it seems. Captain Lawrence pointed this out to me when I suggested he get a man to the train depot to be on the lookout for Mr. Lynch as the trains came in, so that he could be escorted here."

"Good idea. So what is the problem?"

"The problem, my dear D'Arcy, is that Ottawa is a difficult place to get to even by the world's most progressive and efficient mode of transport. I hadn't realized this but McMicken's man canna actually take a train directly to Ottawa! I'm not sure that at the time he sent his wire from Toronto he was aware of this appalling fact, although I will wager he is by now."

"For heaven's sake, why not? Are there not any other branch lines along the Grand Trunk that connect to the capital?" McGee asked, not quite believing it either.

"Yes, the Ottawa-Prescott line but it was sold at a public auction last year and has been idle ever since, according to Mr. Lawrence. And the only other one – the Brockville-Ottawa line – reaches only as far as Arnprior or thereabouts – that's a good thirty to thirty-five miles from here. He'd have to come in by cutter. I suppose we could arrange to have a man meet him there and bring him here with all due haste. Undoubtedly, he'll take this route – his only recourse really. I expect a wire to that effect shortly but—"

"I see your point," McGee interjected. "Time is of the essence and we are rapidly running out."

"Precisely, D'Arcy, and that's not the worst of it."

"Oh?"

"I hear that there is a dandy snowstorm blowing from Port Hope to Kingston, which might delay travel even further. All I'm saying is that he'd better arrive soon to substantiate his alarming dispatch. And quite frankly D'Arcy, I have my doubts."

McGee's eyebrows shot up in surprise. "You mean about Mr. Lynch's information?"

"Aye, point three. I didn't get an opportunity to tell you before the meeting but I had just received word from George in Montreal. The authorities there are convinced that the Fenians are planning something foul. And to me that seems a more likely place than Ottawa somehow."

"Did he mention any specifics?"

"Nothing concrete at the moment but he'll wire me as soon as he knows."

"Hmm," McGee pursed his lips. "A complex, tangled web. Could the Fenians be planning action in both places?"

"Are they that well organized?"

"I wouldn't have thought so," conceded McGee. "Nevertheless, it was still prudent to have called this meeting and taken the precautions we have."

"I suppose so," Macdonald said sourly. "As much as I dislike McDougall, though, he may have a wee point about being unduly alarmist. After all, our actions are based on one mysterious telegraph from the equally mysterious Mr. Lynch."

"What are you suggesting? That it is some sort of ruse?"

"No ... no ... hell's teeth! I don't know," Macdonald said exasperated.

"We must assume it's genuine and act accordingly," McGee stated. "We cannot do otherwise."

"Aye, you're quite right," Macdonald sighed.

"And you be alert, John," his friend admonished gently. "Make sure your back is guarded. If indeed the Brotherhood intends to strike in Ottawa, you're a prime target."

The Minister of Militia laughed good-naturedly. "No more than yourself, D'Arcy. Your public denunciations of the Fenians make you a more likely candidate than I."

"Perhaps, but you're a much larger target."

***

Macdonald woke up with a start, perspiring. He had been dreaming. A huge Irishman dressed in bright green had been chasing and shooting at him. He had been desperately running and ducking. He had just tripped over a shamrock when his eyes popped open.

A soothing hand touched his brow. "What is it, John?"

Macdonald blinked a number of times, re-orientating himself to the surroundings. He was in Luce's bed viewing the contours of her body against the sheets silhouetted in the subdued moonlight pouring through the window onto the fancy bed replete with burnished posts, which stood out in stark relief at their feet. "Just a dream, Luce. Just a dream." He lay back against the pillow.

"Do you want to tell me about it?" she whispered, snuggling up close to him.

Macdonald had been uncommunicative about his day's activities all evening. Not that he didn't wish Luce to know but he didn't want her to worry. Thus, he mentioned the Fenians as little as possible. Certainly, he couldn't explain why on his next visit to her he would be practically escorted to the door by a military nanny in charge of his health.

The more he thought about Luce and himself the more the idea of a militia man chaperone rankled him. He hated to admit it but McDougall had a point. Public appearances were one thing but to have someone lurking in the shadows, even with the best of motives, while one was engaged in

169

private affairs was another. Luce and he were not quite ready to emerge into Ottawa society as a couple. She made that clear and he agreed, fearful of the unwarranted gossip that would run wild at soirées in certain circles. It was a matter of form and decorum, although he wasn't exactly known to abide by either in the past. He half toyed with the idea of dismissing his assigned man on his next visit to Luce but thought better of it. It would set a bad example to the others if word got out, especially since he was the one who proposed that such measures be employed. Best to play it safe but he would impress on his guard the need for total discretion.

Macdonald truly valued his and Luce's privacy. So much so that even McGee had to drag Luce's address out of him. "Someone has to know," McGee cajoled. "What if you had gone courting and an emergency arose? I, for one, would like to know where the Minister of Militia can be reached. And since you totally refuse to refrain from seeing Luce for the next few days – not that I blame you ..."

Macdonald relented. "Mind you, D'Arcy, keep it to yourself," he told him earlier that afternoon in the anteroom to the Privy Council Chambers.

"You can count on me. Only in the most dire circumstances will I disturb you," promised the Minister of Agriculture.

"Maybe I shouldn't have told him," Macdonald muttered to himself.

"What?"

"Oh nothing, Luce, nothing at all – thinking aloud is all."

Luce sat up, her hair shimmering in cascades over her shoulders in the bluish moonlight. "You seem troubled tonight."

"Nay, not really. Must have been the rich food, which brought on a nightmare."

"Why don't you tell me about it?"

"Sure you want to hear?"

"Of course, anything you wish to tell me."

"Well, there I was," he turned more fully toward her, "in this forest of giant green ferns when suddenly, I was attacked by this leprechaun!"

Luce produced a disbelieving laugh.

"The little snot gave me kneecaps a severe beating just before I woke up ..."

CHAPTER SEVENTEEN
Washington

Seward's jaws tightened as he read the dispatch that Baxter had given him. "Well, well, well. Those crazy bastards! I really didn't think they were capable of such an audacious scheme!"

"They are rather brazen, sir – to attempt such a thing."

"Why it's almost akin to assassinating the President!" Seward saw his secretary cringe slightly. The comment hit home what with Lincoln's murder still vividly etched in the minds of many (including his own).

With a scowl that pinched and puckered his face, Seward slowly rose from his chair and ignoring his walking cane, with deliberation paced over to the window, a habit he had acquired when he needed to sort out his thoughts. "This could have serious repercussions," he declared, turning to his stooped shouldered secretary. "Is there any possibility that our agent, ah ..."

"Matthews, sir."

"Yes, of course, Matthews may be wrong about his information?"

"I don't think so," Baxter replied frowning. It was obvious that that thought had not occurred to him. "He seems confident that he got it right and he's been dependable to date."

"And industrious it appears."

"Yes, sir."

"The question is: What are we going to do about it?"

"You do have a meeting with the British Minister in an hour and—"

"Yes, yes I know," Seward snapped. Baxter could be very irritating at times with his incessant reminders. "He wants to talk about the Fenians as a matter

171

of fact and this government's attitude towards them. I had planned to assure him that the Fenians will be prosecuted to the full extent of the law if they commit any criminal acts and that this administration will issue a statement to that effect but as to this matter … well, we're under no obligation to do anything really until a hostile act has actually been perpetrated."

Baxter arched his eyebrows. "Then you won't be informing the minister of Matthews' intelligence, sir?"

Seward started pacing from the window to his desk and back again. "If their security were any good then they would know themselves by now."

"Yes, sir but—"

"Wire Matthews," Seward abruptly cut in. "Commend him on a job well done. He is to continue to observe the situation but until he receives further instructions he's to take no action of his own."

"Sir," Baxter straightened somewhat. "If I may be permitted to speak frankly."

"Of course, Baxter."

"Time is short. Should you wish to amend agent Matthews' orders, he may not be able to act before this … this assassination is to take place."

Seward sighed. "I understand what you're saying and my sentiments mirror yours – it is a revolting act – but this administration's official position is that we not interfere in the internal affairs of another state. And after all, this Fenian madness is not to be carried out on American soil."

"But we know about it. And American citizens are involved, sir."

"This would-be assassin, ah …"

"McCloskey."

"McCloskey is not American."

"McQuealy is and it's in this country where the conspiracy was hatched," persisted Baxter.

"Ah, the roving Fenian ambassador. Is there anymore news about his whereabouts?"

"Not since he eluded Matthews in New York, sir."

"Hmm …"

"I think you should reconsider, sir."

"Your concerns are duly noted, Baxter. Americans may be involved indirectly but not with our sanction. No, I'm inclined not to allow Matthews to interfere in this matter. It would be unwise …" Seward finished off lamely.

After Baxter left, Seward sat at his desk and reread Matthews' dispatch. In two days' time, if the Canadians had not uncovered the plot, an assassination would take place, which conceivably could bring the United States and Britain to the brink of war. In less than an hour he would either inform the British Minister and let the Canadians take matters into their own hands or let events take their course …

***

They followed the same pattern as before. Baxter arrived early, procured his liquor and sat in the shadows at the same table he had previously. Trench entered a short while later, proceeded to the bar, bought a drink and after a leisurely survey of his surroundings, made his way to Baxter. The 'Potomac Hideaway' was not quite as boisterous as it had been during their last tryst.

"Not as lively tonight," Trench said glancing around. "Wonder what happened to the little accordion man?" He eyed the small platform that had served as the musician's perch during their previous visit.

"May be it's his day off," offered Baxter.

"Or he got run off."

"I wouldn't doubt that either," agreed Baxter.

"Wish he was still here though – would make our conversation seem less naked somehow," commented Trench as he put his glass down and pulled up a chair opposite his counterpart.

"I thought you couldn't drink that stuff." Baxter eyed the Englishman's glass.

"I can't but appearances you know. Wouldn't want to get on the wrong side of management." Trench jerked his head toward the stout, swarthy bartender with his hands folded, looking out on his domain. "Won't do for him to be wondering why I'm here and not indulging in some of this establishment's swill." He brought the glass to his nose. "Whew, as bad as the last batch." He then lowered the glass beneath the table and with a flick of the wrist directed the contents into a dark corner. "There now, let's start over."

He reached into his coat and produced a small silver flask, unscrewed the top and poured some into the glass. "Brought my own stock. Care for some twelve-year-old whiskey?"

"No thank you."

"Right, down to business. What have you got for me, Mr. Baxter?" Trench produced the familiar white envelope and shoved it across the table. "I do hope that this time it lives up to the ambassador's expectations."

"It will, Mr. Trench," Baxter said pocketing the envelope. "The particulars I promised are as follows," he continued formally. "The exact location is St. Lawrence Hall, a well-known hotel in Montreal. The perpetrator is one Murdo McCloskey, well known to the locals apparently." Baxter then went on to provide the date and the intended victim. "The only item yet to be determined is the manner in which the deed is to be done," he concluded.

There was a long pause as the Englishman, steady eyed and with an amiable smile frozen on his face, received and digested the information.

"There it is then," he finally said. "And there is nothing else you can add?"

"I have given you the full particulars as far as I know them," Baxter reaffirmed.

"Very well then. I can say with confidence that the ambassador and Her Majesty's government is most grateful for the service you have rendered – to both our countries."

Baxter only nodded.

"Our business then has come to a satisfactory conclusion."

"I can only trust that it has," Baxter intoned quietly.

"Rest assured, Mr. Baxter," Trench stated, sensing his counterpart's unease over what he was compelled to do. "Well, I best be off. Again, we sincerely do thank you and I hope that our contribution, in turn, will in some measure aid in your son's recovery."

"It will. Thank you ..." Baxter hesitated, seemed to collect himself and added. "I only wished that your ambassador had received this information directly from my superior."

"Perhaps he did," Trench said, gathering himself up from the table, "but it's not my place to say. Good evening to you, sir."

With that cryptic comment, Trench departed, leaving the bureaucrat to finish his drink in reflective thought.

CHAPTER EIGHTEEN

It wasn't until he entered the Kingston Station that Lynch discovered that the best laid plans of mice and men sometimes can go awry. He had planned to purchase tickets for Molly and himself on the most expeditious train bound for Ottawa from the Grand Trunk main line. Alas, he found out, much to his chagrin, that there in fact was no rail service to the capital!

"There was one from Prescott," explained the bespectacled clerk somewhat apologetically peering out at the detective through the wicket, "but it's been out of commission now for almost a year – ever since it got auctioned off."

"I don't believe this!" Lynch snapped in frustration. "So how does one get to the capital without snowshoeing up the Rideau Canal?"

His sarcastic outburst seemed lost on the stone-faced official who rubbed his chin and leaned over to inspect a yellowing schedule sheet on the wall to his right. "Well, let's see. Your best course of action would be to catch the Brockville-Ottawa train, which departs at noon today from Brockville," he added redundantly perhaps thinking that the gentleman before him needed very explicit articulation.

"I thought you said that there are no trains to Ottawa?"

"There aren't – the Ottawa referred to is the river not the city."

"And this rail line will get me to?"

"Arnprior."

"Arnprior?"

"Of course, you could also disembark at Almonte."

"Which will get me closer to Ottawa?"

"Hmm ... not much difference really – about thirty miles from either. Arnprior will prolong the train ride, though."

Lynch sighed. "From which town then can I most readily reach Ottawa? Perhaps hire a horse and cutter?"

"Don't rightly know," responded the clerk blinking rapidly through his spectacles.

"Can I make the Brockville-Ottawa connection today?"

The clerk took a quick glance at the large clock on the wall from across his cubicle. "Most certainly – with time to spare."

"Good. Two tickets to Arnprior then," Lynch said making a rapid decision. They might as well stay on the train as long as possible, he thought, if the two towns were roughly equidistant from the capital.

"Sorry, I can't do that. We sell only tickets for the Grand Trunk. Brockville-Ottawa is a different company. You'll need to purchase those at the Brockville station."

Lynch returned to the main passenger area of the station and spotted Molly sitting alone on a bench. There were only a few scattered individuals about waiting, no doubt, for the 'all aboard' call. She had gotten off with him at the Kingston stop over to stretch her legs.

"Another problem has arisen," he said with resignation as he sat down beside her. "It appears, although I can scarcely believe it, that Ottawa hasn't any rail service – at least not directly from this end of the province." He explained the situation as related to him by the clerk.

"So what do we do?" she asked calmly.

"We're going to Arnprior. When we arrive in Brockville I'll wire the Attorney General – request that transport be arranged, perhaps have someone meet us there. Otherwise, I'll hire a driver or a horse and sleigh."

As they again boarded their coach, Lynch was feeling particularly out of sorts. Erratic schedules, delays because of snow covered tracks and "minor" repairs, added to his cramped bowels and mile after mile of dreary, wintry countryside had taken a toll both on his body and his sense of humour.

Fortunately, there were no more nasty surprises. The 4-4-0 chugged into Brockville in good time. Lynch was able to send off his telegraph to Macdonald and the Brockville-Ottawa departed as advertised. For the next couple of hours the locomotive made its way northward with relatively brief stops at Smith Falls and Almonte before rolling into Arnprior.

In the coach, Lynch puffed on his pipe and stared out at the relentless sea of white that blanketed the landscape. In his mind he reviewed what had transpired to date with a mixture of horror and relief. He hoped that as a result of his dispatch from Toronto, the authorities in Ottawa were duly alerted and had taken some preventative measures. His last minute decision to visit Sergeant Major Dixon also appeared fruitful. He caught the policeman at his modest home in his nightshirt ready for bed but he was nonetheless pleased to see him. "Mrs. Dixon can wait!" he remarked with a wink.

Over a glass of brandy, Lynch detailed his adventure in recent days and enlisted his help. "Old Sarge" was, in fact, quite eager to do his part, promising to be on the first available train to Windsor the next day where he would apprise McMicken directly of the situation and of Lynch's suspicions that the Chief of Detective's secretary might be a Fenian spy. He even offered to personally interrogate Mr. Spense. "If he's our spy, then he'll spill what he knows, that I promise," Dixon averred.

Of that, Lynch had no doubt. He had witnessed on more than one occasion, the tough policeman browbeating hardened criminals and Spense didn't strike Lynch as all that resilient to the kind of heavy handed pressure Dixon could exert. Of course, the Chief of Detectives might want a word with his secretary as well. "Do what you need to do," Lynch told his former boss "I'll leave it to you and Mr. McMicken. Telegraph what you have found out as quickly as possible to Macdonald in Ottawa."

The only disappointment as a result of his late night sojourn was back at the hotel. By the time he returned any thoughts of a romantic evening with Molly had literally been put to bed. The lady was fast asleep. Rather than awaking her, he proceeded to draw his bath after which he, too, feeling quite exhausted, fell asleep on the ornate sofa, which seemed almost as inviting as Molly's bed.

The locomotive pulled into the Arnprior depot mid-afternoon. *Must be a slow day for the travelling folk,* thought Lynch as he surveyed the little waiting room. There were no more than about a dozen adults and a couple of children milling about and one wailing infant whose frantic mother was trying to rock into silence. The detective had no idea whether there would be anyone to gather them up so he decided to linger around until most had dispersed and make inquiries of the station master as to where he could hire a driver to take them on to Ottawa.

It didn't take long for the arrivals to take their leave including the mother and infant (less vocal now) who were met by her husband, Lynch presumed, with a brood of bundled up youngsters in tow. The Canadian detective was ready to conclude that either his wire had not been communicated in time to the Attorney General or that Macdonald couldn't make suitable arrangements for conveyance to the capital when a small man in an overly large fur coat and astrakhan hat walked in. He gave the depot a careful look over, spied Lynch and purposefully marched over.

"How do you do? I'm Angus McCrimmon," he announced in a distinct Scottish accent. "You'd be wanting transport to old Barrack Hill in Bytown?"

"How do you do... er, Mr. McCrimmon," Lynch said peering down at a friendly weather worn face, half hidden by the astrakhan and fur collar. "I'm Oliver Lynch and indeed I had hoped that there was an arrangement made to get me to Ottawa. I'm not sure about Barrack Hill."

"I'm your man then – Barrack Hill is where Parliament sits now. I was told that's where you'd want to go."

At that moment Molly emerged from the ladies lavatory and made her way over. Lynch introduced her simply as Molly.

"You'd be wanting a ride as well?" McCrimmon turned to her and then back to Lynch.

"Yes, we're both going to Ottawa," Lynch affirmed.

"I wasn't told that two were going," the man said flatly.

"No one knew," explained Lynch. "Is there a problem?"

McCrimmon thought for a moment and gave them a toothless grin. "Oh, I suppose not. We can manage. It's just that my cutter is built for two but we'll squeeze in and be cozy and warm for a couple of hours or so."

As it turned out, McCrimmon's vehicle, a basic surrey painted black with cracked red leather upholstery and rails instead of wheels, was quite compact. It would indeed be a tight fit for three, particularly with two suitcases wedged between their feet and the front board.

"Here's a couple of blankets," McCrimmon said, taking neatly folded grey bundles off the seat and handing them to Lynch. "Make yourselves comfortable and we'll put these over our knees – a wee bit nippy today."

Once the seating arrangements had been sorted out with McCrimmon in the middle and Lynch and Molly on either side, McCrimmon took up the reins and gently told 'Nellie' to go. The chunky mare apparently knew where, for soon they were sliding along a road to the steady sound of a couple of jangling bells fastened to the harness.

"How did word get to you to pick me ... er, us up at the station?" Lynch asked raising his voice against the steady swish of the cutter moving through the snow.

"Local magistrate received a wire and naturally fetched me. Nellie and I do this quite regular for folks who need transport to surrounding communities. Bytown – can't seem to get used to the name Ottawa – sounds kinda strange don't it – is on the outer fringes of my route but I go there often enough. Too bad, though, had I'd known there were two of you I would have hitched up my bigger sleigh although Nellie prefers this one ... but no matter, we can manage, eh?"

Lynch nodded although not entirely sure. He was pushed against the round back and turned sideways. It wasn't going to be a particularly comfortable trip. Still, he was grateful.

As the powerful horse pulled them along, Lynch discovered that McCrimmon was an incessant talker – to the point that the detective almost wished the driver was one of the those dour Orkneys he had encountered in the course of his days with the Hudson's Bay Company. They usually said little as they went about their business, although that too had its drawbacks – being amongst them was like attending a silent pray revival meeting. But there was no denying that McCrimmon was a wealth of information giving them a capsule history of Arnprior from its founding by the despotic Scots laird Archibald McNab in 1823 to its growth as a substantial lumbering and textile town. He seemed to know just about every family that settled the area and kept up a steady chatter about each as they passed by.

It was cold, but not unbearably so thanks to some moderating cloud cover and no wind except that created by their motion. Lynch leaned across and asked Molly how she was doing. She smiled that all was well but said little, seemingly lost in her thoughts.

About an hour or so into the trip, McCrimmon pulled up into a lane and gently urged Nellie on through deeper snow to a farmhouse. "We'll be stopping at Tooley's place to warm up. Mrs. Tooley will provide us with some 'tea and crumpets' as the English would say and it'll give Nellie a rest and a quick munch at the barn."

Although Lynch was anxious to make Ottawa as soon as possible, he supposed that this was a sensible course of action; most certainly it was McCrimmon's usual way station. As if to illustrate the point McCrimmon announced that they were roughly half way to their destination.

For the next three-quarters of an hour Mrs. Tooley, a large, bustling woman, fussed over her guests, plying them with baked goods and tea. In the meantime, McCrimmon disappeared to take care of Nellie. Like their driver, Mrs. Tooley was talkative – everything from her husband's eating habits (he apparently had gone out hunting with his dog) to her life's story. Lynch let Molly carry the conversation while he smoked his pipe. They finally extracted themselves from their gracious host with many thanks and the plea that they needed to get to Ottawa before nightfall. "Quite a talker, ain't she?" remarked McCrimmon with a laugh as they once more emerged onto the main road. Lynch could only smile.

It was getting on to the supper hour by the time they reached the outskirts of the capital. The temperature had dropped considerably as Lynch's toes could attest and he was thankful they were almost there. Having negotiated a number of twists and turns in the road McCrimmon crossed a narrow bridge over the Water Works Canal and soon Nellie was moving along Wellington Street on the last leg of the journey past the looming spire of Christ Church Cathedral and toward the newly-developed neighbourhood of Sandy Hill. Although the cold, orange sun had begun its descent below the horizon, they could still see the outline of the city. To the east lay the squalid, closely packed huts of Lower Town while in the west set against the fading light was the Chaudière waterfront dense with sawmills and foundries.

A jewel of the Canadas Ottawa was not. Aside from the lofty heights of Barrack Hill where the Parliament building and its two flanking structures rose triumphantly in stone, cornice and plaster, the capital very much reflected its humble timber town origins. Wooden shanties, outhouses and back sheds provided an incongruous landscape to the pretentious castle above.

"Down in those shacks," McCrimmon spoke to Molly, pointing with one hand while holding the reins loosely in the other, "live Bytown's working classes – Irish and French mostly."

Molly nodded sombrely. "Doesn't look like an appealing neighbourhood – rather sordid really."

"Aye, not a place you'd want to be visiting, 'specially now with winter still upon us. Times are hard. The unfortunates down there are desperate. Discord and violence is rampant."

"Violence?" Molly questioned

"Aye, between the races. A long history of it going back to the 1830s when Irish navvies, hundreds of them, left unemployed after the completion of the Rideau Canal, tried to displace the French firmly entrenched in the timber trade. You've not heard the stories then?"

"No."

"Oh well," McCrimmon gave her a wide smile, turning slightly toward her and shoving his astrakhan further back on his head. "A quick history lesson then – the shiners against the French Canadian shanty men—"

"Shiners?"

"Aye, that's what the Irish gangs were called – supposedly got the name because during canal construction they'd polish their shovels 'til they shined – to cook on them."

Molly laughed. "Oh come now."

"Well, perhaps that story is a little far-fetched. Another explanation is that they slicked their hair back with homemade soap."

"Whatever for?"

"For courtin' of course! Make themselves presentable to their lasses."

"Oh."

"On the other hand," McCrimmon expostulated with a teasing grin, "it could've come from *cheneurs*."

"*Cheneurs?*"

"Aye. Shiners – *cheneurs,*" he emphasized, rolling his r's. "Means oak cutters – a term of degradation applied by the French to the Irish on account of they cut hardwood. Apparently, it was deemed lowly work."

"I don't quite understand."

"Well, neither do I, if the truth be known — except that for many years the Ottawa Valley was embroiled in vicious gang wars with shillelaghs and limerick whips meeting clubs and fists from the French shanty men. It spread from the backwoods camps to the streets of Bytown leaving broken heads and destroyed property in its wake. There was no law to stop them."

"Surely that has passed?"

McCrimmon shrugged. "Aye, perhaps. Now they're hovelled together, poor and sullen, hurling insults at each other, pilfering each other's woodpiles and competing for employment in the lumber mills. A most wretched lot they are."

Lynch, who had kept silent to this point, decided to intervene before their escort got engrossed further in his story. "Mr. McCrimmon, it occurs to me that before I go about my business on Parliament Hill we should stop at a hotel not too far from there — if it's no trouble. It's been a long day and," he leaned over to Molly, "we might as well make arrangements for accommodations before proceeding further."

"Oh, that would be most welcomed," Molly exclaimed.

McCrimmon was happy to comply and in short order he pulled up to the Russell Hotel. As Lynch took the two suitcases from the cutter he told the little Scotsman that he could find his way to Barrack Hill since it was so close.

"Very good then," McCrimmon said. "Glad to be of service."

"And we are most appreciative. But what about you?" Lynch asked not imagining that he would return to Arnprior that same night. All told it had taken over three hours to complete their journey.

"Oh don't worry 'bout me and Nellie. We'll be taken care of. Stay at a friend's house just on the outskirts of Bytown. Fine barn for Nellie and a good warm bed for me." He smiled.

Although Lynch knew that McCrimmon would be paid by Her Majesty's government for his service, he insisted that the man take a rather generous tip. After a very short and tepid protest McCrimmon accepted the money with the remark, "Well, I am a Scotsman after all."

Lynch once again registered them as Mr. and Mrs. Lynch and escorted Molly to their room which, although not as stately as the one they shared in Toronto, was nevertheless more than adequate. He then took his leave and hurried up the hill to the East Block where he expected to meet with the Attorney General for Canada West.

***

Lynch had to produce his credentials as a member of Her Majesty's detective force twice – once to a sentry outside and once to one inside the main foyer – before he was escorted to the second floor and into a side chamber where an operations centre of sorts had been established to coordinate the protection of the province's leading politicians. Upon entering he saw two men hovering over a table covered almost completely by a large map of Ottawa. As they turned to him, he noted that neither was the Attorney General. Although Lynch had never had the pleasure of meeting Macdonald, his distinctive face was readily recognizable by any citizen who bothered to read a newspaper.

Lieutenant William Lawrence of the Civil Rifles was a narrow, lanky man with an oval head topped by black, thinning hair. His most prominent feature, however, was a drooping moustache that curved to meet a heavy-set jaw. He had the bearing of an efficient officer who knew his business. "Pleased to meet you, Mr. Lynch," he said extending his hand and staring purposefully at the detective. "I'm Lieutenant Lawrence." They shook hands. "May I introduce the Honourable D'Arcy McGee."

Lynch turned to a rather flat faced small gentleman in a dark frock waist coat.

"Mr. Lynch," greeted McGee in a rich, melodious voice. "Glad that you have arrived." He too, Lynch noted, had a firm handshake.

"Glad to be here finally," he said frowning slightly. "I thought that I was to meet with the Attorney General?"

"That's true," McGee said quickly. "Mr. Macdonald, however, had not anticipated the lateness of your arrival and had a previous engagement this evening. He extends his apologies for not being here in person."

"I understand. I encountered a number of unavoidable delays." Lynch said by way of explanation.

Lawrence cleared his throat appearing anxious to get started. "If I may, Mr. Lynch, I can bring you up to date as to activities here and perhaps you can add to any gaps you may be aware of in our information."

"Very good."

"Yes, well based on your dispatch from Toronto precautionary measures have been put into place to safeguard the ministers that are presently in Ottawa."

"What kind of measures?"

"Discreet surveillance – bodyguards if you will for members of the cabinet. Each has a shadow as it were. Of course, the ministers have been warned to restrict their movements until this affair is over. We are also watchful of any suspicious characters who have suddenly appeared in the city but given our meagre resources and the volume of traffic that presents certain difficulties."

Lynch nodded. Lawrence cleared his throat again and continued his officious remarks. "In the temporary absence of the Attorney General and because he has a great familiarity with the Fenians, Mr. McGee is acting as the government's liaison in this operation, so to speak. We are most anxious to hear the details of your investigation thus far."

"As far as any further useful information," Lynch began, "there is not much I can add to what I have telegraphed." The detective went on at length to relate his activities to date including his harrowing experience with O'Dell on the train. Shock registered on both men's faces as he concluded.

"And where is Ms. Malone now?" asked McGee

"Comfortably settled in the Russell Hotel."

"Good," declared Lawrence, his mind elsewhere. "And this notebook you mentioned?"

"Yes, the notebook." Lynch fished around in his breast pocket for a few seconds before producing a small, black tome, which had curled at the corners. "As I said, I read it until my eyes were crossed – many parts are simply illegible – but it supplied no useful information. Some names and notes about events in Buffalo but nothing relating to the reason for our meeting here, I'm afraid."

"May I see it?" Lawrence asked, eyeing it with evident curiosity.

"Of course." Lynch handed it to the captain who began leafing through it. "I see what you mean—"

Just then there was a knock on the door. A young clerk came in carrying two envelopes. "Telegraphs marked urgent for the Attorney General. Mr. Hewitt thought I should bring them here straight away." He stood before the three men not sure who should receive them.

"Thank you," McGee responded, relieving the clerk of the envelopes. As Macdonald's stand-in it was only proper that he accept delivery.

"What do we have here … a wire from Monsieur Cartier in Montreal and one from Mr. McMicken," McGee announced. "Well, this is dramatic that two should arrive instantaneously while we meet," the Minister of Agriculture continued as he opened Cartier's first. His eyes widened as he read. "My word! What do you make of this?" He gave the telegraph to the lieutenant who quickly scanned it with Lynch looking on.

"Well now, what does this do to our deliberations here if Montreal is the nexus of the Fenian conspiracy? In a perverse, diabolical way, it's more logical – no offence intended," Lawrence glanced at McGee as he said this, "kidnapping a politician, even a prominent one, is one thing, assassinating his Lordship is quite another."

"I agree entirely," said McGee unperturbed. "We may be on the wrong track in which case it's in the hands of the Montreal authorities. The information seems genuine enough; according to Monsieur Cartier it comes directly from the British Ambassador in Washington … Mr. Lynch?"

"First I've heard of this," he said perplexed.

"Is it possible that the Fenians have altered their plan?" pressed Lawrence.

"I am confident that my information is correct," said Lynch frowning.

"Perhaps it is an attempt to misdirect us into thinking that Ottawa is where they would strike," speculated McGee.

"No, that doesn't make sense," countered Lynch. "O'Dell told me this in the full belief that I would not live to report it."

"Perhaps he didn't know. He wouldn't be the first to be used as a decoy by his superiors," Lawrence suggested.

"Or there are two plots – perhaps even independent of each other," volunteered McGee.

"What about the telegraph from Mr. McMicken? It too is marked urgent," said Lynch.

"Right." McGee opened it and read aloud.

LYNCH ALLEGATION CONFIRMED/ SPENSE, MY PRIVATE SECRETARY IS A FENIAN INFORMER/ YOU ARE THE INTENDED VICTIM/ REPEAT: JOHN – YOU ARE TO BE ABDUCTED AND HELD UNTIL CERTAIN FENIAN DEMANDS ARE MET/ SPENSE CAN PROVIDE NO MORE USEFUL INFORMATION/ NO NAMES OR OTHER DETAILS GIVEN/ BEWARE YOUR LIFE IS IN DANGER. SIGNED: GILBERT MCMICKEN

"My God!" exclaimed McGee hoarsely.

"Where is the Attorney General at the moment?" asked Lawrence, reaching for his coat lying across a chair.

"He has gone to a private residence – a Mademoiselle Beaudry or is it Beaudoir? I know the address!" McGee turned to the map spread on the table. Daly Street ... there!" His finger pointed to a spot on the map. "He's at 24 Daly Street, not far from his own dwelling."

Lawrence was already at the door loudly summoning one of his militiamen who appeared forthwith. "Get a carriage and a driver," he ordered. "Have them at the front steps now!"

"Yes, sir!" The soldier turned smartly and marched briskly down the hall.

"When did Mr. Macdonald leave?" Lynch asked McGee as he walked rapidly down the corridor in step with the other two men.

"About an hour before you arrived," responded the Irish politician. "Two hours in total."

"There was a guard assigned to him?"

"A man was with him," affirmed Lawrence as they rushed through the doors into the chilling night air.

"Well, thank God for that!"

"Aye," agreed McGee, "but he'd be dismissed once their destination was reached. This was ... a private visit."

"I see," said Lynch as Lawrence's closed carriage came speedily down the street.

"Do you know where Daly Street is?" Lawrence barked at the driver as he pulled up to the steps of the Parliament building.

"Yes, sir."
"Get us there with all possible speed – 24 Daly."
"Yes, sir!"

CHAPTER NINETEEN
Ottawa

"Thank you, Albert," Macdonald said cheerfully, alighting from the carriage in front of Mademoiselle Beaudoir's abode. "You have done your duty for tonight."

Albert wasn't so sure. The young Canadian militiaman had accompanied the Attorney General from Parliament to this address and now he was being politely dismissed. He stepped down from the hansom and surveyed the street. It was quiet – deserted in fact. Still, he was reticent to leave. It just didn't sit well with him. "Are you certain, sir? Maybe I should remain close by—"

Macdonald shook his head. "That won't be necessary. Trust me. Once inside I will be safe enough. "Mr. Buckley," he motioned to his coachman who was waiting stoically in his seat atop the parked vehicle, "will give you a lift back."

Against the pale light of the street lamp, Albert shifted uneasily, his face expressing some doubt. "Sir, I have been ordered to be on the lookout these next few nights."

"I appreciate your diligence," countered the politician smoothly, "but I assure you, the person who lives here is as concerned about my well-being as you are. "*She*," he stressed the gender, "would be most uncomfortable, as would I, with a third party in the house. And it's too cold a night to be loitering about outside."

Albert cleared his throat, "I understand, sir."

Jaroslav (*Jerry*) Petryshyn

Macdonald smiled good-naturedly and gave the militiaman a conspiratorial wink. "I thought you might."

Albert watched Macdonald proceed to the door, knock and be let inside before he turned and walked by the snorting horse, impatient to receive the 'giddy up" command. "Mr. Buckley, would you mind if we went around the block a couple of times before starting back?"

"Not at all," came the muffled reply from the driver who was well attired against the elements including a large woolen scarf, which covered the lower half of his face.

Macdonald stared with pleasure at Luce adorned in a frock of black lace lined with red silk. "The sight of you is enough to make a man's heart flutter and indulge in sinful thoughts."

Luce laughed lightly. "I shall take that as a compliment."

"Indeed, it was."

They embraced with Macdonald giving her an affectionate kiss on the cheek. "You're late!" she admonished mildly disengaging.

"Aye, I was held up."

"Anything serious?"

"No, waiting for a meeting that never materialized. I'm famished." He rubbed his hands together, discarded his outerwear and accompanied Luce into the parlour.

"Hope you like stuffed quail," she said, reaching for a glass of sherry sitting on the little serving table.

"Sounds marvelous. Canna recall the last time I had quail."

He accepted the sherry gratefully. "I see you had it ready for me," he said with a twinkle in his eye.

"Un petit apéritif." She poured herself a glass from the decanter.

"Aye, just what I needed." He took a healthy swallow and sank deep into the sofa closing his eyes momentarily. Luce took a tepid sip from her glass and observed the politician closely. He looked haggard, a little worse for wear.

He caught her stare. "Forgive me, Luce, I am being somewhat inattentive ..."

"Just sit a spell, John. Drink your sherry. Supper will hold for a few moments."

"What shall we drink to?" he suddenly brightened. "I've got it! To beautiful lasses – to one beautiful lassie in particular ..." He raised his glass to her. "To your soft hazel eyes, your apple blossom cheeks, your—"

"To us," Luce interjected, raising her glass also.

"To us then."

"You just relax and sit there for a time," she whispered. At least it sounded like a whisper – a sweet, lyrical whisper. He smiled, feeling his face going numb. He drank more of the sherry, his hand quivering as he brought the long-stemmed glass to his mouth.

"I – I must confess ..." he started to say, then realizing that Luce was slightly out of focus. "Luce, I—"

"Finish your drink, John."

It was with some effort that he swallowed the remains of the sherry. His throat started to burn and he felt very warm. He struggled with his cravat and high collar in an attempt to loosen his constricted windpipe. "My God I – it seems warrrum in here."

Luce said nothing but maintained a frozen smile on her face.

"Luce ..." Macdonald began, but found the effort too great. He was starting to feel nauseous. "I – I think the sh-sherry has done me in ..." He was slurring his words, having trouble controlling his speech. *Strange,* he thought, *normally it would take a two or three day drinking binge to effect such a state.*

"Just relax, John."

He heard her voice fading away. He gathered his remaining strength and tried to lift himself from the sofa. He could not. Instead, the glass fell from his grasp and with a distant tingle shattered on the wooden floor. His head tilted drunkenly to the side. *God help me,* his mind was increasingly sluggish. *I'm – I'm dying? No! I canna be dying...*

The room darkened and images became watery or was it his eyes. Again, he tried to focus with no success. "Luce," he attempted, stretching out his hand but the effort was beyond him. He saw his mother – a generous, wide smile and dark eyes gazing at him. He was a boy again trampling down the country road to the school at Adolphustown – then Kingston – the sober limestone shops and houses seeming huddled together against the chilly westward winds that blew from the waters of Lake Ontario. For a fleeting moment he pictured Moll, his older sister and Lou, his youngest – then they were gone, lost in a consuming darkness …

Mademoiselle Beaudoir surveyed her handiwork. Macdonald looked like a ragged straw man collapsed on the sofa. "You can come down now, Mr. Reese," she called.

A neatly dressed man somewhere in his mid-thirties, wearing grey herringbone tweeds with a folded overcoat and soft grey hat across his arm, descended the stairs. He possessed a hard, albeit handsome face sporting a carefully trimmed moustache and topped with sandy hair combed straight back. The only untoward blemish on his face was externally inflicted – a particularly nasty gash over the bridge of his nose now scabbed and well on the healing process. It was a blow delivered in New York by an unknown assailant. Reese hadn't quite figured out the incident; it could have just been an unfortunate happenstance or more likely, something more perfidious. He couldn't be sure.

At the bottom of the stairs he draped his coat over the banister and affixed his hat on the rounded end of the rail. Taking only a perfunctory glance at Macdonald he focused his attention on the woman before him.

Reese had met with her exactly three times before this night. The first encounter was two months previous when she arrived in Ottawa. He provided the details of her assignment identifying Macdonald as the chosen 'mark' and set her up in the current residence as Mademoiselle Beaudoir. The other two brief trysts were arranged in order for her to pass along any information obtained from the Attorney General, which might prove useful to the Fenians.

"I'm your sole contact in this cloak and dagger game that we are playing," Reese had told her but that was all she knew or cared to know. She never asked who he was, about the Brotherhood or even what plans they had for their mark as long as she got the agreed to compensation.

"Well done," he said with a smile that exposed a fine set of teeth. "Most impressive."

Luce smiled, "As promised – the mark delivered." She nodded at the prostrated figure on the sofa.

"As I said, I'm impressed." Reese bowed his head slightly in acknowledgement.

Oddly enough, he didn't know who she was really. Only certain members in the innermost circle of the Brotherhood might possibly. Yet, she was trusted enough to be paid from the Fenian war treasury in advance! His coded letter of introduction, which she matched with hers on their first meeting, came directly from Thomas Sweeny, the Fenian Secretary of War.

Nevertheless, Reese had his suspicions. He had heard of an exotic young French-speaking Confederate agent and courier known as the 'French woman' to some and the 'lady in the veil' to others (which might have accounted for the lack of a clear description or photograph). Apparently, and he could only surmise, her name was Sarah Gilbert Slater although she employed a number of aliases – Miss Thompson, Mrs. Brown and now (perhaps) Mademoiselle Beaudoir. She was a known associate of John Wilkes Booth and had made several trips to Montreal with him, some suggesting that she spent much private time with Lincoln's assassin. They were seen either travelling together or rendezvousing at fine hotels in a number of American and Canadian cities.

Reese knew this from the long detailed newspaper accounts of those con-spirators on trial for Lincoln's murder. She kept popping up in the testimony under her various aliases – although it seemed that Sarah may have been her proper given name. It was known that she met with Booth in Washington in early April '65, a month or so before the young actor did his deed. Thereafter, she simply vanished while on a mission to Montreal carrying a large sum of money for the Confederate Secret Service's Canadian operations. The authorities never found her or the funds.

With the Civil War over, whether she believed in the Confederate cause or not had, perhaps, become a moot point for her. She was now a freelancer for hire and obviously had cultivated those clandestine connections that brought a spot of adventure and a great deal of cash – in this case from the Fenians' war chest – or so thought Reese. Yet, he knew that he could not ask her outright (or get a truthful answer); that simply was the nature of their busi-ness however much he was intrigued and would have liked to nurture their acquaintance further.

Instead, he asked, "What did you give him?"

She smiled – the cryptic smile of a temptress beckoning. "Now why would you wish to know that?"

Reese shrugged, "Curiosity mostly. It takes exacting knowledge and great skill to render a man senseless with a potion in his drink I should think."

"My particular 'Mickey Finn' as you might say, is not overly unique but effective nevertheless. With the proper mixture of laudanum, poppy heads and chloral hydrate in the whiskey or sherry an average man will succumb to sleep within a half hour," she said matter-of-factly. "And", she added, "stay that way for quite some time."

"So I'll not fear that Mr. Macdonald will wake up anytime soon or unexpectedly?"

"It will take a couple of hours to wear off," she assured him, "and he'll be feeling his head for much longer than that."

"Well, you are a most clever woman to get the Attorney General into your confidence and pull off this charade."

"He was susceptible."

"I'm sure he was," Reese mused, eyeing her shrewdly.

Just then, Macdonald moaned and shifted on his side. He was in danger of tumbling to the floor. Luce hurried over to the distressed politician and impeded his further involuntary movement. "Here, let me help you," Reese said, taking a couple of rapid strides to the sofa. Together they lay the politician more securely on his back with Reese swinging the limp legs over one end. Macdonald was breathing shallowly but quite regularly.

"Poor John," she remarked with genuine contriteness in her voice. "He really is an honourable older gentleman. I do hope you treat him as such."

"We're not barbarians. Mr. Macdonald will be treated well enough. Flanagan should be along shortly to take him down to lower town where he'll find himself in comfortable custody while certain communications are made to the government and the citizens of the Canadas."

"I'll have to take your word for it then," she stated flatly.

"Tell me, and this is pure curiosity on my part," Reese said, sticking his hands in his pockets, "what are your motives in all of this?"

"What do you mean?"

"Well, aside from, let us say a certain excitement of having successfully completed this elaborate ruse, is there something else at stake? You're a mystery lady. I don't even know your true name or where you're from."

"That was part of the arrangement."

"Yes, yes. What I mean is, in taking this assignment are you avenging someone? Perhaps a relative – brother, father, lover perhaps, dispossessed or expropriated or maybe sent to the gallows by the English in the old country, let's say? Or is it your historical sense of justice that compels your actions – a strike at three hundred years of British tyranny?"

Luce laughed. "None of what you mentioned has the slightest bearing, and certainly not your scheme to seize John there and hold him for ransom until you get whatever it is you want – setting Ireland free, is it?"

"Something like that," Reese conceded.

"I am here because your Irish Republican Brotherhood paid generously for my services. This is strictly a professional contract to obtain information and deliver the goods."

"And that's it? A mercenary then – a most unusual profession for a woman, that is."

"It does provide me with certain advantages."

"I can image." He appraised her again, his eyes revealing a glint of desire. "I should like to discuss this further at a more … shall we say at a more convenient time and place?"

Luce smiled. "Can you afford me, Mr. Reese?"

"Ah," he chuckled, "the professional indeed."

"Mr. Reese, I can perhaps appreciate your interest but after what has transpired tonight Mademoiselle Beaudoir will no longer exist and I will be as far away from this fair town as possible. I'm sure you would agree it's the safest course of action."

"Of course," he performed a slight bow.

At that moment there were three rapid knocks on the door. "I do believe that Mr. Macdonald's transport has arrived," he said, going to the window, drawing the curtains slightly and peeking out. "Right on time."

Reese opened the door just enough to let a large figure squeeze through. "I'll be right with you, Mr. Flanagan – just get my coat and we'll help Mr. Macdonald to the carriage," Reese informed him.

Mr. Flanagan glanced around nervously but said nothing.

As Luce looked on Reese donned his coat and hat and motioned Flanagan over to the resting politician. "Well now, let's get him up. You support one side and I the other."

With relative ease Flanagan lifted Macdonald by the shoulders and stood him up awkwardly. The Attorney General moaned as his head dropped down toward his chest. They then proceeded to haul him toward the door, his feet dragging behind.

"Dead weight," Reese muttered. "This won't do. Mr. Flanagan, perhaps it be best if you simply carried him."

Flanagan didn't object but with a grunt lowered his torso and swung Macdonald over his right shoulder.

Luce, meanwhile, came over and handed Reese Macdonald's winter apparel. "Wouldn't want John to catch pneumonia."

"Right you are," Reese mused, a sardonic smile forming on his face. "Well then, Mademoiselle Beaudoir," he said formally. "I bid you adieu."

"Good night, Mr. Reese."

"All's clear, sir," Flanagan spoke for the first time, opening the door and peering out in both directions.

"Good. Let's make this quick."

Luce watched as Flanagan strode purposefully toward a closed carriage. Reese swung its door open while the big man unceremoniously spilled Macdonald inside. At that she gently closed her door and sighed. "Time to take my leave as well."

CHAPTER TWENTY
Montreal

St. Lawrence Hall, Matthews discovered after some judicious inquiries, was regarded as Montreal's finest hotel. According to one talkative doorman it had a bit of a history, at one time serving as the headquarters of the British Military Staff and more recently, as a rather posh nest for Confederate spies and conspirators during the Civil War. "Yep," he said, winking at Matthews (the agent couldn't tell whether it was done purposefully or whether it was the result of a peculiar eye affliction) "them Southern boys would plan and plot in one room while the unionists would counterplot in another, all very civil like. Mind you, the proprietor, Mr. Hogan, had a reputation for running a neutral establishment which gave discreet service to either. Course, we had our own spies watching them both! Had our fair share of Yankee business we did."

Matthews didn't doubt that at all. While the conflict raged, Canadian hotels such as St. Lawrence Hall became the sites of numerous intrigues by Confederate agents who naturally had to be closely watched by Washington's agents – such as himself. The circumstances had changed but somehow it seemed apropos that he was there now, albeit on a mission that left him wondering what course of action he should take next.

At that moment, Matthews stood in front of the Bank of North America directly across the street from the hotel. He took some time to survey the edifice and its nooks and crannies. There were three basic elements to its architecture – the main block roughly three hundred by one hundred feet, he judged, and three storeys high and two lower lateral wings on either side.

The central portion was built of cut stone and featured massive Corinthian columns supporting a portico that ran the length of the structure. Above the cornice that separated the first and second floor were five huge Venetian windows behind which was the dining salon where the honoured guest was to deliver his banquet address. More cornice differentiated the third level, which had smaller windows bordered with ornate trim reaching to the roof on which was mounted a lengthy pole supporting a rather lethargic Union Jack barely bestirred by the cold winter's breath. The adjunct wings were less impressive with unembellished exteriors. Overall, St. Lawrence Hall was a most imposing and commodious house, decided the American. On this day, however, with the sky a dull grey and the snow blanketing the surroundings it had a sombre, forbidding quality – not unlike his disposition.

Matthews stomped his feet and shivered – time to circulate. He crossed St. James Street to the front steps, there he fell in step with the other arrivals who alighted from the bevy of carriages that paraded through. In the main foyer Montreal's Who's Who gathered; like solitary islands, they huddled in little groups, no doubt, discussing their latest acquisitions, business deals and the inevitable social gossip. Matthews took in the knowing nods, banal smiles and worldly airs. They were a comfortable, smug lot, quite beyond the realm of Griffintown, which he had absorbed a few hours earlier.

Security seemed incredibly light; there wasn't a gendarme in sight, a fact that troubled the agent. Surely, the Canadian authorities through their own intelligence service would have at least an inkling that something rotten was afoot? They had to be aware that this presented the perfect opportunity for the Fenians to make history. Perhaps he should have continued to follow McCloskey, and shadow his movements to the hotel, but that would have been extremely risky, he had decided, exposing himself beyond reasonable bounds. The man would certainly be on the alert. The question was how and when was he going to do it? Matthews had no idea. No doubt it was a carefully planned assassination with an avenue of escape. McCloskey would not have accepted money from McQuealy just to become a martyr. A feeling of heightened anticipation and anxiety gripped Matthews. Normally a man of action, in this case, he was ordered not to intervene. He wasn't sure he could play the role of an omnipotent observer, unobtrusively stationing himself from a vantage point and simply watch a man die.

Wrestling with his conscience, Matthews made a slow circle of the large foyer catching bits of conversation here and there and keeping an eye out for McCloskey or the guest of honour. The banquet was scheduled to start within an hour, and thus far neither had appeared. Starting to sweat profusely, he ascended the broad marble staircase on the second floor for a better view. As expected, *'les demoiselles de service'* were awhirl with motion and chatter as they prepared the elaborate dining salon for the stately group gathering below. Venturing into the dining area he saw nothing or no one remotely suspicious amid the white of the table clothes and crystal pendants of the chandeliers flashing in the gas light. *Maybe I should have followed McCloskey after all,* he berated himself again, *instead of waiting for him to arrive.* Since the man was nowhere to be seen perhaps the assassination was planned in such a way as to eliminate the dignitary before he entered St. Lawrence Hall. There was nothing from the evidence surveyed in McCloskey's home that suggested with certainty that the deed would actually take place inside the building. And yet, subconsciously, he assumed that to be the case.

Silently chiding himself for his sloppy reasoning, Matthews descended the stairs back to the foyer. How would his Lordship arrive? By carriage of course! He then could be easily done away with as he stepped down from the vehicle. There, in all probability would be no more than his attendants and a constable or two about. Or, further – on the steps of the hotel. A well-placed shot from a reasonable distance would buy all the time McCloskey needed to make good his escape. Damn his orders! It suddenly became imperative that he be there to prevent McCloskey from pulling the trigger, if indeed, that was his intent.

Halfway down the stairs Matthews almost missed a step when he caught a glimpse of a plump figure rounding a pillar. Michael McQuealy, dressed in a sober gentleman's costume and looking very self-satisfied, was chatting to a smallish man sporting a very pensive expression as he listened. Matthews had a feeling that McQuealy would show up but had quite forgotten about him until now. With McQuealy on the scene, there was no question that foul play was in the offing. In all probability, surmised the American, the dastardly Irishman was seeing first hand that he got his blood money's worth from McCloskey. As the Fenian bagman he might even have arranged to personally convey to McCloskey his second instalment on completion of the job.

Matthews edged his way toward McQuealy. Close enough to hear, he judiciously cast a sidelong glance at the cherubic features of the Irishman and listened.

"... No," the other man was saying, "I have never met the Governor General, but by all accounts Lord Monck is a formidable gentleman, keenly interested in Canadian affairs."

"That I don't doubt," McQuealy agreed smiling.

"I am most anxious to receive his views on the proposed confederation. I am most hopeful that it will come about – confederation, I mean."

McQuealy pursed his lips as if giving the matter some thought. "A weighty question," he finally said. "Of course there are some who would argue against it."

"Ah, the maritime politicians – they do seem to have the upper hand at the moment but I have heard that there are cracks developing in the anti-unionist forces in New Brunswick."

"What about the Fenians?" McQuealy asked placidly, retaining his pleasant smile. "They too have declared their intentions to prevent this federation of the colonies."

The man laughed. "I wouldn't put too much stock in their utterances. Bombastic rogues – they'll receive a knocking if they try. Let us hope their ilk won't become a nuisance come St. Patrick's parade tomorrow. Lord Monck may well have something to say on the subject being an Irish peer himself."

"Perhaps he will at that," McQuealy replied smoothly. With that he tipped his hat and excused himself, melting into the assemblage.

Cunning fellow, thought Matthews, *sweet with words, gracious in matters but malice in his heart.* It would be worth a month's salary to corner him against a stone wall in a narrow, dark alley and beat the tar out of him. But at the moment McQuealy, Matthews realized, was not the main concern.

Out on the steps of St. Lawrence Hall again, Matthews lit a cheroot and observed the street in either direction. Presumably the Governor General's regal carriage would be jingling along at any time now and still no sign of McCloskey. He scanned the mansard roofs, the dormer windows and the various services and openings of the stone façade of the buildings near the hotel, remembering the ensign rifle in McCloskey's closet. If the assassin fancied himself a marksman perhaps he would station himself at an appropriate elevated point. But where? It would take an incredible shot indeed if it were across St. James Street ... still ...

Matthews was about to take a more thorough reconnoitre of the area when he heard what sounded like a loud thunderclap about a block away around the corner. An explosion? Throwing his cheroot into the gutter, he hurriedly made his way toward the source. The first scene before him was a runaway horse and cab followed by a very agitated man in full pursuit. Matthews grabbed the man's arm nearly upending them both. "What going on?"

"That's me 'orse," sputtered the man puffing heavily. "Me livelihood is disappearin' down the road."

"What happened up there?" he gestured in the direction the man had come.

"Don't rightly know ... Looked like some bloke blew 'imself up. Scared the nag out of 'er wits."

Matthews released his hold and increased his pace up the street.

"Oh God!" The agent felt the taste of bile as he came upon a substantively charred hole in the cobblestones and the fragments of a body scattered all around. A couple of constables had just begun to diligently pick their way through puddles of blood rapidly congealing in the snow and little heaps of scorched clothing. They looked grim and no wonder. It took a certain fortitude not to violently empty the contents of one's stomach on the spot.

"Seal off the area and let's clean up the mess." The authoritative voice was that of Deputy Chief Constable John Clancy, walking briskly to the site of the carnage. "Fetch a couple of shovels," he ordered a young, fair-haired constable whose eyes and agape mouth testified to shock and incredulity.

"Yes, sir," he recovered sufficiently to squeak. Then he hurried off.

"Poor bugger," Clancy shook his head at the same time noticing the approaching American. "Ah, Mr. Jakes, is it? Had a feeling we'd meet again."

Matthews broke his stride and nodded. "Deputy Chief Clancy."

"I don't suppose we'll find all of him," Clancy sighed.

Matthews cleared his throat and swallowed, "Who ... who was he?"

Clancy raised his eyebrows in mock surprise and then frowned. "He was Mr. McCloskey."

Matthews said nothing. Clancy took another look around and turned up the collar of his coat. "I wonder what happens to a man's soul when in a flash of a light his body disintegrates?" the Canadian muttered.

Matthews shrugged. He had witnessed worse during the Civil War although one never really got used to it. "I have not given much thought to the mysteries of the spirit after death."

"Not a religious man, Mr. Jakes?"

"Nor a philosopher."

"Well, it was a bad choice. He should've known better for a military man," the Canadian policeman said matter-of-factly. "Some sort of bomb ... homemade I'd bet. It's a wonder he didn't blow up anyone else."

A bomb. Matthews had not considered such a possibility. Certainly, he had not found any materials at McCloskey's home that suggested explosives but then, they could have been kept at the Canteen. "What happened?"

"That I suspect we'll never know precisely," said Clancy, "other than the obvious result. Faulty construction, a detonator that went off prematurely. Could have been nitroglycerine – very unstable stuff and much more powerful than gunpowder." He paused and seemed to appraise Matthews with a critical eye. "Why are you here, Mr. Jakes?"

"I heard the explosion and—"

Clancy waved his hand in annoyance. "Yes, yes but why are you really here? Look, let's you and I make a bargain."

"A bargain?"

Clancy nodded. "I'll satisfy your curiosity if you satisfy mine."

"I don't quite understand—" Matthews started to object.

The Canadian cut him off. "I think you do, Mr. Jakes. You see we were informed of an assassination plot on the Governor General."

"I see," Matthews said.

Just then a police wagon pulled up and stopped in front of them. A couple more constables jumped down brandishing shovels.

"Right," Clancy said smartly to the constables who looked rather unsure of themselves. "I want this ... er ... mess cleaned up – every bit of him. Put the remains in sacks. The medical examiner may want to sort through the pieces."

"Yes, sir."

"And seal off the area. I don't want any curious citizens being sick. And no comments as to what occurred here to anyone – especially the newspaper men."

"Yes, sir."

"We'll have to concoct a story later…" he muttered more to himself than anyone in particular. "Gas leak or something to that effect, which unfortunately claimed one victim – the well-regarded proprietor of a certain Griffintown tavern."

As the constables hustled off to perform their sordid duties, Clancy motioned Matthews to walk with him. They slowly made their way back toward St. Lawrence Hall. "As I was saying, Mr. Jakes, we knew of the assassination plot against Lord Monck."

"How, may I ask?"

"By a very circuitous route actually. The British Minister in Washington was informed. Apparently, the American secret service had found out about McCloskey's intentions." Clancy glanced sideways expectantly at Matthews. When this produced no response, he continued. "We, of course, took the necessary precautions. The Governor General arrived earlier, clandestinely shall we say, and has been seconded in the Hall for a couple of hours now. Indeed, he should be beginning his speech at any moment. McCloskey was put under surveillance. Meanwhile, we had to ascertain if the information supplied to the Minister by the Americans was reliable."

"Obviously it was," Matthews stated flatly.

Clancy nodded. "It appears that he was waiting for the Governor General's carriage where at the appropriate moment he could hurl his bomb and escape while attention was riveted on the exploding carriage. We had a decoy carriage coming along – fortunately it didn't come to that or I would have lost a couple of good men. At the last instance, it was decided that we should apprehend him before any overt action on his part – his intentions seemed clear enough and at any rate the evidence of his intent would be on his person. I can only surmise that when he saw the constables he became nervous. Error in judgement, perhaps, or as I said malfunction of the detonator if he used such a device – it could have been suicide even, if he believed he was cornered. If he was foolish enough to employ nitro … well simple body heat could have set if off."

"Fate then was with you. Explosions of such force usually result in a much greater catastrophes," Matthews stated sombrely, again remembering his war experiences.

"Quite."

The two men walked on in silence for a few paces.

"Now, Mr. Jakes." Clancy seemed to have made up his mind about something.

"What is your connection in all of this? And don't feign innocence please. Tell me here or accompany me to headquarters for a tiresome interrogation."

"You put me in a delicate situation, Deputy Chief Clancy," Matthews replied evenly.

"Yes, I suppose I do. You see, the British Minister hinted in his dispatch that Washington may have a man up here."

"That might cause some diplomatic difficulties if that were true," Matthews said in a neutral tone.

Clancy gave Matthews a thin smile. "It could, but then it wouldn't be the first time, would it? I agree, however, questions would be raised. Still, as I said a few moments ago, satisfy my curiosity – unofficially you understand."

"In that case, your deductions are correct – unofficially."

"Yes, well, I thought as much when I saw you at the Canteen."

"You couldn't have possibly known about the plot then," Matthews countered.

"Quite right ... not about the specific plot," Clancy assured him, "just some suspicions. No, but you were terribly out of place and we've had some experience with visitors from the south in our recent past."

Matthews said nothing. Perhaps he had underestimated the Canadian intelligence service after all.

As they approached the steps of St. Lawrence Hall, Clancy was puzzled by one more aspect of the case. "On your own now, what would you have done to prevent this crime?"

"I was under orders to do nothing," Matthews stated truthfully.

"I see."

"It appears," Matthews added quickly, "that my superiors thought it best to let the local authorities handle this ... situation."

"So it appears," agreed Clancy. "Still if you were in a position to act?"

Matthews shrugged. "That thought had crossed my mind. I believe that it would have been against my conscience to simply let it happen."

Clancy nodded apparently satisfied. After a moment's pause the Canadian said, "I am glad that we had this chat – unofficially. I suppose this finishes our business."

"Not totally," Matthews asserted.

"Oh?"

"Unofficially there is one other piece of information that you should know."

"I'd be glad to receive it – unofficially."

"There is one American visitor connected to this plot who is at this moment listening to the Governor General and no doubt wondering what went wrong."

"Ah, now that's interesting," Clancy rubbed his hands like a child presented unexpectedly with a new toy. "What's his name?"

"McQuealy – Michael McQuealy. He appears to be a bagman for the Fenians. Most certainly, he hired McCloskey to do your governor in. Luckily, he did not pick his talent well."

"Don't judge McCloskey too harshly," Clancy mildly chided. "I don't profess to know the motives that got him into this but he did some good in Griffintown. Ah, what a sad business. I rather liked the man."

"I won't argue the point."

"Yes, well, about this fellow McQuealy, I would need to impose on you one more time."

"Certainly, if it doesn't compromise my unofficial status."

"Not at all. Would you kindly point him out?"

Matthews smiled. "It would be my pleasure.

"Good." Clancy gestured to a constable stationed beneath one of the massive columns like a frozen doll with cap and cloak at the top of the stairs. Suddenly, Matthews noted, there were lawmen all over the place.

"Yes, sir," the policeman answered smartly.

"Come along with us."

"Yes, sir."

No doubt the young constable would have been happy to follow his superior into the warmth of the hotel, however, as fate would have it, it proved unnecessary because McQuealy suddenly appeared. It was safe to assume that he knew something had gone awry and that it was time for him to make a swift departure.

"Speak of the devil," Matthews remarked, nudging Clancy, "there's your man."

McQuealy stopped, scanned the constable and two men beside him and nervously adjusted his silk scarf and top hat. He then turned and briskly began making his way down the stairs.

"Mr. McQuealy," yelled Clancy, "a word." The Fenian managed a faltering step and then increased his speed.

"Stop that man!" Clancy ordered the constable.

"Yes, sir."

The race was on. At the bottom of the steps the constable caught up to his quarry only to stumble and come crashing onto the icy ground aided by a wild swing from McQuealy who just managed to elude the grasp of the younger man. Hatless now, the silk scarf stiffing out against a sudden breeze, McQuealy ran toward the spot where McCloskey had involuntarily or otherwise detonated himself. When he saw the coterie of constables now just about finished with their grizzly work, he halted momentarily, his face contorted with exertion, confusion and consternation. He was about to make a dash across the thoroughfare when Matthews grabbed him by the sleeve, whirled him around and clipped him solidly in the chin with his right fist. Even with the glove on, the American knew he had bruised his knuckles again – but it felt good. McQuealy dropped like a soggy sack of rotten Irish spuds, doubling over in the snow.

"I say, a good connection," puffed Clancy slightly winded from his run.

Matthews nursed his fist. "That's the second time I've done that in recent days." He recalled his overhand right to the nose of McQuealy's associate in the chess rooms in New York.

"Constable, secure this man," Clancy ordered. "I'll be with you in a moment."

"Yes, sir," answered the young gendarme somewhat peevishly, not fully recovered, at least in pride, from his tumble at the bottom stairs of St. Lawrence Hall.

"Her Majesty's government thanks you again and so do I – unofficially."

"It was my pleasure, especially this last part."

As Matthews hailed a cab to the American Hotel, he felt a certain gratification – both for his work and for his government, which saw fit in the end to do its part in the whole affair. He now looked forward to a long bath, a leisurely meal and one last visit to Giselle.

CHAPTER TWENTY-ONE
Ottawa

"Whoa," Buckley commanded, bringing the hansom to a halt. He got down from his perch just as Albert opened the door.

"Why have we stopped?" the militiaman inquired looking around puzzled.

"To warm my bones," responded the older man. "I don't know about you – of course you're cozy in there," he added with a touch of bereavement, "but it is a frigid night and if we're to continue trotting around in circles by Mr. Macdonald's present address, then I'd be wanting a few moments beside a fire and I know just the spot!"

"Terribly sorry to put you out," Albert explained as they entered a local pub, "just want to be sure that nothing is amiss – I am responsible for the Minister's well-being."

"Yes, yes I know," Buckley said gruffly. "And your dedication is admirable but I shouldn't worry about anything being amiss tonight. There's nothing out of character. 'Tis been Mr. Macdonald's habit of late to pay his lady friend these evenin' visits. Sometimes he walks, you know – just lives a couple of blocks away."

"Speaking of which, who is she?"

"I haven't the foggiest and I don't ask. He's a bit touchy about people finding out too much. But then he's a politician, right, and I suppose he'd be wanting to avoid scandalous gossip and what not."

"I take your point."

"Are you armed?"

"What?"

"You're not in uniform, are you? And I see no rifle attached anywhere."

"It was decided that we be discreet. I do have a weapon on me."

"Just wanted to know in case. It's good though, that you're not in uniform, that is. Wouldn't want the locals here thinking I was suddenly hobnobbing with the militia."

Albert was about to ask why but decided to let it go, suspecting that he wouldn't like the answer.

The establishment they entered had a decided dearth of patrons but a small fireplace was crackling and they went directly to it pulling up chairs close enough to warm their backsides.

"Ah ... that's better," said Buckley, taking off his gloves and unwinding his long scarf.

A young woman with a full bust in a tight bodice materialized before them. "Good evenin', luv."

"Good evening, Mr. Buckley – you're late tonight."

"Couldn't be helped," he gave Albert a pointed glance. "I'll have my usual."

She smiled and turned to the militiaman. "And you, sir?"

"Huh, I'm on duty so perhaps a cup of —"

"Bring 'im the usual too," Buckley interjected. "A wee drop of rum will do 'im good."

"Ah ... yes, in that case."

"Very good, sir." She turned and disappeared.

"Friendly lass," Buckley said, "daughter of the proprietor, you know."

They sat in silence for a few moments until the drinks arrived.

"If I may ask, did Mr. Macdonald instruct you to come back at a certain hour tonight to pick him up?"

"No. He never has. Why should he?"

"Just wondered."

Albert settled back and enjoyed the heat and the rum, which he had to admit was as functional as the tea he would have ordered. Perhaps he was being overly conscientious about his assignment or disturbed, rather, that it had been so abruptly curtailed. It was, after all, the Minister's prerogative and if he chose to have a private evening with his lady with no civil rifle about, well, Albert couldn't really blame him. And Buckley had just confirmed that the Attorney General in all likelihood would remain sequestered inside until the morning.

After a half hour or so with their toes toasty, they were back outside. Buckley agreed to swing by the house one last time. As the hansom rounded the corner onto Daly Street, Albert spotted another hansom parked directly in front of the residence in question.

"Mr. Buckley," he called, "could you hold up, please."

"Whoa," came the command from the coachman. The horse stopped some distance from the stationary vehicle ahead of them. Albert stepped out of the cab. "What would you make of that?" He pointed to the hansom seemingly left unattended.

Buckley shrugged. "What should I make of it?"

"Rather peculiar," Albert muttered to himself.

The appearance of the cab, although probably innocent enough, justified his remaining, he decided if only to satisfy his curiosity.

"Thank you, Mr. Buckley, for indulging me and your patience. I think, however, that I shall remain here a while longer. But I won't detain you," Albert added quickly. "You've been most accommodating."

"Are you sure?"

"Quite sure."

"Suit yourself then," Buckley said brusquely. "I'll be saying good night then."

"Good night, Mr. Buckley."

With a flick of the reins and a "giddy up" the hansom lurched forward and down the street.

Now, Albert had a decision to make. Should he wait for the owner to come along or should he risk annoying the Minister by knocking on the door to check on his well-being? Before he could come to any firm resolve, the call of nature was upon him. Since he couldn't think under pressure he ducked into an alley to relieve his protesting bladder.

Albert had just finished his business and stepped out of the alley when he saw a bulky man deposit what appeared to be a body into the cab. It was a body! He could see the feet sticking out! The hansom sagged to one side as another man was struggling to hoist the limp body onto the seat.

"My God!" he croaked and started to run toward the jiggling cab.

At that instant, a carriage came careening around the corner behind Albert. The hansom, meanwhile, with its cargo now more or less securely stowed inside was taking leave, the big man scrambling up on his seat and urging the steed on. Albert was almost at the residence when the carriage pulled up alongside. He recognized the distinctive features of his superior. He did not know the two other gentlemen with him.

Lawrence stuck his head out. "What's going on here?"

The militiaman collected his wits about him. "Mr. Macdonald, sir. I believe he has met with foul play – that cab," he pointed to the receding hansom, "he's inside!"

"Check the house," Lawrence ordered. "See who's inside. Detain them and be careful!"

"Yes, sir."

"After them!" Lawrence shouted to his driver. "Don't let them get away!"

With that Lawrence and his companions sped down Daly Street in hot pursuit.

Albert, slightly flustered, took a deep breath, fumbled for his revolver and gingerly tried the door handle. It turned and the door swung open. Cautiously, he entered.

A very attractive, finely dressed lady with slightly disheveled hair stood before him, one hand on the sofa and the other clutching a crumpled handkerchief. Albert quickly put his revolver away.

"Are you the gendarme?" she asked with agitation evident in her voice.

"Y-yes in a manner of speaking," he replied, realizing that his status was not exactly that. He assumed that he had the authority to act as one but he certainly did not belong to the Ottawa constabulary. There was, however, no point in bringing up such a fine distinction at that moment.

"Oh, I'm so glad you're here," she wailed. "Two men burst into the room, knocked Mr. Macdonald senseless and dragged him out – it was horrible!"

"Calm yourself, please," Albert said awkwardly as he took in the surroundings. "There is no one else here?"

The lady shook her head.

"And you have not been injured?"

"N-no," she said. "Just a little shaken and frightened."

"Entirely understandable. But there's no need to be alarmed," he assured her. "The situation is well in hand. Is there anything I can get you?"

"Actually, I'm quite all right," her voice seemed to gather strength. "It was the initial shock of ... I'm fine now."

Albert nodded thinking hard. Undoubtedly, Lawrence would come by eventually, hopefully with Mr. Macdonald in good health and the kidnappers in tow. Then he would have some explaining to do to his superior. In the meantime, he should get some particulars from the lady. He asked her name.

"Luce – Luce Beaudoir."

"Miss Beaudoir," he tried to sound official, "I shall need a statement from you as to what occurred here. A description of the men who broke in – you said there were two?"

"Yes."

"And whatever else comes to mind. Did they say anything? Identify themselves in any way?"

"N-no. Not that I recall. Constable, I'll endeavour to answer your questions but if you don't mind I think I could use a little sherry to steady my nerves."

"Of course. I can—"

"No, please," she interjected giving Albert a wan smile, "allow me."

She walked over to the table with the decanter of sherry and poured a small amount into a long-stemmed crystal. "Oh, where are my manners?" She turned to him. "What can I offer you? Whiskey perhaps?"

"Well I—" Albert hesitated.

"You do look chilled. Can't hurt now that the excitement has passed." she replied.

"I suppose it can't at that," Albert agreed, thinking that the rum with Buckley did go down rather well.

"I'll be right back," she said walking into the adjoining kitchen area. A moment later, she called out, "is whiskey satisfactory then?"

"Yes, fine, thank you."

Luce came out with a stiff glass of mellowed Irish whiskey and handed it to him.

"I still can't believe this has happened," she said wide-eyed.

"Nasty business all right," Albert commented taking a gulp of his drink. It burned all the way down his throat making his nose tingle and his eyes water.

"If you could …ah, Mr. …"

"Oh, I'm sorry, I hadn't introduced myself Albert – Albert James."

"Mr. James, if you could excuse me for a moment – I need to visit the ladies room."

"Certainly."

"And do have a seat," she gestured to the sofa.

Mademoiselle Beaudoir went upstairs and directly to her bedroom. From the closet she took out her suitcase packed well in advance. She then took off her evening attire and put on a plain white chemise and a coarse brown skirt more suitable for travelling. After inspecting herself in the mirror and combing her hair she calmly donned her coat and gloves, took up the suitcase and made her way down the stairs.

As expected, Mr. James was sprawled out on the sofa, the empty glass on the floor. He was conscious but hardly in any position to get up let alone stop her. She paused near the helpless man, smiled and said "Sleep tight – sorry I can't tuck you in."

At the door she pulled on a pair of long leather boots and walked out, gently closing the door behind her.

***

"We'll get them," Lawrence confidently predicted. "We have the advantage of four wheels and two steeds – those two wheelers are notoriously hard to handle and manoeuvre at speed."

"If-f you s-say s-so," McGee chattered, hanging on for dear life. The little Irishman was bouncing about on the seat, feeling like he was riding a bronco in some Wild West show he had read about once.

"Conditions are treacherous," remarked Lynch, noting that the hard packed snow made for an icy roadway. *Mr. McCrimmon's cutter would have been more suitable for this escapade,* he thought, but kept this to himself.

They were still on Daly approaching the intersection of Ottawa Street, and definitely gaining. The fleeing hansom got through the intersection cleanly.

Unfortunately, their coachman at the last moment had to pull hard on reins of his thundering horses to avoid a spectacular collision with a wagon ponderously making its way up Ottawa.

"Damn!" Lawrence bellowed, his head stuck out the window as they were thrown roughly to one side. "That was close! Keep it moving," he shouted to the grim-faced driver on top.

As Daly turned into Baldwin the distance between the two vehicles had lengthened to about a quarter mile. On Nicholas, the kidnapper's cab made a sharp left turn, its two wheels skidding sideways almost tipping the light rig over, the attached horse pulling mightily, barely keeping its legs. The larger carriage followed, taking the corner somewhat more gracefully. They were now heading south paralleling the Rideau Canal.

"Crazy bastard," Lawrence sneered.

"Th-this can't go on much longer," observed McGee. "If-f one of the horses stumbles …"

Lynch couldn't agree more, suddenly wishing he was back on the train.

They had rushed by Albert, Slater and James when at the last possible moment the hansom attempted a right turn onto Theodore Street.

"They're heading for the canal bridge – oh shit!" Lawrence shouted.

"What?" McGee and Lynch both exclaimed in unison.

The hansom did not complete the turn. Its right wheel hit a hard snowbank and sheared off, spinning down the road. At the same time, the horse went down as the cab listed violently and came to a jolting stop. The momentum thrust Flanagan forward and he was thrown into the air like a rag doll, his progress abruptly arrested by a lamp post. Their coachman was much more fortunate; pulling on the reins of the heaving horses he finally got them under control, overshooting the Theodore intersection by a few yards.

The three men scrambled out of the carriage and started toward the wrecked hansom and the struggling animal, which was gallantly but unsuccessfully attempting to rise. At a distance they could see the hansom door suddenly swing open and a man staggered out. It took but a few seconds for Reese to assess his situation before he fled (albeit with a pronounced limp) into the darkness.

"I got him," Lynch hollered, running after him.

Lawrence and McGee raced for the hansom. Behind them, their coachman calmed his horses and slowly turned the carriage around onto Theodore.

McGee, puffing heavily, climbed into the cab with Lawrence on his heels. Macdonald lay wedged in the corner, his long legs askew, arms limp at his sides.

"John … John," McGee croaked. He stared at his friend's ashen face and grabbed a limp wrist searching for a pulse.

"Is he – is he dead?" Lawrence asked anxiously.

McGee almost jumped out of his skin when the Attorney General, his eyes still firmly shut, said "Not quite – but I dinna feel so good."

"Don't move just yet, sir," Lawrence advised, "'til we're sure nothing is broken."

"Ooooh – no fear of that – not until my head stops dancing."

As McGee, having got his heart rate under control, administered to Macdonald, Lawrence hurried over to the splayed figure lying under the lamp post. It didn't take long to ascertain that the man was beyond first aid. A broken neck, the lieutenant surmised on closer inspection. He then walked over to the coachman who was beside the downed horse speaking softly to reassure the distressed animal still feebly struggling to rise.

"Shattered leg I'm afraid," he said.

"Too bad. I suppose we better put it out of its misery."

Lynch heard the loud report of a revolver disturb the night air and wondered what had happened back at the hansom. He hoped that there was no further confrontation – perhaps with the driver of the hansom. However, he couldn't worry about that at that instant. His quarry was somewhere in front of him in the dark, garbage-littered back lanes off Theodore Street.

In the immediate area there were no private dwellings to be seen, only large commercial buildings separated by narrow gaps. Straining his eyes in the pale light of the moon, Lynch thought he caught a glimpse of someone entering one of those alleys off to his left. Revolver in hand, the detective hurried in that direction. He paused at the entrance – a most uninviting lane – sandwiched between what seemed to be warehouses. A dog barked in the distance but otherwise all he heard was his boots crunching in the crystallized snow. This one appeared to have no exit with a fence of some sort at the far end, although it was difficult to be sure. Indecision gripped him. Should he go blindly down the alley, placing himself at considerable risk or should he stay put assuming that he had his man boxed in?

Lynch decided to play it safe and wait for Lawrence who undoubtedly would come along in due course. As the detective turned back to reposition himself nearer to the entrance of the lane, he heard the distinct creak of a door opening followed by the click of it swinging shut at the far end of the alley. That settled it. If his quarry could get into the building then he could find another way out. There was no choice but to pursue.

Hugging the brick wall of the large building, Lynch made his way toward the source from which the sounds had come. Careful not to create undue noise himself, he worked around debris and other indeterminate objects in his path until he was at a door — the only door, as far as he could tell, on the west side of the structure. Apprehensively, he tried the knob. The door opened with the same ominous creak. He entered in a crouched position his revolver poised for action. The building was relatively empty of content — an abandoned factory of some sort with odd bits of machinery silhouetted against the poor light of the night sky through the high windows. He was at a great disadvantage, he realized, literally fumbling in the dark. Taking a deep breath, he began feeling his way around the perimeter of the edifice. Sweat seeping down his back, his pulse racing and his senses heightened, the detective strained for any sight or sound that would give him the edge in the cat and mouse game that was being played. Then he heard it — a shuffle and the distinct clang of a foot hitting a hollow tin object. Straight ahead and very near.

Lynch widened his stride, stepped over a long pipe and spotted a figure, his back to him, stooped as if picking something off the floor. Positioning himself squarely behind the man, his weapon ready, Lynch announced his presence brusquely. "Stay where you are and slowly turn around."

His adversary gave a startled yelp and stumbled forward and started to run. Lynch aimed and fired. The shot reverberated in the empty cavity with a deafening loudness. The man dropped to his hands and knees.

Lieutenant Lawrence heard the discharge as he approached the alley. His pistol drawn, cautiously he proceeded into the dark abyss. He saw the door open and two men emerge. With a sigh of relief, Lawrence noted that Lynch appeared to have the situation well in hand. "That our man?" he asked as he approached still somewhat wearily.

Lynch shook his head. "Afraid not."

"Oh? Who's he?"

"Meet Moloch here – case of mistaken identity."

The grizzly faced man with decidedly ragged clothes hung around him said nothing. He was visibly shaking – terrified in fact.

Lynch said to him, "You're free to go now."

Without a word the man hurriedly departed up the alley and around the corner.

"Street person," Lynch said by way of explanation, "looking for shelter and firewood. Bad luck he crossed my path at the wrong time and in the wrong place."

"You fired a shot?"

"Yeah, over his head to stop him from running. Poor beggar."

"Lucky bugger, I'd say."

"Gave him a couple of dollars for his ordeal. Should keep him fed and warm for the night."

"If he doesn't drink it away." Lawrence commented uncharitably.

Lynch shrugged. "Either way, our man is long gone by now."

CHAPTER TWENTY-TWO

St. Patrick's Day went off without 'troubles' as McMicken put it in his report to Macdonald and the ten thousand or so militia men that Macdonald had ordered mobilized along the border and major towns did not have much to do. The St. Patrick's Day parades throughout the Canadas also proved relatively tame without the Irish Protestants and Irish Catholics confronting each other in riots or the spectre of some Fenian induced murder and/or mayhem.

In Montreal, where McClosky had involuntarily blown himself up the day before, St. Paddy's parade proceeded smoothly making a circuit from Place d'Armes to Rue St-Denis, marching down rue Saint-Jacques over any tiny bits of McClosky not scraped up and stopping in front of St. Lawrence Hall where a nonplussed Governor General gave a brief but buoyant speech on behalf of the queen as if nothing had occurred.

It was, perhaps, somewhat tongue in cheek that after thanking the cheering crowd Lord Monck added, "I accept this demonstration as evidence on your part to your sovereign, of attachment to the institutions of our land and as a protest against the principles of wicked men who would disgrace the name of Irishmen and desecrate the birthday of her patron saint by a wanton attack on a peaceful, prosperous and happy country."

In Ottawa, John A. would have said much the same thing were he not tucked in his bed at his lodgings still recovering from the spiked drink he had consumed a few hours earlier. His head hurt, his mouth was exceedingly dry and his stomach was roiling again. After the doctor had gone, prescribing plenty of rest and no visitors, McGee came for a visit and an update.

"I've been in a worse state," Macdonald commented, propping himself up on a large pillow. "'Tis like intoxication – the brain is dulled, the tongue thickened, the eyelids heavier. But then, I've delivered some of my best retorts under such conditions. Thank God I dinna have to today ..." He paused tilting his head forward a little. "So has the news of this gotten out?"

"No, not a peep," replied McGee. "The incident has not been recorded on any official document or reached the newspapers. Those involved have agreed to remain silent for now. It is as if this Fenian plot never materialized."

"Good, this best be buried," Macdonald said weakly letting himself sink back into the bed. "If Mr. Brown and the *Globe* ever got wind of this ..."

The decision to suppress Macdonald's abduction and harrowing rescue was reached in Lieutenant Lawrence's chambers in the small hours of the morning. Those involved in the chase and its aftermath solemnly agreed that no word of what transpired should be revealed publicly.

"There would be too many recriminations and accusations," McGee argued. Not to mention, he thought but did not voice, John A's embarrassment or worse at being duped by a Fenian 'femme fatale'.

Lieutenant Lawrence concurred for different reasons. "We would be questioned about our state of preparedness and competence if all the facts came out. If it weren't for Mr. Lynch's diligence and timely arrival, I dare say, the plot would have succeeded."

"Aye, best let it lie undisturbed, at least for now." McGee reaffirmed. "Can the ... ah ... evidence be easily dealt with?" he asked turning to Lawrence. There was, after all, still the matter of a corpse.

"It can," Lawrence responded grimly. "It will be recorded as an unfortunate traffic accident – common enough and which, in a manner of speaking, it was. Of course, we should try to identify the deceased – no such luck on his person. Given the circumstances, I should think that no one will come forth to claim the body so he in all probability will be laid to rest as an indigent soul in an unmarked grave."

Silence filled the room. A consensus was tacitly reached with nodding heads, the full details best left in Lawrence's hands.

"Then there is the matter of the fellow that Mr. Lynch chased. What of him?" McGee asked. "I never got a proper look at him," Lynch said. "Made a clean escape into the darkness. Didn't look that he was injured to any significant degree, despite the violence of the crash. Most assuredly he had other accomplices and now is safely hidden licking his wounds."

"Can't have the Civil Rifles scouring the town even if you could describe him," Lawrence remarked. "We can't very well say that no plot was afoot and then give credence that indeed one was."

"A conundrum then," said McGee "that cannot be circumvented, it appears."

"The same applies to the woman," Lawrence continued "Miss –"

"Beaudoir," McGee filled in. "An alias I suspect. No doubt, Mr. Macdonald can provide more information when he's up to it."

Lawrence frowned, "As can Albert – he had a good look I am sure before she rendered him unconscious with some sort of potion in his liquor which," he added, "he should not have been drinking. But, as I stated, the same logic holds does it not?"

"A description and any other particulars would still be useful for Mr. McMicken's files," Lynch interjected, "for future reference. We may run across this mysterious lady again."

As the discussions continued, Lynch found that he was suddenly spent with little else of substance to contribute. Indeed, he was grateful that Lawrence had jumped into the breech, so to speak, to take care the particulars of the affair. As a matter of course, he would report what transpired to McMicken and leave it at that. If so finally determined, McMicken could be counted on to make sure that this sordid episode never saw the light of day. The other person that would have to be told was Molly since she knew that a dastardly plot was in motion. He would omit some of the more contentious details however.

By the time the meeting was over Lynch could hardly keep his eyes open. He was tired, cold, hungry and looking forward to getting to the Russell Hotel where there was running water and the spectre of a hot bath. Afterwards, he hoped to enjoy a late breakfast with Molly. Sleep would have to wait.

***

Shortly after the demise of McClosky, Matthews telegraphed an encrypted message to Mr. Seward's secretary stating what had happened with a note that Canadian intelligence was aware of the plot and seemingly had the situation in hand. He left out, as a form of judicial self-censure, his role in the capture of McQuealy. He was there strictly as an undercover agent supposedly unknown to Canadian authorities. Best let that puzzle be, he figured.

Matthews had no intention of prolonging his stay in Montreal. Still, he registered at the St. Lawrence Hall Hotel to be on hand for the parade and any other planned (or unplanned) events. Thus, the next day, he loitered around the hotel lobby, listened to Lord Monck's address and managed to spot the diligent Canadian gendarme, Mr. Clancy – or at least the back of his head – in the surrounding crowd. Later, with the day proving to be quite uneventful, Matthews decided to revisit Griffintown and make Giselle his last port of call.

The next morning he caught a tram to Bonaventure Station. It was time to bid adieu to Montreal and get back to his abode in New York. There was a dispatch or two to complete and in all probability some new instructions awaited him. His plan was to board a southbound train to the border, connect with the Central Vermont, which would take him alongside the frozen white expanse of Lake Champlain down to Albany where he would catch the New York Central into New York City.

Bonaventure Station was a large, imposing limestone structure with what looked to Matthews like an odd pekoe pagoda on top. It was a crisp morning with a light layer of snow that had fallen overnight. A good number of people were already bustling about but nothing compared to Grand Central Station he mused. It took a few minutes to get his bearings and find the wicket window where he could purchase his ticket. Alas, he was in for a lengthy wait before the next scheduled southbound train. His one battered brown suitcase in hand, he cast around for a comfortable place to sit and study his connections when he caught a glimpse of a vaguely familiar figure apparently having just disembarked from a Grand Trunk locomotive arrived from the east.

"What's he doing here?" Matthews muttered to himself in surprise. The Texan needed to move closer just to be sure that indeed the man in the pack of gathered people was who he thought he was. A smaller hombre than himself, he nevertheless seemed almost shrunken in a heavy dark coat and a pork pie hat of indeterminate fur that sunk around his forehead and ears. He was travelling particularly light, Matthews noticed, without even a satchel or handbag of any sort. Moreover, he sported a pronounced limp as he made his way to the same wicket window that Matthews had bought his fare a few moments earlier. In all probability, he too was returning to New York.

Careful not to be seen, he slid behind a massive support column deciding what to do next. Matthews realized that the fellow may now be of no consequence – as far as the U.S. government was concerned, he amended. So a choice had to be made – let the matter drop or pursue it – at least to a point. Matthews decided on the latter – if nothing else for the sake of his own curiosity. There was a high chance that he would end up on the same train and if Matthews recognized him, then most assuredly the reverse would be true. Besides, he didn't want to leave a stone unturned – might be safer that way.

"How's your nose?" Matthews enquired wryly just as the man turned from the wicket window.

Reese was caught off guard, his face registering shock, surprise with a measure of fear as it turned pasty white.

"See you've collected a couple more bruises since we last met," Matthews noted the patch above the left eye and a recently lacerate cheek, "as well as a limp."

Reese steadied himself seemingly to debate his options and deciding, it seemed to Matthews, that it was no use pretending that they hadn't had an encounter. He gave the Texan a crooked smile. "How's your chess game?"

"Never got a chance to play did I?" Matthews quipped.

"Ah," Reese nodded "so you didn't …"

"Obliged to leave in a hurry if you remember."

"So you did," Reese rubbed the scar on his nose. "And what is your game now exactly?"

"I would ask the same of you," Matthews retorted.

"You have approached me not to rehash old times so who are you and what is it that you want of me?" Reese asked in a low edgy voice.

"We didn't quite finish that conversation did we?" Matthews said evenly trying to take the measure of the man before him. Instinctively, they moved away from the flow of traffic in the main concourse into a more secluded section.

"Are you here to arrest me or accost me?" Reese put his right hand into his coat pocket as he spoke while Matthews warily lay down his suitcase.

"There's a perfectly workable derringer pointed at your gut," he added, his eyes lowering.

Matthews held up his hands in a placating gesture. "No need for anything that drastic. I have no jurisdiction or inclination to arrest or accost you, besides it appears that someone had beaten me to it – if you pardon my saying so."

"Had an unfortunate fall," Reese stated flatly, his eyes narrowing.

"Can never be too careful I suppose"

"What is it that you want?" Reese reiterated more urgently.

"For the moment, we're just two gents with a slight but eventful history about to take the same train."

Reese shifted his weight slightly which Matthews hoped was not a prelude to the use of the derringer. Matthews continued: "A mutually agreeable chat is all I'm after. Look, there's still quite some time to kill," he winced at his choice of words, "before the train departs. A truce and a drink perhaps at a nearby establishment might pass the time in a more productive and agreeable way."

Reese hesitated.

"There'd be no harm in hearing me out," Matthews pressed on. "As I said we have got time on our hands."

"All right, I'll humour you," Reese said evenly taking a step back to keep his distance. "Lead the way – keep your hands out of your pocket and off that revolver I know you have."

They walked across the street to a fashionable saloon on rue McGill that Matthews had spied on his way into the station. Reese kept pace a couple of steps behind, favouring his right leg. Neither said a word.

Matthews bought two whiskeys and they settled comfortably into ornate armchairs opposite each other away from the long mahogany bar and seating area that most patrons appeared to prefer. Reese grimaced reaching for his glass. To Matthews he appeared to have sustained more damage than just what was seen externally but he doubted that Reese would tell the truth of how his injuries were inflicted.

"Well then, I ask again, who are you and what do you want of me?" Reese took a sip of his whiskey and gingerly fingered his glass, waiting.

"A trade of information for curiosity's sake … mine and possibly yours," Matthews replied, "after which we can both be on our way with an understanding that would not necessitate our paths crossing again."

Reese cast a furtive glance around that Matthews judged signified a degree of nervousness – like a man on the run.

"What kind of information?" he asked

"To start, what brought you to Canada for instance?"

"Business – I'm a businessman."

Matthews gave him an annoyed look. He was getting very tired of all the verbal sparring he had engaged with on his trip to Canada from reluctant bankers to cryptic Montreal policemen.

"Mr. – I never did catch your name?"

"Nor I yours," Reese countered.

"No matter, let's cut to the chase shall we? Then we can depart without having any reason to encounter each other again and," he emphasized, "not have to look over our shoulders on the train."

When Reese said nothing, Matthews continued: "I very much suspect that the business that brought you here was connected to the same business that brought me to this fair place as well, so I'll start. Your business was with a man I followed from your meeting with him to Montreal or rather I followed his money trail. Mr. McQuealy and his associates, as you no doubt have by now surmised, failed in his venture. I won't bore you with the details. My question is where do you fit in?"

After a long pause, Reese seem to relent. "All right, I will meet you halfway. My business," he cleared his throat uneasily, "was in Ottawa."

"Ottawa?" Matthews knew nothing of any Fenian activities in Ottawa. In fact, he had only heard the place mentioned once or twice in passing. "Go on," he urged.

"I'm returning home disappointed," Reese stated without elaboration.

Matthews let that sink in. It sounded true enough. He was pretty sure that he would have heard if the Fenians managed to pull off something nasty in Ottawa or elsewhere in the Canadas for that matter.

"But you're not going to explain further the nature of your business," Matthews pressed, "just to satisfy my curiosity?"

"No. That would be imprudent of me."

"But I can assume it was of a similar nature?"

"You can assume," Reese replied curtly.

"Then let me relay one more piece of information, which you may not be aware of. You are luckier than Mr. McQuealy. At least you get to go home."

Reese's face remained neutral, "Oh?"

"Yes, not only was the game played discovered but Mr. McQuealy has been detained by Canadian authorities."

"Are you a Canadian spy of some sort?" Reese asked abruptly.

"No, if I were you'd be facing more dire consequences, I imagine. No, I'm looking through the spyglass from the opposite direction observing the ebb and flow, as it were, of your organization on either side of the border."

When Reese said nothing Matthews continued, "I just want to satisfy myself that the particular game you and McQuealy played is now concluded and I won't be chasing you from the shadows."

"I can say with a high degree of certainty that this game is over," Reese replied simply.

"Glad to hear that. Despite your refusal to divulge what the game in Ottawa was, I've sufficiently satisfied my curiosity. I trust we can be on our separate way – or least separate coach compartments – without any cause to trouble each other again."

"I do appreciate that," replied Reese.

EPILOGUE

As it turned out, the Fenians were far from done in creating "troublous times" for the British North American colonies. Persistent rumours of impending invasions were still rampant. Finally, one of sorts came in mid-April targeting New Brunswick, the key province to Macdonald's confederation scheme. A few hundred Fenians gathered in the seaport of Portland, Maine rather openly bragging that they were there to launch an assault on the colony with the aim of not only preventing its union with the Canadians but provoking a British-American conflict.

The plan was to take Campobello Island in the Bay of Fundy just off New Brunswick's shore and use it as a base from which to attack. Two British warships from Halifax and about five thousand British regulars and New Brunswick militia effectively discouraged it. As a show of bravado more than any sound military strategy, a boatload of Fenians raided Indian Island, a tiny slip of land not far from Campobello Island, where they managed to torch a Customs House before rowing back to the U.S. side to resume their drinking from the night before.

Meanwhile, the announced Fenian goal of preventing the "obnoxious" confederation project was a godsend to Macdonald in Ottawa and Tilley in Fredericton for it strengthened measurably their arguments for unity in matters of defence and resistance to American annexation. The pro-confederation forces carried the day in the June elections that followed.

A more egregious threat materialized in Canada West, however. At the stroke of midnight June 1, the Fenians launched what was dubbed the 'Canada Plan'. Approximately fifteen hundred men crossed the Niagara River from Buffalo in small boats and assembled on a wharf not far from Fort Erie. Led by a former Union colonel and fervent Fenian, John O'Neill, they seemed prepared and well informed as to the terrain and the forces they would likely face. O'Neill proudly announced that he had seized Canada West in the name of Ireland.

The following day the Queen's Own Militia, some nine hundred or so volunteers, including University of Toronto students, engaged them at Ridgeway, a village near Fort Erie. Well entrenched on higher ground and more experienced in battle tactics, the Fenians were victorious with the Canadian militia forced to retreat leaving fifteen of their own dead or dying.

As word of the defeat spread, other communities mobilized defence volunteers throughout the province. In Windsor, McMicken received mounting reports of a large Fenian force in and around Detroit ready to cross the Detroit River to invade Windsor and/or Sandwich.

In the general alarm, McMicken was chagrined to discover that Spense, his traitorous former private secretary had managed to escape from his Windsor jail cell. How that occurred was vague, although it appeared that it was less an escape than release thanks to a suspected Fenian sympathizer in the Windsor constabulary.

"No doubt," McMicken wrote in his report of the incident to Macdonald, "the little worm has by now gotten across the river. The only solace is that he could pass on limited intelligence since his arrest and detention in March precluded any further opportunities for spying. Still, quite galling that he got away," McMicken concluded.

Fortunately for the Canadians, the invasion was a forty-eight hour affair since the reinforcements and supplies that O'Neill counted on did not arrive. Larger issues overshadowed O'Neill's initial success. Seward, who remained mute and inactive while the Fenians effectively broke U.S. neutrality laws, was forced to act – or least his boss, President Andrew Johnson did for the sake of improved Anglo-American relations. Four days after the Battle of Ridgeway, Johnson issued a proclamation stating that the Fenians had indeed violated the country's neutrality statutes. Further men and supplies were not allowed to cross the border. Moreover, those Fenians making their way back across the Niagara River were detained midstream by an American gunboat and summarily put in the brig on an accompanying steamer.

This in turn created another problem. Incarcerated Fenians – loyal American citizens most of whom had fought in the Union Army – were suddenly becoming a political liability for the government. As Seward told Baxter, "I need to get these stupid Irish men freed! The adverse publicity will cost us dearly come voting time."

The Secretary of State suggested that they be allowed to escape as a possible solution. Baxter thought that a dubious course of action instead proposing that they be simply released on bail. "That would be less sensational in the press and neutralize to a great degree their capture and detention, which makes for a more positive news story I should think," Baxter argued.

Seward immediately warmed up to the idea directing Baxter to begin the process of making it so. "That should stop most of the bad publicity," Seward agreed with his private secretary, "and relieve some of the President's anxiety." *Not to mention possibly saving my job,* he thought privately.

However, not all the Fenians managed to make it back to Buffalo. About one hundred or so were captured by British regulars and local militia. They were shackled and transported to Toronto jails where they were officially charged with "entering the province with the intent to levy war against Her Majesty", an offence punishable by death.

Feelings were understandably running high and none too charitable toward these invaders. When the Canadian legislature reconvened in the newly-built Parliament building, Macdonald was in a feisty mood and so were his colleagues who agreed on a number of provocative measures. 'Habeas Corpus' was suspended, which meant that the detainees had no redress to the normal judicial system and indeed they were to be tried in a military court. Macdonald, meanwhile, ignored Seward's requests that the said American prisoners be deported.

Seward was beside himself. "Dastardly, blood thirsty Canadians!" he thundered to Baxter. "This will not do!"

Baxter shuddered inwardly. It wasn't his place to tell his boss 'you reap what you sow' but the Secretary of State was right, this couldn't possibly do and some dramatic action was needed for the sake of the current administration. With the Irish vote key to Andrew Johnson's victory and mid-term elections going badly, it was imperative that Seward find a way to bring these stranded Fenians home, especially since a belligerent Congress passed a resolution demanding that the President do whatever it took to get these 'Americans' freed from Canadian jails.

Jaroslav (*Jerry*) Petryshyn

Seward spared no expense "for our citizens" as he told the reporters to provide legal representation. He was then absolutely "floored" to learn that twenty-five Fenians had been found guilty and that sixteen were sentenced to hang! "Declare war if necessary. We must prevent Canada from giving these men hemp neck ties!" he bellowed to Baxter.

Baxter suggested a personal appeal to the British Minister in Washington. Seward calmed down long enough to conscript Baxter into penning such a draft for his perusal. The final document contained such words as "tenderness, amnesty and forgiveness," necessary Baxter insisted to "set the correct tone". Seward found it quite humbling, tantamount to begging. Still, he supposed Baxter was right and begrudgingly signed and sent it off.

For his part, Macdonald too was under enormous pressure but from London to assuage Anglo-American relations by granting mercy to all prisoners "under the sentence of death." After due discussion and consideration Macdonald commuted the sentences to twenty years in the newly-refurbished Kingston Penitentiary.

Seward still fumed but at least no Americans would be swinging from Canadian gallows. As it turned out, all incarcerated Fenians were released and deported within six years – each receiving five dollars for train fare.

Included in the amnesty was one particular Fenian who was not put on trial – Michael McQuealy. After his apprehension in Montreal, he was whisked away to Toronto for rather diligent interrogation regarding his Fenian activities. McMicken wanted names, codes, locations and finances. The Canadian chief of detectives thought that his prolonged visit to Toronto was well worthwhile, telling Lynch in one of his rare joking moments "We got more from Mr. Quealy than the standard $1.50 per diem rate that informers usually get. In fact, he would have earned a handsome bonus for the information he related had he been on our side …"

After his prolonged (and secret detention) McQuealy was surreptitiously released when Macdonald commuted the Fenian death sentences. He was allowed to flee across the border as quickly as he could arrange transport. The Fenians' unofficial ambassador returned to New York and within a month was found shot dead in an alley not far from the 'Fenian Hall' (and chess club) that Matthews had followed him to. New York police concluded that it was a violent robbery although rumours swarmed within Fenian organizations that it was retribution for talking too much and for either pocketing or allowing Canadian authorities to lay their hands on a good portion of Fenian operational funds in Montreal and Toronto banks.

McQuealy's co-conspirators, although they worked in different circles and independently, soon dropped out of sight including Mr. Reese. Quite shaken by his conversation with the American agent/spy, he didn't know exactly which, Reese concluded that he would be on report and potentially flagged as a dangerous rascal at the very least. Then there were the many intricacies and intrigues of the Fenian groups themselves who were not happy with events as they had unfolded. There was no bold, dramatic action as promised. The coordinated 'Canada plots' though carefully designed and richly financed, for one reason or another – he couldn't quite put his finger on it – proved a miserable botch. The Fenian Brotherhood was in disarray and he needed to cut his losses and move on. Real estate and local politics seemed a ripe undertaking for an enterprising Irishman like himself who could continue to the support the cause in a more acceptable and less dangerous way.

In a strange twist, Matthews would have appreciated Reese's logic and change of direction, if not heart. While the Texan did his work exceptionally well and received commendations for such, he still felt that he had been left dangling out there, subject to the whims of his superiors, his range of actions limited and with no real sense of purpose. He stayed with the government's nebulous (and extremely secret) 'secret service' for a couple more years before moving on to join a better known organization – Allan Pinkerton's Detective Agency.

He spent a number of years operating out of the New York branch office (he didn't want to move to Pinkerton's headquarters in Chicago) ensuring the security of wealthy businessmen, ambitious politicians and their often mercurial wives/mistresses. He heard "low muttering" of all kinds and spent many hours in the city's saloons and well-furnished drawing rooms trying to separate the wheat from the chaff, the grains of truth from the drama and bull. For the most part, he encountered those with 'dark purposes' on their minds but without the steely will or the necessary skills to actually follow through. Meanwhile, New York and the cities of the east in general, began to wear thin on his western spirit.

One day he realized that he preferred riding horses to train travel. This epiphany took a while to fester and sink in before Matthews gave the agency his notice, packed his bags and headed for the Lone Star state. Within a short time, he was back in "law enforcement" as a Texas Ranger.

North of the border, Lynch too rethought his peculiar line of work. Having done his part in thwarting Fenian designs on Canada, early in the new year he resigned from McMicken's team of agents and returned to Toronto and his old job with the Toronto Police where he quickly rose up the ranks to Chief Constable of Station House No.4 in the heart of the city. In large part, his decision was motivated by his courtship of Miss Mahone, which had reached a critical junction – a proposal of marriage. She had secured a position at the Toronto Public Library to supplement her small government stipend.

***

London, December, 1866

It was a beautiful wedding with over eighty guests, among them prominent members (and their wives) of the British cabinet. Indeed, Lord Carnarvon's son acted as one of the groomsmen while Emma, Jesse and Joanna – lovely daughters of Sir Charles Tupper, William McDougall and Sir Adam Archibald – acted as bridesmaids. They were attired in pink crepe bonnets and long tulle veils that were of the latest fashion and which greatly impressed the groomsmen. The bride, wearing a white satin gown with the wreath of orange blossoms and a veil of Brussels lace, appeared serene and content. But the happiest of them all was the groom. Standing before the magnificent St. Georges altar, John A. Macdonald couldn't believe his good fortune, especially after the events of a few months ago. Who could have imagined that not only was confederation assured but that he would be coming back from England with a wife!

Macdonald, along with the other fifteen delegates had gone to London for the final conference preceding the union of the British North American colonies. He had but one objective on his mind – the realization of his political objective. One day while taking a walk along Bond Street who should he bump into (quite literally) but Agnes Bernard and her mother. Agnes had refused Macdonald's marriage proposal while in the Canadas and had left for England late in 1865 thereby indirectly contributing to his ill-fated entanglement with Luce. However, within weeks they renewed their earlier courtship and just before Christmas he once again asked her to marry him. This time, she accepted.

Sitting in the hansom, on their way to the Westminster Palace Hotel after the ceremonies, Macdonald's thoughts strayed to the recent past. The assassination and kidnapping attempts had failed; both the Montreal and the Ottawa affairs had been judiciously hushed up from the press and the public, although, of course, there were rumours and a corpse and the scattered remains of another to discreetly dispose of. The St. Patrick's Day parade had gone off as scheduled with only a few, trifling incidents but certainly no massive assault by the Fenians on the Canadas as feared. Whether that had anything to do with the two doomed plots was a moot point.

True, the Fenians did attack at the end of May along the Niagara frontier and the New Brunswick-Maine border. And although casualties were sustained by the Canadian militiamen, the Irish gangsters had been thoroughly routed. Indeed, their invasion proved a blessing in disguise for in New Brunswick the anti-confederation government had fallen in no small part due to their folly. The actions of the Fenians had convinced the voters to elect the pro-confederation party of Leonard Tilley. *Nothing like an external threat to promote internal unity,* John A. thought smiling. It had all worked out for the best. Still, in moments of solitude and reflection he couldn't help but think of the mysterious and bewitching Luce Beaudoir and whatever happened to her ...

AUTHOR'S NOTE

This is a work of fiction set against historical events. In marry-ing fictional characters with actual personages, I have tried to be as accurate as I could in regards to the latter. The same is true of events, many of which did occur as described. In researching and writing the novel, I discovered that often the truth is indeed stranger than fiction; some of the historical figures had a more unbelievable story than I could have imaged for my fictional characters. Finally, the fictional characters are just that, and any resemblance to anyone living or dead is coincidental.

I wish to thank my academic colleagues, Dr. Duff Crerar and Dr. Tom Enders who read an earlier draft and provided useful feedback; my wonderful daughters, Alisha and Halyna, who vetted the manuscript and gave insightful critiques; the Friesen Press editor who "tidied up" the work, particularly my attempts at French and Irish accents; and finally, my wife Diane, who encouraged and cheerfully put up with a pen swinging historian turned novelist.

Ultimately, errors of commission and/or omission, along with any incongruities in plotting and structure are entirely my own.

Printed in Canada